Wildfire

JOHN CUTTER
WILDFIRE

A VINCE BELLATOR THRILLER

LUME BOOKS

LUME BOOKS

Published in 2021 by Lume Books

ISBN 978-1-83901-427-7

Typeset using Atomik ePublisher from Easypress Technologies

www.lumebooks.co.uk

For all the fans of The Specialist books.

"Everybody has a plan until they get punched in the mouth."

--Mike Tyson

FROM THE FBI DOSSIER ON VINCENT BELLATOR
Rough Summary
Agent Richard Chang, FBI
Classified

…As a captain in the US Army Rangers, Bellator was the recipient of numerous medals and commendations. Bellator's record is unblemished. He is not known to have engaged in any form of friendly fire, or to have harmed non-combatants.

While de-infiltrating from a Rangers mission in Syria, Bellator was captured and tortured. He escaped, and later returned, killing his captors… Eighteen months later he was recruited into Delta Force, under the aegis of the Joint Special Operations Command. As a Special Forces Operator with Delta Force he engaged in a number of classified missions, most of them anti-terrorist, killing significant al-Qaeda and ISIS commanders as well as their bodyguards. One-hundred and seventy-one kills, carried out by Captain Bellator alone, were recorded by his support team.

After several years with Delta Force he resigned, declined to reup with the army, and took a job with a private-military contractor, ProActive Security, operating in the Yucatan jungles of Mexico in actions against narco cartels. The operations were part of a cooperative project between the DEA and Mexican Federales and private military cadres. He became disenchanted with ProActive Security after his best friend from the Rangers, Christopher Destry, died due to the company's intelligence failures, and he resigned.

Taking up residency on Harstine Island in Puget Sound, Northwestern Washington State, he built a four-bedroom two-story house, largely on his own. On a subsequent trip to Georgia to meet Christopher Destry's family, Bellator stumbled onto a domestic terrorist operation. On his own initiative Bellator infiltrated the Neo-Nazi group, The Germanic Brethren, in order to find and release Christopher Destry's younger brother, Robert Destry, who was being held prisoner by the domestic terrorists. There, Bellator made contact with undercover Bureau agent Dierdre Corlin, who was disguised as a Germanic Brethren "Shield Maiden". Together they learned of a plot to kill numerous black-caucus US senators as well as massacre a large crowd, during a Civil Rights commemoration at the Lincoln Memorial. Dierdre Corlin's cover was compromised and she was taken prisoner by Germanic Brethren. In order to save Agent Corlin from torture and execution, Bellator killed somewhere between twenty and forty domestic terrorist operatives (estimates differ, due to possible internecine combat) inside the Brethren bunker. He went on to intervene in the planned attack at the Lincoln Memorial, stopping the attack with a minigun-style machine gun mounted in a helicopter piloted by Agent Corlin… He is suspected of killing the leader of the Germanic Brethren in a separate attack…

Vincent Bellator went to ground immediately afterwards but is believed to be in Arizona seeking the head of the "Fallen Angels" cartel, (*Angeles Caidos*), on a mission of vengeance linked to his experiences in the Yucatan…

See Dossier 8767.2B for full details.

Chapter One

Santo Virgil, Arizona

Vince Bellator was sitting at a small chrome table in a medium sized Airstream trailer, cleaning a gun.

He removed the chrome barrel of the .50 Desert Eagle, and peered through it toward the trailer park outside, toward the afternoon light shining through the window…

That's when the memory came rushing back to him.

Looking through the barrel of the big automatic pistol, Vince was suddenly seeing through the scope of the SCAR combat rifle he'd carried that early morning in the Yucatan, focusing on the main house of the henequen plantation down the hillside. He was lying on his belly in damp leaves, at the crown of the hill, wreathed in soursop and tamarind foliage; it was foggy, raining lightly, and the three heavily armed men standing in front of the sprawling plantation house weren't looking his way. They were focused on the five prisoners stumbling out into the open concrete area between the brush and the house. The prisoners were two adults, a teenage girl and two small boys. Just a man, his wife, their children.

1

Beyond the house, Vince could see the rows of spiky henequen, and a sentry, a rifle on a strap over his shoulder. The henequen plantation was now a cover for a modest little heroin processing factory.

Their arms bound behind them and blindfolds over their eyes, the six prisoners stumbled into one another as they stopped at the order of a tall, lanky man in a white straw hat.

Lopez.

And Lopez gave another order. A stocky, muscular man with long curly black hair, a Herstel Mark 48 machine gun cradled in his arms, stepped out from the others, and...

Vince closed his eyes, shook his head, forcing the memory away. His hands were only trembling a little as he looked, again, through the gun barrel, to check it for dirt, and...

The machine gun leapt like a vicious dog in the big man's arms, one long strafe tearing the family of five apart...

Vince fired on instinct at the gunman but the guy wore a Kevlar vest and it was too late and the screams cut short as...

"No!" Vince snapped. It was an order—a command he gave himself. He reset the focus of his mind, as he'd learned to do long ago in Afghanistan, and quickly—angrily—put the gun back together.

The memory withdrew to the dark recesses of his mind. He ran his fingers through his new beard, took a deep breath and stood up, thinking if he'd aimed at the gunman's head, that morning—maybe, just maybe, he could have saved them...

Vince had been onsite to do recon. He'd known the family was there. Five innocent people. They hoped to figure a way to rescue them.

Angel Lopez had ordered the execution. He had forcibly taken the plantation over, had kept the family as workers—prisoners, enslaved really—till they tried to escape. And other workers were watching from the field had to be shown what happened if anyone tried to leave....

Lopez. Who'd killed Vince's close friend Chris, too.

And Lopez was now operating in the USA. Even here, in Santo Virgil, in southern Arizona…

Vince heard a familiar rumble outside the trailer. The sound of Dutch Becker's Kenworth big-rig. Relieved to have the distraction, Vince put on his sunglasses and went to the door. He opened it to the crisp December day and looked out to see his friend climbing down from the big semitruck's tractor.

Dutch was a ginger-haired trucker somewhere in his thirties, with a broad forehead, a neatly cut russet beard, an abundance of freckles and a wide, infectious smile. A fellow veteran, Dutch had also decided he wanted to be a help to Vince in his self-appointed mission.

"I see you grew a beard," Dutch said, coming over to shake his hand. "It figures, I guess."

"My mug was on too many news clips. You drop off a load of TVs or something?"

"Heaters, up in Tucson. You'd think they wouldn't need 'em much in Arizona."

"Gets cold in the winter, at night. If you're ready, we can talk about a little something you can do for my mission—you and your truck."

Dutch put on a doubtful look. "Not a chance… Unless you've got coffee and donuts. Then—fine."

Vince grinned. "Both in copious supply. Come on in."

Diego Juan Fernandez was out behind the QuickShop store, scrounging cans and scrap metal to sell at the recycling, when the boy Pascual approached him and said, in Spanish, "A man was here looking for you over on Yuma Street. A *big* man."

Diego shoved a handful of energy drink cans into the fat plastic

3

bag and asked in the same language, "Is it that guy from the Veterans Administration? Short, skinny man with glasses, wears a suit?"

Pascual shook his head, rubbed his runny nose, and said, "No, I told you. Tall and... big. He said to tell you he is from 'Delta' and you know him. Says from when you were in 'Blue Barrel'. What is this Delta and Blue Barrel?"

Diego froze, staring at the boy now. "You sure? Delta?"

"He said you helped him. In the Army."

Diego rubbed his eyes. Could it really be him? Captain Bellator? "What color were his eyes?"

Pascual shrugged. "Did not see."

"Did he give you a... a message for me?"

"He said the Airstream at the Sedona Trailer Park." Pascual stuck out his hand, expecting to be paid.

Diego snorted. "He already paid you."

"He said you would pay me more."

"Now you're lying, Pascual Vasquez. I remember when you were a good kid. Your mama gave me work, and I saw you helping her. Now you lie to me! Why? Because you work for the cartelitos! Lying—that's what the Sinaloa teach you."

Pascual's eyes widened and he pointed a finger at Diego. "Renaldo will know if you say those things!"

"You going to tell him?"

The boy looked away. "No. But he will hear, somewhere. Because you talk a lot! You get on the glass chimney and you talk crazy, man."

"I stopped taking that drug. I am telling you this about the Sinaloa because I know you took their shit over the border, you carried it in a backpack. They ruin so many boys." He spat at the asphalt. "It's a sickness, Pascual. You should go to Father Campos and talk to him."

4

"You owe me five dollars," the boy said, compressing his lips, furrowing his forehead and pointing once more at Diego's face.

Diego slapped his hand away. "Go home to your mother, and stop trying to act like a gangster, boy."

Turning away, Diego finished filling his bag with cans, wondering if he could bring himself to face Vincent Bellator.

But was it him? Captain Bellator, the same man who killed all those white supremacists in D.C.? Wasn't he a wanted man?

Diego chewed on a knuckle. Part of him wanted to leave the area, to hide. Who knew what Captain Bellator wanted from him? Maybe he was loco, killing all those people. Bad people, sure, but... that *many*?

He had saved Captain Bellator's life once, when they were both in the Blue Barrel project in Iraq. And the captain had never forgotten. Vince Bellator had tried to help Diego, when he got sick from the dreams; when he went two weeks without sleeping.

Hijo de mil putas, Diego muttered.

What did Bellator want?

Diego decided that he had to know.

"So it's this guy Lopez?" Dutch asked, shifting in his seat. They were both crammed into the small chairs on either side of the Airstream's little fold-out table. "That who you're going after?"

"Angel Lopez? Yeah, he ordered the missile launch that killed my best friend," Bellator said. "Lopez was one of the executioners, and then became a lieutenant for the Zetas in the Veracruz state, down in Mexico. They killed hundreds of people, just to keep them quiet, and buried them in the desert." He picked up his coffee cup, drank a little, looked down into the swirling blackness in it and said, "They even killed young girls forced into their big sex parties. Because the governor of Veracruz was at the party."

5

"I read something about it," Dutch said, toying with a piece of plain donut. He grimaced. "Lot of bodies buried out in the desert."

"They killed twenty-seven journalists, too, over sixteen years. People just trying to do their jobs. They either disappeared or the bent cops said they were 'victims of a burglary gone bad'. Lopez got money from somewhere to start his own business—we're not sure where he got it, but we've got a suspicion. He set up his own system for refining and smuggling dope in the Yucatan. Called his outfit *Angeles Caidos*. The 'Fallen Angels'. Or just the Caidos. Things got too hot in Southern Mexico so he moved up around Nogales, and southern Arizona. Including this town. Seems like he's getting investment capital from outside the cartels..."

"There's a suspicion about that, you said. Who's Angel's angel?"

"You can't talk about it, if I tell you what we think..."

"When you say *we*—you mean Dierdre Corlin?"

Vince sighed. "I should never have told you about her."

"We friends, or not?"

"Yeah. We are."

"Does a guy talk about girls with his friends?"

"Not necessarily. And hey—she's not a girlfriend. She's a federal agent. I happen to know her."

"The tone in your voice when you first told me about her—"

"You're reading too much into that," Vince growled.

He saw Dutch suppress a smile. "Sure. Listen, about Lopez and his backers—I'm not going to tell anyone, anywhere, what you tell me."

"Not even your old lady?"

"Nope."

"On your honor as a soldier?"

"Yep."

Vince nodded. "It's just that—if a whisper got out on the internet, it'd alert them. They'd cover their tracks. And it could put certain people at risk." Like Dierdre.

Dutch gave a single nod. "I get that."

"Looks like it might be the Russians. Putin's intel people. Dierdre says Putin is obsessed with hamstringing America—gutting it, in time, so he can take it over. Interfering with the elections was just the beginning. He wants to undermine the country anyway he can. So he's established connections with the narco cartels. And basically—his agents started his own little cartel."

"It sounds like somebody's crazy theory to me," Dutch said.

"Yeah," Vince conceded. "So far it is. But money for Angel Lopez's enterprises came to a shell company from a bank in Brazil—a bank that's controlled by a Russian Oligarch. Who's close to Putin. And there's another thing—a guy believed to be a Russian agent has been spotted with Lopez, more than once. A businessman, supposedly an import-export guy. Calls himself Pavel Krupin."

"Sounds like your… *contact*… has been telling you a lot. You don't think you're pushing your luck, chasing this down, Vince?"

"Probably. What else is new?"

"After what happened in D.C.…" Dutch looked at the Desert Eagle, lying casually on the small table, next to the coffee carafe. "Sure, there's *talk* of your being pardoned." He sat back and spread his hands. "But killing all those terrorist assholes from a heli with a damned *machine gun,* for Chrissakes! Some people are saying 'laws are laws' and you broke a lot of 'em. Got me worried."

"Worried about hanging out with me?"

"Hell no!" Dutch looked offended. "Worried about your ass being dragged to some federal prison!"

"Okay, take it easy, buddy." Vince cleared his throat. "My legal status, I'm told… depends on what department you're talking about.

7

It's complicated. Behind the scenes, the DIA and the CIA are both in favor of a pardon. They don't cut their people off easily, especially not Delta Force. But some congressmen think I'm a loose cannon, and the new Attorney General's hung up on the politics of it all. The FBI is hemming and hawing but privately most of them are with me. The public seems to be on my side."

"Way I hear it, you're still a wanted man."

"Not that many people actively looking for me. But…" Vince shrugged. "I've got to lay low. Meanwhile, Dierdre's a liaison on the Lopez-Krupin connection, between the FBI and the spooks at the CIA—and she says they're very interested in what I find out. Only, they don't want me to take any action on what I find out."

Dutch snorted. "You? Like you would *act on your own*, unilaterally? *You?*" He laughed.

Vince gave him a crooked, rueful smile. "I will do just that, yeah. It's personal. You know about Chris. But when I was on a recon mission in the Yucatan…"

Dutch listened closely as Vince told him about the family he'd seen executed by Lopez's order.

"Angel Lopez has killed a lot of innocent people," Vince said, at last, pushing the carafe toward Dutch in case he wanted a refill. "But right there in front of me… those kids…" Vince picked up a paper napkin and balled it up tight in his hand.

"You opened up at the shooter—and then what?"

"Then…" Vince tossed the ball of paper across the little room, into a waste basket. "The Caidos chewed up the hill with about three hundred rounds from the Herstel and AKs. I barely got out of there with my hide intact. And I was way forward of my support team…"

"Your support," Dutch scoffed, seeming a little amused. "You really think of those private-army dweebs as that organized?"

"No. They weren't. Taking the job with Pro-Active Security was a big mistake—contrasted bigtime to the Rangers and Delta Force. I guess it was them interfacing with the CIA, the DEA, that made me go for it. What they really wanted, I think, was to get Perez in custody, make him turn on the Zetas." He shook his head. "It got to be three kinds of ugly working for PASI. Long story."

Dutch freshened his coffee from the carafe. "You think Lopez is here, in Santo Virgil?"

"He controls people operating out of a number of places. Seems to have a small mansion in South Tucson. But he's not there much. Hard to pin down where the guy is, at any one time."

"So—he makes his money with cocaine?"

"Crack cocaine, meth, fentanyl and heroin. And trafficking in human beings."

Dutch's eyes hardened. "Give me any chance to help you stop that guy—and I'm in."

"I don't want you on the firing line. But there's a thing or two you could do, without much risk…"

Renaldo Silvano was more than nervous to meet Angel Lopez in person.

Renaldo had been appointed as Lieutenant for the Caidos, in the Santo Virgil barrio, just two months ago, while Lopez was on a trip to Brazil. He'd been given the job by Jorge, the Columbian who did much of the boss's organizing. A guy Renaldo had done a lot of work for.

Renaldo was scared. But he did everything possible to hide his fear, to look confident but respectful, as he glanced at the clock over the cash register of the little corner store. Eleven-thirty a.m.

Any minute now…

Lopez's bodyguard came into the bodega first, to vet it for the boss.

9

The bodyguard was a broad-shouldered man in a sharply tailored cream-colored suit and gold rimmed sunglasses; but his most striking feature was the mane of glossy black curls falling thickly about his shoulders. His nickname was Rizado, Spanish for curly. His handsome face was clean shaven except for a little black soul patch.

Renaldo had met Curly Estrada before, and found him intimidating. Renaldo had Aztec ancestry, and he looked it. Curly was almost a foot taller than Renaldo, and had a face that women liked. Often fatally.

Renaldo had once tried to date a native girl from the Tohono reservation, but she said he had "a nose like an eagle's and a stomach like the eagle just ate a whole bear".

Curly's shades swept the two-aisle store. Then a customer started to come in—a young, acned waiter, wearing his greasy apron, from the taqueria across the street. Here for cigarettes, probably.

The bodyguard stepped in the waiter's path and pressed a forefinger into the center of the man's forehead, stopping him in his tracks. Then he gave a little push. The man staggered slightly, then turned and hurried from the store. Renaldo was glad he'd gone peacefully. When he needed to be, Curly was a *sicario*.

Curly turned to frown at him. "And your name?" he asked, in Spanish.

"Renaldo Silvano."

"You work the cash register yourself?"

"I own the place. But I sent my cashier out for lunch early. Because of the Jefe coming."

Curly gave a short approving nod. He went to the door to the backroom, moved the curtain, glanced through. No one back there.

Then he went to the door and murmured to another Caidos. Renaldo could only see the guy's arm and shadow.

Another minute of waiting and Angel Lopez strode in, gaunt but energetic. He had a Benson & Hedges cigarette in one hand, the other

10

hand in the pocket of his Gucci black leather horse-bit jacket—that jacket retailed, Renaldo knew, for around four grand American.

Angel looked slightly stoned, on something, to Renaldo. He wore small Gucci rose-colored glasses over his deep-set eyes; his sunken cheeks were neatly shaved, just enough to leave a little carefully shaped decorative fuzz. He had a Panama hat that went with his cream-colored Gucci Credoman pants. Nice black shoes—Renaldo thought they were Italian.

"Curly," Angel said, not even looking at Renaldo yet. "You check the backroom?" "Sure. No one."

"Because you know what happened to that whore-son Emilio. It was a place just like this."

"Sure. Guy hiding in the backroom. One shotgun shell. Boom, no face." Curly chuckled.

Renaldo had heard about it. The Sinaloa had been displeased with one of the Caidos for trying to hire a street woman away. So they killed him. Not only was Angel Lopez reluctant to get into a war with the Sinaloa, he had to apologize to them, though they'd killed his man. To save face he told people he'd said, *Hoy por ti, mañana por mí.* An old Latino saying: "'Today is for you, tomorrow for me."

He also claimed Emilio hadn't been following his orders. Unlikely. But he told the Sinaloa he'd have executed Emilio himself if they hadn't done it, for breaking turf rules.

So now Angel was looking for ways to show his strength again. He was going one by one to his lieutenants, like Renaldo, and throwing his weight around.

Now he pointed his cigarette at Renaldo. "You—you're selling here, or someplace else?"

Renaldo knew he didn't mean groceries. "We make contacts here. We sell it another place. 'The Plaza'. I am up to date, Jefe."

11

"I decide if you are up to date with me! Find an extra five hundred American dollars for me *right now*, in cash. Right fucking now!"

Renaldo was only a little startled. He'd half expected something like this.

He had an envelope in a drawer ready, just in case. It contained a thousand American. There was no graceful way to take only half of it out...

Renaldo simply said, "No problem, Jefe." He took the envelope out, took out the money, and put on a sad face. "I'm sorry, Jefe—I can't give you five hundred. Only a thousand." He handed it over.

For a moment he felt a chill, with the way Angel looked at him. Then came the grin, the flash of whitened teeth. Angel waved the money at him. "It's a good thing the joke you made had another five hundred for a punchline! I don't like people making fun of me!"

"*Never*, Jefe. I got too much respect for you to do that."

Renaldo was trying to show camaraderie, in a submissive way. But inside he was cold, because Angel Lopez had a reputation for killing people out of hand, when the whim took him.

The Jefe counted the hundred-dollar bills, peeled off three of them, and stuck them in the side pocket of Curly's jacket. "You—buy some better shoes."

Curly looked like he was a little offended, and about to defend his taste. But then Renaldo saw him relax. He had thought twice. "Thanks, Angel."

"What else can I do for you, Jefe," Renaldo said, keeping his voice even. "Anything in my power!"

"You can step up and show people we're not fucking around! I want you to find someone who's showing disrespect for me. I don't know who it is—I'm just hearing it happens sometimes! I want you to find someone like that, and I want you to kill them, just like you'd

12

shoot a rat in your yard. Just speaking disrespectful about me or the Caidos, that's enough. You do that, in your territory, and you let people know why. Right away! Every lieutenant is getting this order, and everybody better follow up, and pronto."

Renaldo said, without hesitation, "I will take care of it, Jefe. Pronto!"

But as Lopez and Curly left, Renaldo wondered just who he could find to kill.

Who in Santo Virgil would have the cojones, the huevos, the massive balls, to speak disrespectfully of Angel Lopez, or the Caidos?

Renaldo shook his head. He'd just have to find someone who needed killing and claim they'd said the wrong thing.

He sighed. It could be messy.

Chapter Two

The barrio in Santo Virgil was relatively small. A row of shops on Cesar Chavez Avenue, and fifty square blocks of neighborhood. There were Hispanic neighborhoods scattered throughout Southern Arizona. Most of them were economically stable. Some were even affluent. And there were many successful Latin businesspersons living in formerly white neighborhoods. But most of the houses in this barrio looked lower-middle class.

The poor are always with us, in any community, Vince thought, sitting beside Dutch as the semitruck rumbled down Chavez. The much-dented Airstream trailer he rented stood on blocks in a run-down trailer park chiefly occupied by underpaid white folks. That whole desert-adjacent part of Santo Virgil was a hodge-podge of crumbling adobe-style tract homes from the 1970s and trailer parks, mixed in with bars, liquor stores, and Dollar Discount outlets selling crap that cost a dollar though it wasn't worth ten cents. Vince had already noticed meth dealers in the trailer park; twitchy gap-toothed white guys, riding bicycles instead of the fancy cars of top dope dealers. He had persuaded himself not to wring their necks.

The barrio that the truck was driving through seemed, on the whole, tidier, more maintained than Vince's hood in Northeast Santo Virgil. There were some appealing restaurants—he hadn't had lunch yet—and there were beauty shops, manicurists, candy stores, botanicas, toy stores; there was a clinic, a bookstore, a bodega…

Was that Angel Lopez and his bodyguard in front of the bodega, walking to a brand-new Cadillac CD4?

But the semi kept rolling and a parked delivery truck blocked Vince's view. With a grind and whine of hydraulic brakes, the Kenworth pulled up at the red light.

Vince had the Desert Eagle holstered under his thigh-length brown leather jacket. He thought: *If that was Angel Lopez, I could jump out, run down there, shoot him and the other prick down, and split. Just get the hell out of Dodge.*

Maybe Vince would get away, maybe he wouldn't. But he'd have done what he'd come here to do.

But even if it was Lopez, he couldn't kill the guy, right now. Because of Dutch. Someone could see Vince get out of the truck. *"I saw the man who killed Senor Lopez and his friend! He got out of a truck driven by a red-haired guy and I wrote down the license number."* It could happen that way. Dutch would be arrested.

No, he had to be careful to keep this all on him, on Vincent Bellator, not on Dutch.

Vince looked into the right-side mirror. He could see the new Caddy pulling out into traffic. But only the driver, some Latino he didn't recognize, was visible.

"So where to now?" Dutch said.

Vince ran it all through his mind once more and sighed. "Turn right up here, Dutch. I'm going to a neighborhood where a friend of mine's been crashing. And I want to check out the scene there. I heard he'd been threatened…"

"Who you looking for, Vince?" Dutch asked, as he pulled the big rig over on a side street lined by small, ordinary houses, some of them with adobe fronts and flat roofs. There were children's toys tossed aside out front of the nearest house. It was early December and Christmas vacation hadn't started yet. The kids were at school. Except Pascual probably blew it off.

"There's a local boy who knows my friend," Vince answered, "And a lot of other people."

"You could've come out here in a taxi."

"I need the cover." He hooked a thumb at his shirt, which Dutch had given him—a utility shirt, tan, and somewhat too small for him, with *Becker Trucking* sewn across the breast. "You got somewhere to go?"

"No, I was just curious. You don't share a lot, bro."

"Safer for you that way. The kid lives on this block. Name's Pascual."

"How do you know this kid?"

"A friend of Dierdre's at the VA gave me the last known address of my friend—Diego Fernandez. This block. I asked around, nobody knew where he lives now. Except the kid said he saw him sometimes. Made me pay him to carry a message."

"Hustler already, huh?"

"Yep. And there he is."

Pascual was booking along the sidewalk, hands in his pockets, his hair slicked back, scowling as if daring someone to mess with him.

Vince smiled.

He opened the truck's passenger-side door—and froze, seeing a low-slung sedan screech up to the curb next to the kid. It parked crookedly as the kid backed away toward the houses and two men got out; one was a tall man in a tan leather jacket and cowboy hat; the other was shaped like a barrel and wearing a blue jean jacket and pants, and snakeskin shoes. Vince recognized them—Dierdre had sent him a DEA list of local Caidos gang operatives, via burner phone, including pictures. They stalked toward the boy. Pascual turned to run—and tripped over a little kid's scooter.

The tall one, the guy in the cowboy boots and cowboy hat, lifted Pascual up by the collar and shook him.

"Where you going, boy?" the man said in Spanish. "You've been sneaking out on us!"

Vince, striding toward them, had no problem understanding. He'd made a point of picking up as much Spanish as he could during his time working in Southern Mexico. He had one hand under his coat on the Desert Eagle. He didn't want to fire it—at this range the bullet could go right through his target and into one of the houses. He didn't even want to draw the gun unless he had to—that'd pull way too much attention his way.

Cowboy Hat lifted Pascual up by the neck and shook him like a rat. "You know a man who was talking shit about the Caidos. Where is he?"

"I don't know!" the boy said.

Cowboy Hat viciously back-handed the boy, splitting his lower lip. Blood trickled onto the boy's chin. "I said where is he!"

This was pissing Vince off.

"Let go of the kid," Vince said, striding up.

They turned, scowling. "Shoot this gringo if he gets in the way," Cowboy Hat said, in Spanish. Vince understood him quite well.

His uppercut caught Cowboy Hat on the point of the chin and pitched him backwards. His hat fell off as he lost his grip on Pascual who sprawled, dazed, to Vince's right; to his left the short-round guy

17

was pulling a gun as Vince swung to him, left hand closing over the man's gun hand, his right punching him the throat.

The short guy gagged and his finger must've contracted on the trigger of the gun still partly in his waist band—the gangster's gun went off, sending a bullet into his upper left thigh, shattering flesh and a bone.

Blood spurted and as Vince ripped the gun away the man cringed and went to his knees, making a thin shriek down in his windpipe. His throat was closed up pretty badly, he could barely breathe.

"Look out, gringo!" the boy shouted.

Vince turned in time to see Cowboy Hat sitting up, raising a gun.

But the gangster was in kicking range. Vince kicked out and struck the same bruised chin with a vicious upward kick. Vince felt the guy's jawbone crunch; felt it right through the tip of his hiking boot.

Cowboy hat slumped back, out cold, the gun clacking to the concrete. Pascual was up, swaying, staring open mouthed at Vince. Then he turned to run.

"Pascual!" a woman shouted as she trotted down the sidewalk toward them, her small red purse pendulating from her wrist. She was a short plump woman with pony-tailed black hair and large, lustrous, frightened brown eyes. She wore a pink waitress's uniform, its skirt going down to midthigh, and she wore white server shoes. There was an emblem of some restaurant franchise on the blouse's collar.

"Mama!" the boy shouted. He rushed toward her, yelling in Spanish, "We got to get out of here!"

The woman stared at the unconscious man and then at the other gangster—who was groaning and bleeding. And then her gaze swung to Vince. Her eyes widened when she saw the gangster's gun in his hand.

"I'm not with them, ma'am!" Vince said in Spanish. "I was trying to help Pascual!"

"They were beating me, Mama," the boy said. "He…" Pascual stared at the fallen men, then at Vince, with a sort of awe. He finished in English: "He kicked their asses."

"Oh no, Pascual!" She pulled the boy to her. Her expression told Vince she was angry at Pascual and deeply worried about him at once. "What did you do!"

"I didn't do anything—!"

Sirens were blaring from maybe a quarter mile away, if that far. "I was afraid they were going to seriously hurt him, Senora," Vince said. "I've seen that bunch…" He had seen them murder a family. He didn't want to tell her about that.

It occurred to him that maybe he'd stepped in too soon. He had no qualms about taking down drug cartelitos but maybe his timing had made things even worse for Pascual and his mother. He had picked up a little about them from his last visit to the barrio. Pascual's father had died during the pandemic. His grandparents were dead, too. Pascual's single mother was all he had. No one else to protect them. And now Pascual could be blamed for Vince's attack on the Caidos thugs, simply by association.

Vince realized he was still in the emotional sway of that PTSD vision—seeing a family mowed down by Angel and his thug Curly.

Now he was responsible for these two… and that was not PTSD. *It is how it is.*

He took a deep breath and said, "Look—let me help you, Senora…" The sirens were close. "Come along in the truck—there's room. I'll take you somewhere safe, both of you."

19

"We got to, Mama!" Pascual said. "They're going to look for me now! They'll blame me!"

"Can you trust the local cops?"

She winced and shook her head and said in English, "No, this is where Officer Fuentes runs things. He's a police sergeant working with the Caidos!"

"No reason you should trust me, ma'am, you don't know me, but if that's true about Fuentes, then you two'd better get in the truck."

"Come on, Mama!" Pascual said, tugging her by the wrist. "Fuentes will give us to the Caidos!"

She shook her head but let herself be tugged along to the truck.

"Ma'am, I'm Vince Bellator. That's Dutch driving. I've met Pascual—"

"Lupe Velasquez," she said breathlessly, looking down the street. "They are coming."

"Climb up in back!" called Dutch.

Vince lifted the boy in; he clambered in back, his mother squeezed in the bunk area beside him, muttering her doubts about this. "And where are we going? How do I know you are not... not..."

"We're *not*, ma'am, I swear on my life and in the name of Jesus," said Dutch, putting the truck in gear. "I guess we'll take you to Vince's place and from there we'll figure the safest place for you to go."

"What about Superro?" the boy said suddenly as Vince climbed into his seat and closed the door.

"Superro?" Vince asked. The truck was easing into the street. Around the corner. The sirens shrieked into the street they'd just quitted. Had the cops noticed the truck? Was it part of the report?

"For Super-Perro," his mother said. "Super Dog. Our chihuahua."

"Oh, *Superro*," Vince said. He smiled. "Sure! He's a legend! I'll

20

come back on my motorcycle for him. I've got a helmet completely covers my face. I can stash him in a backpack. Just give me the address."

Vince turned and looked at the boy, crammed in by his mother in the sleeping compartment "What did they ask you, Pascual?"

"They were trying to find Diego. Same as you were!"

"Not the same. I wasn't knocking you around, and I want to help him. I'm guessing they don't plan to do that."

"He's in trouble, he's been talking shit about the Caidos. Telling people they should go to the federal police. I heard him say it too."

"Pascual!" his mother said sharply. "Did you tell the Caidos what he said?"

"No! But I heard people talking about it."

"Did they hurt you?"

"A little. They scared me—but I could have handled them. I could tell them something. But then he came—" He pointed at Vince. "—and beat their asses. Now we're all in trouble!"

Vince looked back at the road. "Yeah. Seemed like they knew you and this Diego were acquaintances." He glanced into the passenger side mirror. Saw no police lights behind, no one following.

"Diego was a handy man. Used to be a carpenter. I would give him work. Sometimes I could only pay him with food, if I didn't have any money. He fixed up my place and we got to be friends... He used to take Pascual to the park... But then..."

Vince's phone rang.

The burner phone in his pants pocket had never rung before. He'd used it to call a special corresponding phone in D.C. Vince shrugged and answered. "Who's calling?"

"Hey, Vince." FBI Agent Dierdre Corlin's voice. "Who'd you think it was going to be? Anyone else have this number?"

"Nope. But someone could get it. Thought maybe the president was calling to tell me 'Fat chance' on the pardon."

"That your way of asking if there's any news on the pardon?" Dierdre said, a bit of a tease in her voice. "Because there isn't. Just rumors. Some rumors say yes, some say no. No one says, 'fat chance'. She's a new president, remember, she's not thinking pardons so much. Not quite a year in office."

"I thought we were supposed to call only one way, me to you?"

"That was your idea. I never signed on to that."

"I just thought it might…" *Might protect you.* But he didn't want to say that.

"No one's going to be listening, not on these burner things, Vince… Listen—I'm coming out there. There are complications on the whole Caidos investigation. We just got a bigger sense of what might be going on. We have someone who has some knowledge of Krupin. She's in southern Tucson. She got in touch but she won't give the information we need except for money and in person. I volunteered to go and interview her. So I'll be in the general area…"

Vince wondered if she had more than one motive in coming out to Santo Virgil. He hoped so.

Then he thought, *If she and I really got involved, I'd just get her dragged into something ruinous again. Her career barely survived the last time.*

She'd flown the heli as he'd fired the minigun from it; the machine gun he'd used to cut down scores of domestic terrorists. Sure, they'd saved hundreds of lives, stopping the Neo-Nazis in mid-attack on a big crowd. But he had no authorization whatever and she'd been acting without orders.

She was on working probationary status as the feds argued in back rooms about what to do with her case—she was still skating on thin ice. More association with him could wreck her career with finality.

But there was no way he was going to try to talk her out of coming here. He didn't know how much time he had left. His chances of survival weren't very high. If he could just see her again

"Okay, Dierdre. When you coming out here?"

"Day after tomorrow. Ten a.m. We'll talk by phone, figure where to meet. Meanwhile, you hear anything on the street about Pavel Krupin?"

"Not a word. All I know is what you already told me about him."

"You hear the name Lorvec?"

"Never. Another Russian?"

"Oh yeah. An enforcer associated with Krupin. DEA got a picture of Krupin meeting a guy at the airport. When we share his face with the CIA, they I.D. him as Boris Lorvec. His passport's good. We don't have the goods on him but he's believed to be a dangerous man."

Vince nodded. "I haven't found out much, Dierdre, except I heard from a guy on the block that Angel Lopez is throwing his weight around more than usual. Like he's trying to draw attention from something else, maybe. Why don't you just arrest the son of a bitch?"

"Lopez? He's actually got a legit work visa. Perez claims he came here to invest in local business. Convenience stores."

"Where would Angel Perez get a goddamn work visa?"

"Somebody got paid off, we assume. He's not officially wanted for anything in this country and in Mexico they only have hearsay. Or maybe they have more—but there's a lot of bent cops in Mexico. We have Lopez under observation when we can. He's slipped away from us more than once."

Vince snorted. "I had him under observation for about twenty seconds within the last half hour. I saw him in front of a bodega on Cesar Chavez, here in town. Situation prevented me from..." He didn't finish the explanation. But he didn't have to.

"You'd have killed him except for, what, possible collateral damage?"

"Essentially."

She sighed. "Vince. We asked you not to go after him that way. You can help us with intel. That'll help bring him down. You don't have to kill him."

"It'll take forever your way. And at the first sign of trouble Perez will go to ground. That's his pattern. If people are giving him work visas, here, then he could have strings on somebody in the State Department. And I don't think you ever found the guy that Gustafson was working with, there."

The line crackled for a few seconds. Then she said, "That's our bailiwick, not yours, Vince. We'll find him."

"How many people would have died at the Lincoln Memorial if I'd listen to the 'let us handle it' advice?"

"Oh, Vince. Now you're just being a... pain in the ass."

"What was the epithet you were going to use before you chose 'pain in the ass'?"

She chuckled. "Not telling. I'll call you. Develop your sources, Vince, and don't get all crazy on anyone."

"Yeah, well..." He cleared his throat. "I should tell you I just had a run-in with a couple of Caidos assholes."

"Oh Jesus. Are they still alive?"

"Yeah. No gunplay. But..."

"Hospitalized?"

"On their way there, yeah."

"And this was absolutely necessary, *why?*"

"You had to be there, Agent Corlin. They were beating up on a kid who—never mind. You guys know about a dirty cop named Fuentes, works the Chavez precinct here?"

"Oh sure, change the subject, Vince. Umm… Fuentes? Doesn't ring a bell. I'll look it up. Does he have form?"

"Don't know. Just heard Lopez has him in his pocket."

"Good to know. See? You can… wait, did you beat that information about the cop out of these guys?"

"No! came from a reliable informant."

"And who would that be?"

"Rather not say if I don't have to. He and his mom are in the truck with me and Dutch here."

"Okay, that's—wait, *what?* His *mom?*"

"Yeah. We're almost at my trailer. Listen, any word on your situation?"

"Justice Department's letting me work until there's a final decision. I have to keep a low profile. You could help me do that by keeping one yourself."

"You going to call me when you come in?"

"I will. Wednesday morning."

She ended the call and Vince wondered what would happen if, at the right moment, if there ever was a 'right moment', he actually made a pass at Dierdre. Would she say, "*Hell No?*"

That'd be the smart thing to say. And she's a smart woman.

Another five minutes grinding along, and then the truck pulled ponderously into the trailer park, Dutch steering with exquisite care. Vince had one of the bigger lots and there was just room for the truck and its trailer.

Dutch had told him he could stay in town for maybe five

days, then he had to pick up a truckload in Phoenix to take up to Seattle. From there he'd try to get a delivery back to the Southeast, and home.

"Dutch," Vince said, as the Kenworth ground to a halt in front of the silvery trailer, "you could find some place to store the trailer for a few days, make it easier to get around, and…" He broke off, seeing a haggard middle-aged guy wearing a cammie jacket sitting hunched over on the porch of the trailer. It took Vince a couple seconds to recognize him. Actually, he was only about forty. He only *looked* at least fifty-five.

It was Diego Juan Fernandez.

Vince climbed down from the truck cab. "Diego?"

Diego looked up, squinting—and then stood bolt upright. "Captain!" He began a salute then cut it short when he remembered they were both no longer in the Army.

They'd spent just four months working in Blue Barrell together; Green Berets supporting Delta Force inserts. Each man had impressed the other.

Vince walked up to Diego and stuck out his hand. Diego took Vince's hand. Vince could feel the trembling in them. "Good to see you, Diego."

They shook hands and dropped them and Diego said, "I heard you were looking for me. How come, Captain?"

"You can call me Vince, brother, we're not in the army anymore. I had two reasons to look for you—looking for two kinds of information. First, about you—I heard you weren't so well, so I went to see for myself. Second, I was hoping you might have some intel for me."

"You working for the spooks now?"

"Not exactly. Sometimes we exchange information. FBI too. But…"

"Oh I saw your face on a newspaper. You killed a bunch of terrorists." He shrugged. "Same old Cap Bellator."

Vince grinned. "I didn't want to get into anything, uh, extra-judicial like that. But they didn't give me much choice."

"That's what the president thinks about you." Diego showed his gap-toothed smile, and then self-consciously closed his mouth. "That you didn't have much choice."

"She does? You're more informed about me than I am."

"President says it's being talked over, still. What to do about you."

"She tell you about this, did she?"

"Ha! Naw, I saw it before I came over here. Read this morning's paper when I unwrapped some old cheese in the trash can." Diego grimaced. "That about sums me up now, Vince. The guy who eats dried out cheese from the trash."

"Sounds like a soldier out of rations scavenging in the field, to me. People throw away stuff that's still good. It's a damned shame."

"Pascual! Lupe!" Diego burst out, seeing them climb down from the truck. "How many other people in that truck?"

"Just me," Dutch said, coming around from the other side of the truck.

"Diego, how about this man?" Lupe asked, speaking in Spanish. She tilted her head toward Vince.

"Lupe, you can trust Vince Bellator," Diego said in English. "I'd trust him with my life, and I have—and he came through for me in Iraq. Put himself on the line for a lot of people. Even the locals liked him."

"Diego saved my life," Vince said. "I owe him—and I trust him too."

"You don't owe me nothin', Cap," Diego said, looking a little misty-eyed.

"Hey, Mr. Vincent, you going to get Superro?" Pascual

demanded, walking over to him like a supervisor checking up on a subordinate.

Vince grinned at him. "Yep! Dutch, you and Diego introduce yourselves," Vince said. "Everybody make yourselves at home. Pascual here's got me on a mission, Diego. I'm going to get Superro—and see if I can bring us all some lunch back too."

He went around the back of the trailer to his large backpack and Harley.

Lupe had given him the key to the little condo apartment. And it was easy to find the dog. But the dog wasn't so easy.

Superro the chihuahua snarled at him from under Pascual's bed, baring his fangs, his back up.

"Hey, Superro, man. Pascual sent me," Vince said. He was on his hands and knees, feeling ridiculous as he peered under the bed. His backpack was leaning on the bed, beside his opaque bike helmet. "We don't have time for this, pal! Cops going to be here if they're not already."

The little dog snarled in reply.

Vince tried whistling, making kissy noises, and putting out his hand gently so the dog could sniff at it. Superro tried to bite his finger.

Sighing, Vince put on his motorcycle gloves, reached under the bed, felt the bite on his right hand, used his left to grab the chihuahua. He dragged the little dog out as gently as he could. "Sorry Superro, I get you're just doing your job. You're going to go see your family now." He put the dog in the backpack, a tricky maneuver in itself, closed it but left the zipper partway open for air. The dog squirmed and barked as Vince put the pack and his motorcycle helmet on.

Vince went to Lupe's bedroom to get a few papers and a rosary she'd asked for. The dog squirmed and yipped and Vince said, "I'll let you out as soon as I can, pardner."

He was putting the papers into the inside pocket of his jacket when he heard the sound of a police radio from out front.

Had he locked the front door? He hadn't. And now there was a cop's knock on it. "Hello! Police! It's officer Fuentes!"

"Oh, great," Vince murmured. The one Pascual and Lupe had said was bent. Would he bother with a warrant? He'd pretend to have probable cause.

Vince went to the bedroom door, peered around the edge of the doorjamb. The hall opened onto the living room about thirty feet away. He could see a dark, uniformed cop with sergeant's stripes looking around, his cap in one hand, the other on his holstered gun. He was a stocky, heavy-browed guy with a handlebar mustache. Squinting, Vince could make out *FUENTES* on an I.D. tag below the badge.

The guy had his hand on his gun. If Vince ran down the hall, toward the back door and the alley, the cop might shoot him.

Vince pulled his head back into the bedroom and waited. The dog yipped and snarled.

"Hey, *perro!*" called Fuentes coming back. "*Hay alguien en casa*"

Vince listened to the heavy bootsteps as the cop came down the hall, following the dog's yipping. Vince flattened against the wall just inside the door, next to a small shrine to the Holy Virgin, as the cop stepped through, only to meet a powerful uppercut. Vince connected solidly and the cop was knocked off his feet, bounced off the hallway wall, and slid to the floor. Vince looked around the edge of the door. The guy was out cold.

Vince didn't feel good about it. Reportedly bent cop or not, he didn't like hitting law enforcement. He'd never had to do it before. He stepped over the cop's legs and strode to the back door, unlocked it, looked into the gravel alley behind the ranch-style two-apartment building—no cops out back. But he could hear another car pulling up in front of the place. Vince hurried to the motorcycle, climbed on, started it and rode quickly off to the right, down the alley to the next street. No one stopped him.

"Superro!" Pascual shouted as the dog leapt out of the backpack and into his arms.

"He almost took my hand off, boy!" said Vince, with mock severity, as he leaned the pack against the trailer.

Pascual laughed and kissed the dog. "He's a bad ass, that's why!"

"I got some food here in the saddle bags." Vince put the bike's saddle bags down. "Five Subway sandwiches, ten tamales. One gallon of orange juice. I hope nobody's a vegetarian, I didn't get that covered."

An hour later they were all seated in lawn chairs, some of them borrowed, in front of the Airstream. All except Dutch, who was taking a nap in the bed alcove behind his seat in the cab of the truck. Vince could hear him snoring from here. Dutch had gone short on sleep driving out to Arizona. Having eaten half of Pascual's sandwich, Superro was curled up in Lupe's lap, sound asleep.

"You're staying with an ex-girlfriend, Diego?" Lupe asked.

He gave a rueful shrug. "Ex, like from eight years ago. I sleep in her garage on a cot. She's in Narcotics Anonymous—I saw her at a meeting and we got to be friends again. She's got zero romance-type interest in me. She's putting me up 'cause it's part of the Twelve Steps to help me. You know?"

Lupe gave him a dimpled smile. "I don't know much about the Twelve Steps, but it sounds like God is taking care of you."

"How you getting by, Diego?" Vince asked. "She isn't feeding you, from what you said."

"I won't take anything like that from her. I did a little work for her, then I let her feed me a couple times. Otherwise, I get my own. Sometimes there's them food cards." Diego rubbed the raspy hair on his narrow chin. "I get a little SSI payment. Can't rent anything with it. Been looking for a job, Vince, but I don't think I come across like something they'd take a…" He broke off, narrowly watching a red sedan driving by.

"See someone in that car you know?" Vince murmured, careful not to stare after the car.

Diego hesitated then shook his head. "Don't think so. For a minute I thought it was… Nah. Thing is, Vince, on the way here I heard the Caidos are looking for me. Just because I was badmouthing them. Maybe it's just talk. Or maybe I shouldn't have showed my face here. But the boy gave me the message about Blue Barrel… Anyway…" He looked at the street again. The red sedan was gone. "Maybe I'm jumpy now."

Vince nodded. "You did right to come here, brother."

"How we going to get to go back home, mama?" Pascual asked.

"Oh, *Santa Maria*… We've got so little there," Lupe said. "Old junk furniture. TV doesn't work. Some clothes. Not much. Vince brought back your birth certificate and my naturalization papers. I got my I.D. with me. He even brought my rosary and my Bible. I have what I need. I have you and I have my bank account—not much in it, but it's something." She cleared her throat. "And Pascual, I have been so worried about you and the Caidos. You ran off and you broke the law for them. You could be in juvenile detention right now! So maybe this is God taking care of *us*, saying here is a way to get away from these people!"

"Oh, no, that's *mierda!* I got it covered, Mama, I use them they don't use me, I'm going to take care of you—"

"Don't use language like that and don't tell me you can control those people!"

"She's right about the gang, Pascual," Vince said, gently. "The control comes from the top in a narco cartel—always, and only. Once you're in their organization, they'll kill you if they think you have any, you know, *confusion* about who's in charge."

"Huh! What do *you* know about it!"

"I made it my business to learn about them. I fought them in Mexico and I learned. Anyway, what they do is not the work of a *man*. A *man* doesn't prey on weaker people."

"The captain's got that right, boy!" Diego said, slapping his knee.

Lupe nodded. "Yes. It's true."

Pascual shook his head stubbornly. "I could go to Sergeant Fuentes, explain to him. Those Caidos were looking for Diego. I will say I don't *know* where Diego is! I just got in their way and a crazy gringo got out of a truck and—"

"That is not going to work," Vince said firmly. "Trust the adults this time, Pascual. Fuentes would take you to Lopez to find out who I am. Two of their men hospitalized—they'd torture you to find out what you know."

"And where we supposed to go?"

"I think I know a place you could stay, for now," said Vince, his eyes fixed on the road into the trailer park. He was half expecting to see cops or gang punks roll in. "There's a veteran I met about a half-mile from here. The guy I rented this trailer from. He's looking to rent out a room in his house. You and your mom could stay there for a while and think about things, Pascual. Least you can do is give what your mom said some thought, you know?"

Pascual snorted and looked away.

Five men sat in a basement room. Angel Lopez sat on the sofa, Curly Estrada stood behind him, arms crossed over his chest; Curly watching the others carefully.

Pavel Krupin, Boris Lorvec, and Jim Greenwald sat on easy chairs across from Angel. Greenwald was droning away and gesticulating, going on and on about some ship.

It was a *luxurious* basement room. Plush carpeting, comfortable chairs, a sofa with a mahogany coffee table; a big screen television, a full bar with brass fittings, a refrigerator; small but well outfitted bathroom. From a reasonably high ceiling hung a small chandelier of translucent blue glass.

The big flat screen TV was showing a soccer game, Mexico versus Columbia. The sound was off, but Angel Lopez glanced at the game scores, caught some of the action, as he spoke. He had money on the Columbian team, *La Tricolor*.

But the men were not talking about soccer. They were casually discussing treason, and the money to be made from it.

The man Greenwald was talking forth in a very lengthy monotonous way, in English too. It was the only language they all spoke in common. Every so often Greenwald tried to make a little joke, hoping people would like him perhaps. Greenwald was a pale man in a cheap brown suit; he had a double chin, small blue eyes and thinning gray hair and if his hands weren't making dramatic gestures they were wringing. Angel was only tolerating him for the sake of Krupin, who was a man connected in a way that Lopez was not; and this Lorvec, who emanated the quiet confidence and unnerving watchfulness of a professional killer.

"So you see, this vessel is going to disrupt the body politic of

33

America, radically," Greenwald said. "It'll be a major step forward for Libertarianism! It'll create its own overlay, its own reality in media, and it'll have the best hackers available—now, *ha,* you'd be crazy—not that you're crazy, *ha!*—to not *ask,* how will we get away with this *thing* hanging around off the California *coast*? Good question—you didn't quite ask! Well, it'll be outside territorial waters, it'll be really well camouflaged as a cruise ship, and it's using a new technology to hide itself as the source of the transmissions. It's not something I can talk too *freely* about—"

"Very important to remember that," said Lorvec, in a low voice like the purring of a leopard. "That part about talking too freely." He was a thick-bodied man, almost bald, with a square face, a short neck, black eyes; he wore a gray Nike track suit under a matching Nike jacket. There was a gun under that jacket, Angel knew. Normally he would never allow a gun in here. But these men represented a network—an international presence that was far more powerful than the *Angeles Caidos*. The Caidos did not have their own fighter jets, their own bombers, spy satellites, and nuclear weapons. Which was, when he thought of it, too bad. Someday...

Greenwald cleared his throat. "Yes. Very important. Well, it's new tech, *ha,* is all I can say. But you can trust—"

"Stop," said Angel, noticing the wrong team had just made a goal in the game.

"What?" Greenwald said, blinking.

Angel raised a hand, palm outward, between him and Greenwald and turned to Krupin. "Pavel." He kept his voice smooth, polite. "You tell me. Why am I hearing about some ship? What money is there in this for me?"

Krupin shrugged. He was a compact man with dull blond hair,

in a neatly cut blue suit and red tie. He had wide cheekbones and behind his clear-rimmed glasses his eyes were the color of sea ice. "I was opposed to saying this much."

"He has said too much," Lorvec murmured.

Krupin nodded. "Boris is right…"

"*Boris!*" Curly chuckled. "A real Boris!"

Angel knew why Curly was mocking Lorvec. To try to show he was the stronger of the two. A "you don't measure up to me" hint from one enforcer to another.

Boris Lorvec gave Curly a look as focused and threatening as a laser aiming device. Angel could almost see a red dot on Curly's head. Curly returned the look. Laser for laser, but all done in cold gazes.

Krupin went on, "But Central thinks that you should know something of the stakes, Angel. Who controls this ship? Because you will have to see it, when we move it out… And later you'll have to supply it."

"Supply it?" Angel frowned. What was he, a dock hand?

"We cannot have Russian ships supplying it. It'll look better if it's ships with a Mexican flag, and Hispanic sailors. I know that Caidos has a small freighter. You use it to move drugs. It can be used to supply Cupid Cruise."

"Cupid Cruise?" Angel was not sure he'd heard right.

"Yes. That's the ship's name. It has a sort of romance theme cover. It's like *Love Island*."

"Ohhh, I like *Love Island!*" said Curly, rubbing his hands together.

"Jim Greenwald will be on the ship, you will interface with him to supply, and also for security purposes, so it's important you know him. His father is in the cruise ship business and Jim knows the vessels quite well."

"I worked on 'em for years, eventually retrofitted all the ship's computers," Greenwald started eagerly. "Then—"

"Stop!" Angel said, with the hand face-out again.

Greenwald snapped his mouth shut. Angel said, coldly, "Pavel, when you say, I supply, you think I'm going to go on some ship and pass boxes around? I never go on my ships."

"No, of course not, Angel!" Krupin smiled, took off his glasses, and began to polish them with a handkerchief. "You will give the orders. You will have men do it. They must be trusted men. And they must know as little as possible."

"I haven't heard how this pays me," Angel said.

"I wonder if you realize who you're—" Lorvec began.

It was Krupin's turn to hold a hand up for silence. "Boris!" He put his glasses back on, adjusted them minutely, and said, "We will transfer fifty million dollars American to your personal account when the first part is done. Fifty million when the second part is arranged—the supply chain. And it must be carried out, along with some other little favors we need, for the third and last fifty million."

"What is this first part?"

"We will need a major decoy event in the harbor at the port in Long Beach. There must be considerable death, and some explosions. Enough to bring all the resources of the Coast Guard in the area. This will be just as the *Cupid Cruise* is heading out to sea. You can set it all up by remote control, have your people quickly out of there. It is a decoy and also—Central wants us to create some… general domestic disturbances. We have our reasons."

"I don't care what your reasons are," Angel said impatiently. "This sounds complicated. And expensive."

"We will cover all costs."

"And what were these other favors?"

"I'll let you know." The man's arrogance was incredible. Angel had a sudden desire to kill him.

But he had no desire to fight the entire Russian intelligence service.

"Sure," he said. "You let me know."

Chapter Three

Agent Dierdre Corlin...

Vince glanced at the burner phone. No text from her; no call. But then, she'd said it'd be tomorrow. He still didn't know when she was coming into the airport, nor on what airline.

He was sitting astride the idling motorcycle outside the Airstream, waiting for Lupe to give Pascual the go-ahead to ride on the bike behind him. It was getting late, but he'd arranged with Hal Robbins, the guy who rented the trailer to him, to rent out space in his house to Lupe, Pascual and Diego. The old vet, a night owl, didn't care how late they showed up. The little silver trailer couldn't bunk more than one.

Dierdre...

He didn't want to get her involved unless he had to. She could end up in the line of fire between him and the Caidos.

But still... For the sake of Lupe and the kid and Hal and Diego, he had to bring her onboard.

He shook his head. But he called her number on the phone.

"You've reached Agent Dierdre Corlin, but I'm unable to answer right now. Leave a message. If it's Bureau business, call Agent Richard Chang at..."

Vince sighed. He waited for the beep and left a message to tell her roughly what had happened and where he was going.

Maybe it would be okay. No reason the Caidos should know Hal's place.

"My mom says I can ride the Harley with you!" Pascual said excitedly, waving the extra bike helmet.

It was an extra Vince had bought in case Dierdre wanted or needed to go on the bike with him. He resisted the word *fantasized* but he'd *visualized* her on the motorcycle with him, clasping him around the waist.

"Pascual, you keep that helmet on your head," Lupe told him firmly, striding up to them and pointing her finger at him. "Hold on to him tight!"

"I got this, mama!"

"Just do it!"

Pascual put the helmet on and climbed up behind Vince. Lupe watched with a frown.

"Hold on tight, kid!" Vince told him. The boy got his feet on the footrests and clasped Vince tightly around the waist.

Vince smiled at Lupe—then remembered she couldn't see him through the helmet. He waved instead, then gripped the handlebars and accelerated around the Kenworth big rig, as Lupe went over to get into the truck with Dutch and Diego. Vince put the bike in gear, circled around the truck and headed out, slowly at first. Dutch had the address and GPS. He and Diego and Lupe would get there a little after Vince.

The bike roaring and veering through the streets, the boy clinging to him, Vince found himself worrying about this billeting. His move against the gangbangers pushing the boy around had got Pascual and Lupe more in the line of fire than they'd been before. He felt responsible for them now and he had to find someplace safer than the trailer for them to be. But something was bothering him…

It was that red sedan that had driven by, catching Diego's eye. Vince knew Diego was trustworthy. If he'd been *sure* about the driver of that car, he'd have said something.

As Vince reached the little side street Hal lived on, Vince slowed the Harley and stopped at the corner, half a block away from the house. It was an ordinary, fairly quiet side-street.

"Are we there?" Pascual asked.

"Not quite. Almost. I'm just reconning."

The kid said nothing. He knew what Vince meant.

Vince scanned the dead-end block. They were a couple weeks out from Christmas but there were already strings of Christmas lights, blue and green and red, blinking on the dead-end street. A diagonally striped red and white barrier blocked the end of the street. Beyond the dead end was a weedy vacant lot between an old out-of-commission gas station and a closed red-brick automotive repair place. He saw no one on the other side of the dead-end barrier.

Hal's place, an adobe style one-story, was at the very end of the block on the left. His old blue and white Ford pick-up was parked in the short driveway, sticking partway across the sidewalk. In front of the houses across the street from it were a ragtop Jeep, a blue Toyota SUV and a yellow panel truck. No red sedans. There was a beat-up matte-black 1980 Mustang GTO in the driveway of an old wooden house.

Vince didn't see anyone sitting in a car; no one seemed hidden in a doorway or staring out a window.

The roofs? Oh yes, Vince checked the roofs too. Knowing that it was half paranoia; that a man like him, with his combat history, walked a fine line between alertness and PTSD obsession. But today there was a genuine ongoing high-risk situation. With him was Diego

Fernandez, a guy the Caidos cartel was looking for. Just because he dissed them sometimes, and some *Jefe* was trying to prove something. And caught in the same trap with Diego was Pascual Vasquez and his mother Lupe.

There was something else. For weeks, Vince had been quietly asking questions around town about Angel Lopez. Had someone reported that? Could someone have figured out the identity of this overly inquisitive, bearded guy in the Arizona Wildcats ball cap?

Still, the dilemma. Was all this paranoia or peril? A hunch told him to be extra careful right now, and right here. But he knew some of it could be driven by the charge carried by lots of long-time combat veterans. Would he be seeing things that weren't there, next?

Bored, Pascual kicked at the sides of the motorcycle with his heels.

"Don't kick the Harley, Pascual," Vince said distractedly.

He glanced at the roofs again and wondered what he'd do if there was a shooter up there. He had two weapons with him—a Desert Eagle under his jacket and a Glock .45 handgun in a saddle bag. Neither weapon was ideal for shooting people off roofs.

One thing at a time.

Vince took a deep breath and centered himself; then, inwardly, he stepped back from the hard edge of his alertness, and simply checked out Hal's place. A rectangular front window released the twitching light from a television screen over a brick porch. Waist-high cacti seemed to strike poses in the otherwise barren front yard. A junk female mannequin, wearing a Santa cap and a polka-dot bathing suit was lolling on a basket chair on the porch, waving with one chipped hand; the other hand was missing.

"That's the house over there, Pascual," Vince said, as Dutch's truck rolled around the corner behind them. "Last on the left."

"How come that dummy thing is on the porch?"

41

"That's Hal's idea of a Christmas decoration."

A white van pulled onto the street; Vince couldn't see the driver as it went by. He saw *Special Needs Services, City of Santo Virgil*, neatly painted in red on the side. A notification about not passing it while it was picking people up was blocking its back window. It sat there, probably calling in for whoever it was picking up. Waiting for them.

A beer-bellied man with a scraggly beard came out onto a porch to Vince's right, beer can in one hand, staring at Vince and the boy with rank suspicion.

"Can I help ya'll?" he asked, not sounding like he wanted to help.

"We're good," Vince said. "Just waiting for our friends in a big ol' truck coming up."

He heard the rumble of Dutch's truck pulling onto the street. Its brakes squeaked as it pulled up beside him. The Kenworth semi sat there with its massive engine idling, sounding like a large panting animal. Vince waved at Lupe, who was looking at them from the passenger window. She rolled the window down. "Is everything okay?"

Vince grinned. "Pascual rides like a real pro. Hey Dutch!"

Dutch leaned over the steering wheel to look past Lupe. "Yeah?"

"Give me one minute to talk to Hal and then drive that monster on up."

"Gotcha!"

Vince put the bike in gear and rode it past the idling semi-truck, up to Hal's house.

An aged black man, with a modest white afro and short white beard, came out on the porch and nodded at Vince as the bike pulled up into the driveway behind the parked 1970s vintage Ford pickup.

Hal wore gray sweatpants and a sleeveless tee shirt. In his right hand was a drink—rum and coke, most likely. On his right bicep was the faded tattoo of a crowing rooster he had gotten in Saigon, back in the early 1970s. On his right forearm was a US Marine Corp symbol, blurred with age. From the house came the sound of some old baseball game replaying on ESPN.

"How you doing, soldier?" Hal called, as Vince took his helmet off.

"It's kinda fugazi, sarge," Vince said, as he and Pascual got off the bike. "I'm okay but we got us a Charlie Foxtrot." Vince knew Hal liked old military slang. A Charlie Foxtrot was a clusterfuck of a situation. "Need billeting for these people. I can pay you cash in advance. Way past what you're asking. I brought another ex-sergeant along."

Hal looked at Pascual and raised his eyebrows. "Kid looks a little young for a sergeant! But anything is possible in today's military."

Vince chuckled. "Not him, smartass. Diego Fernandez, coming with the boy's mother in that truck."

"What is this, a goddamn VA support group? Where'd this Fernandez serve?"

"Served with me in Iraq. Watched my six. Saved my ass."

"Rangers?"

"Nope, he was special assignment from Green Berets."

"Those fuckers can be loony. He gonna be okay?"

"Yeah. Don't offer him a drink though, he's in NA and AA."

Hal nodded, understanding perfectly. Covering his mouth as he coughed, he watched Dutch's truck pull up now. "You delivering me a new couch? I need one!"

"I'm delivering roommates."

Police Sergeant Fuentes watched on his laptop as Diego Fernandez got down from the cab of the parked semitruck.

Fuentes was sitting in the back of the Special Needs van, parked across the street and down a few houses, watching via a hidden camera in a side mirror. He rubbed his sore, swollen chin, almost broken by the punch from the big man in the helmet. Fuentes wasn't in uniform, because he was off-duty and this little job, for which he was to be paid ten thousand dollars, was not something he wanted associated with the police department, in case someone spotted the van as the town police department's only undercover surveillance vehicle. He had been planning to take the van over to Lupe Velasquez's house to watch for her and the kid. On the way he got the call from Renaldo…

He watched as Diego turned and helped Lupe climb down. The red-haired driver got out on the other side.

Renaldo had been looking for Diego Fernandez. One of his men had spotted him in a trailer park; set up a watch and followed him here. He had called Renaldo, who had called Fuentes.

Fuentes had heard about Diego Fernandez through Renaldo. "Someone's got to die, may as well be that waste of air," Renaldo had said. But there was this other factor, the big guy on the motorcycle. "*El Gran Extrano*"—The Big Stranger—as the gang now called the man. The *cabron* who'd put two of the Caidos in the hospital earlier today; a *gabacho* who was otherwise unidentified. Fuentes figured the man before him now was the same one who'd sucker-punched him, knocked him out or as close to out as mattered, at Lupe Vasquez's place.

This *Gran Extrano* definitely had to go down. Maybe, after all, it would be best to call it in, make up some story, get a passel of police out here. He could get the big guy to surrender, take him in personally, deal with him in the cell. Arrange for him to "commit suicide" in custody.

No. Too many ways people could get curious. Ask too many questions. He was the only police officer in Santo Virgil getting paid by the cartel, as far as he knew. He couldn't take the chance that Chief Skanson would figure it out.

Best let Angel deal with this *Gran Extrano*, and the others. Make it look like a gang hit.

Fuentes got out his special cell phone and made the call.

"Angel?" He went on in Spanish: "The man who sent your men to the hospital, and this Diego Fernandez, who talks shit about you… I know where they are. One of my men saw them, and he set up a watch. Followed them here."

"Who was the man who attacked my people?" Angel asked.

"No identification on him yet. Seemed to have commando moves— that's what Shaker said. Maybe ex-military. Big man. Bearded. Brown leather jacket."

"That is not information. That is shit. I want to know who he is. Maybe when you kill him, you'll find I.D. on the body."

"I can't do that myself, Angel."

"What do we pay you for?" said Angel. "Take care of it."

"Some things I can do for you, some things I can't, not without getting caught. You need me in the job. Send your men. We can blame it on the Sinaloas. I can keep police response from coming right away, I can decoy them till your people get the job done and leave."

There was a silence on the line for about fifteen seconds. It made Fuentes nervous.

Then Angel said, "You make sure no cops show up when we do this. What's the address?"

"You dogfaces don't know how to do a disassemble on basic ordnance no more, is what I heard," said Hal, pointing a finger at Diego. "Now, a Stoner 63, damned good UCW, you wouldn't know what to do with it—"

"You 'Nam jarheads can't handle modern ordnance at all!" Diego retorted.

Jarheads and dogfaces. Marines and Army.

Vince had ordered pizza, and a few minutes past eight-thirty p.m. they were sitting around Hal's living room, talking. All except for Dutch who was sitting on the front steps, talking to his wife on a cell phone.

Pascual was sitting on an old leather-topped footstool, frowning, seeming deep in thought as he fed bits of pizza crust to Superro. Vince sat on a kitchen chair, reversed so he could lean his folded arms on the back. Beer can in hand, Hal was lounging in a patched old La-Z-Boy by the disused old brass-fitted fireplace. He had tubes running from his nostrils to a small oxygen tank leaning up against the chair. Had to use oxygen supplementation sometimes. COPD. Chronic Obstructive Pulmonary Disease.

Diego and Lupe sat on opposite ends of the cracked leather sofa. Talking heads commentary on the ballgame was on a screen in a corner but the sound was turned low, an unintelligible singsong murmur in the background.

"The trouble with dogfaces," said Hal, "is they spend so much time hunkered down like scared kittens they get mud in the chamber of their weapons. Now a Marine…"

Hal started coughing. Diego waited respectfully for him to get it under control.

Vince smiled to himself. Every veteran's group included some bantering and name-calling between the services. All of it lighthearted. Every service was respected—but that didn't mean you couldn't make fun of it.

Sometimes Vince missed being in the military. You knew where you stood, in the Army. You went where you were sent. As a captain he'd had responsibilities, but the big decisions came down the chain of command.

Now he had to make decisions alone. He had started on a course he felt he had to pursue to the end. But the risks weren't just to himself alone, or to soldiers. Now there was a group of civilians around him he felt responsible for. And, for god's sake, their little dog too. Were they really safe here, at Hal's?

He'd paid for a month's rent, paid triple what Hal was asking, because of the risks to the old marine. It wasn't a big financial burden for Vince. Between what he'd saved over the years, what he'd inherited from Uncle Jack Sullivan (not really his uncle, but he'd always thought of him that way) and his pay for working at Pro-Active, he had about $650,000 in the bank.

He wasn't worried about the rent money. He was worried about people's lives.

Chances were, he'd see Dierdre tomorrow. Another responsibility.

But she had the power of the FBI behind her. Or did she? Wasn't she always on the edge of being fired from the Bureau, after what had happened at the Lincoln Memorial, in D.C.? How much back-up were the feds likely to give her?

Vince shook his head. He should try to keep her clear of whatever his next move was.

He knew that Diego, Lupe and Pascual weren't truly safe anywhere in Santo Virgil. It would be best to get them out of town, but Fuentes would have the police looking for them right now. They could be caught on the freeway, or at a bus station on some excuse contrived by Fuentes, and dragged to jail in Santo Virgil. Vince was thinking he might use an offensive action to draw the Caidos away from Diego and Lupe and her son. Give them a safer shot at getting out of town. If they could keep their heads down for a week or so, here...

He needed a confab with Diego, see if he'd picked up anything useful about Angel Lopez. He'd planned to help Diego with his PTSD; see if it could give him another step up toward staying off drugs and drinking and living on the street. He was going to offer Diego a gun, too, because of the Caidos threat, and it was important to know he was sane enough to use it.

Talk in the room had turned to Lupe and Pascual, Hal asking her, "So, you're a waitress?"

"Was. Probably will be again. But I don't think I can go back to the place I was working at now."

Hal nodded. Vince had told Hal about their trouble with the Caidos. He'd half expected Hal to back out of the rental, on hearing that. But he'd seemed more intrigued than worried.

"Maybe it's not safe for you, if we stay here?" she said, looking worriedly at Hal.

"I hate those sons of…" Hal cleared his throat. "Anyhow, you can stay here for now and keep a low profile." He coughed, covering his mouth. "I don't see how they'd know you were here. Anyhow, we'll figure it out."

"God bless you, Mr. Robbins," she said, her eyes misting.

"Must be hard for you," Diego said. "Losing your apartment. Your job. Rootless like this all of a sudden. I'm sorry, Lupe. This is 'cause of me. I ran my mouth."

She shook her head. "It's not your fault what these cartelitos do. In a way, it's not their fault either. I just want to go someplace else. I can always find another restaurant job. Maybe in a little while when they stop looking for us. Then, like Vincent said, Pascual and I can slip away."

"And Superro," the boy said, flicking the Chihuahua a piece of crust.

The dog ate the crust then stared into space, before running behind the sofa to vomit. Hal sighed but said nothing.

"Yes, and Superro," she said at last, looking dreamily at the TV. "My father was a great cook, in Guadalajara. He had his own place. Three stars in the Michelin guide. He studied in Paris! He knew cuisine! French, Spanish, Mexican, Guatemalan, Brazilian."

48

"*Mi abuelo* taught my mom to cook," Pascual said.

"I could never raise the money to start my own place," Lupe said. "But… maybe someday…"

Pascual shrugged. "That's what I was trying to do, when I took that job on the border, to get the money for—"

"I don't want their money!" Lupe said sharply. "They killed my father because he wouldn't pay them off! We had to leave Mexico!"

"That was the Zetas, Mama, not the—"

"Narcos are narcos! Cartelitos are cartelitos!" She jabbed a finger at him and said, in Spanish, "Go clean up the dog's throw-up! Get a sponge and paper towel and do it! Now!"

Muttering to himself, Pascual sulkily went to the kitchen.

Dutch came in then. "Hey Vince? I'm gonna move the truck out of here, it's blocking part of the street. You got your chopper—anybody else need a ride out of here?"

"No, they're staying on here, Dutch. I got your number. You get an 'unknown number' calling it's probably my burner phone."

Dutch nodded. "It's gonna take me a few minutes to get that rig turned around on this street… gotta back to the corner…" He waved at the others and went out to his truck.

"Diego, need to talk to you in your billet," Vince said, standing up.

"Sure thing, Captain," Diego said, standing.

"I got stuff I want to talk about too," said Pascual, coming back from the kitchen with a sponge in his hand.

"Like what?" Vince asked.

"Like plans and shit."

"Pascual!" his mother said, wincing.

"We'll make plans later," Vince told him. "Right now, I need to talk to Diego privately."

Vince led Diego down the short hall and into the room he'd rented from Hal. Diego was quartered in a small bedroom overlooking the alley, furnished with only a rickety folding metal chair and a queen-sized bed, its lumpy mattress covered by a single sheet and a green Army Surplus blanket. The bed was shoved up to one side of a window that looked out on the darkened, gravelly back alley running behind the houses.

"Dogface, he calls me," Diego remarked, looking at the bed. "But I notice he buys blankets at Army Surplus."

"Last I looked there wasn't a Marine Corps Surplus," Vince said, sitting on the chair. It creaked warningly at his weight, but grudgingly held.

Diego sat on the bed. "Captain, you never told me why you wanted to get in touch with me."

Vince shifted his weight on the uncomfortable chair, which groaned in response. "Couple reasons. First, I heard you needed some back-up. I mean, in general. Before this mess with the Caidos. Second, I was just wondering if you had any intel on these pricks. Angel Lopez and his knuckleheads."

"You working with the feds?"

"Halfway. But my mission is my own."

"Like what you did with those Nazi pricks back east?"

"Something like that."

Diego grunted, and gave a single nod. "Risky mission, Cap. The *Angeles Caidos* are at least as dangerous as ISIS, and more than any redneck racists." He scratched at his groin, seemed to realize he was doing it, and stopped. "You heard about Fuentes?"

Vince nodded. "Oh yeah."

"How about *Rancho de los Santos*?"

"Nope. Ranch of the Saints?"

"Yeah. Big spread on a basin a little east of the Sedonas. I had a buddy worked there for a while. They were paying people in money and meth. He decided he had to get clean so he left. Big factory for making crystal meth and cutting Chinese Fentanyl."

"It's Angel's operation?"

"That's what my buddy said. Angel's there sometimes. Mostly a guy they just call Jorge runs it. Some Columbian *hijo de puta*."

Vince nodded. *Rancho de los Santos. Jorge.* Very interesting indeed. "Your friend still in the area?"

"Last I knew. In a place called Stapp about twelve miles from Rancho de los Santos. Don't have his address but it's a small town. His name's Soren Lenger."

"You hear anything else could help me?"

Diego shrugged. "Renaldo Silvano's the boss for the barrio around here. He's got a little grocery store… *Renno*'s, he calls it… on Cesar Chavez. He's the one seems-like sent the *pendejos* around that went after Pascual."

"Hear anything about any Russians connected to the gang?"

Diego's eyes widened. "Russians! Hell no!"

"Okay. Forget I said it. So, Diego… You got a gun, or not?"

"Nope."

"Do they trigger you?"

"Is that a, what you call it, a *pun?*"

"No. You know what I mean."

"Yeah, I do, Cap. Naw, it's not the guns set me off. I just got some bad memories. Mostly still back to that one thing." He closed his eyes and clenched his hands. "Stanny getting his lower half blown off and he's crawling up to me… and begging me to shoot him…"

And you shot him, Vince thought. *Which you had to do, in that place and time. And that was the worst part.*

"Okay, Diego," Vince took the Glock from his coat. "It's loaded, safety set, nine .45 rounds in this piece. If you're okay to have it—and to use it if you need to—take the Glock, just set it down over there on the bed next to you. It's yours long as you need it. I've got another box of shells in my saddle bag for you."

He offered the pistol butt-first to Diego, who reached for it with a trembling hand. But when he took it, his hand steadied. He hefted it, nodded to himself, and put it beside him on the bed. "Anything else, captain?"

"You remember in Bagdad, when I taught you how to move your attention around in your body, and in your mind?"

"That meditation you got from the Sufi guy in Samarra? Sure. I try it sometimes. Hard to concentrate."

"The concentration you need gets built up as you keep doing it. Every morning, half an hour working on it. Do it every free minute, until you've got it. Diego, brother—it's the only thing that's kept me from melting down. I can't control nightmares, but I can control where my mind goes when I'm awake, when the flashbacks come. I learned I could move my attention at will. I didn't have to keep it centered in the flashback, the fear, the rage, whatever it is I'm dealing with. You can learn to see the feeling, the image, from another place, a more centered place, so you're not *in* the state that was fucking with you, you're just looking at it. You objectify it, so it loses its power over you."

Diego was listening closely, his head cocked to one side. He probably remembered most of it from the time Vince had coached him back in Iraq. Maybe Diego hadn't acted on it enough. But he knew it was a lifeline back to a home; back to sanity.

Vince took a breath and went on, "You do that enough times, the flashbacks come less and less. You can stay centered, like that, and go on with what you need to do. Now sit up straight, like this, and center your mind in the present moment. Nothing but the present moment, keep bringing your mind back to it. Just *now*… and now… and now."

They sat together, trying to stay in the present moment, for a few minutes. Then Vince said, "Now turn your attention to take in the tension in your muscles, just see the tension in your mind's eye, and allow your muscles to relax as much as possible. Then, staying in the present, you start moving your attention around in your body, like I taught you before. You feel the inside of your right arm, sense it from inside. Just the sensation, the whole feeling of it."

They continued for almost twenty minutes. He was starting to feel better, feel his muscles relax.

And then the bedroom window exploded inward.

Chapter Four

Before the shattered glass finished spinning and jingling across the room, both combat-conditioned men flattened themselves on the floor, Diego grabbing the Glock on the way. Vince had drawn the Desert Eagle.

"Nice way to end a meditation," Diego said, his voice shaking a little. *"Hijueputa Caidos pendejos."*

Vince saw him flick the Glock's safety off and lift himself up enough to fire out the window.

Vince growled, "Don't fire out that window, Diego."

Diego flattened down and looked questioningly at him.

"Not till you've got a good target with no one's house behind it," Vince went on. "Those rounds can go through back windows in those houses over there. Check your fire. Civilians in houses all around us. Anyhow you'd be framed in that window."

There were shouts from the front room, but Vince couldn't hear what they were saying. The dog was barking shrilly.

Then he heard Hal yelling. "Just keep down! I'm turning off the lights!"

Glad that Hal had thought to turn off the lights in the living room, Vince wondered if anyone was hit. And if Lupe was calling the cops. It would be like calling her enemies to help her, with Fuentes a local police bigshot. It didn't matter—the neighbors would be dialing 911 by now.

Another shot cracked through the empty window and smacked into the wall behind them. Plaster dust spurted.

"Not sure what to do if I can't fire the weapon, Vince," Diego said.

"We just have to pick our targets carefully, and get our people out of here," Vince said, knowing what Diego must be thinking: *But how do we get them out?*

Vince didn't have the answer. More shots came from the street in front of the house. The dog was barking but he couldn't hear much else. Had someone been hit? He hoped the gunmen didn't find his Harley—and then he mocked himself silently. He'd become absurdly attached to that vintage bike. But he was glad he'd moved it, hiding it around the side of the house by the dead end.

A heavy rifle round shattered the window sash. Splinters flew, and Vince felt a stinging on his forehead. "Diego, crawl into the hall, get down in a crouch, check on the living room without exposing yourself." After a moment he added, "If you think it's a good idea. I'm not your C.O."

"Closest I've got to one, Captain," Diego said, crawling to the hall.

Another shot punched through the wall, low down, the bullet zipping past his left shoulder and chunking into the wall behind him—the house was only superficially adobe.

Vince was tugging his burner phone out as he crawled backwards and then turned toward the hall. He had Dutch's number memorized and tapped it in. "That you, Vince?" came Dutch's voice, while two more shots slammed into the room, punching into the bedroom wall by the door.

Still crawling, Vince asked, "You nearby?"

"Had to go six blocks to find a space for the truck. What's up?"

"I've got a big ask, man. We're under attack here."

"What about the cops?"

"Not coming. Someone must've followed us here."

"So that *was* gunshots I heard! I'll be right there!"

"No, don't do that. Not yet. Get close, then turn so you're a few blocks away from here, head north, get to the street on the other side of the tracks from the dead end." He gave him the rest of the plan quick as he could, always keeping an eye on the window in case someone stuck a gun through.

Crawling toward the hallway, it struck Vince that the attack seemed to have stalled. Why? Then he heard voices whispering in Spanish close outside. *"Prenderle fuego!"*

Set it on fire.

Vince stood up in the hall, turned back to the bedroom door and just out of view he shouted at the top of his lungs toward the window, "*Fuego? Tienes pelotuda, cobardes!* Come and get some!" Then he got into a crouch, looked across the room through the lower-right corner of the smashed window, and saw a guy in a hoodie, running up with a Molotov cocktail, fire trailing from a half-gallon bottle; the guttering flame washed the gang-tattooed side of the guy's face with a red light. The gangster's arm was cocked; the firebomb lifted to throw.

Vince stepped out for the angle, fired the Desert Eagle at the bottle. He had to stop the Molotov cocktail right where it was. An easy shot; the gas-bomb exploded with a *whuff* over the guy's head, covering the Caidos thug with burning gasoline. The man screamed and slapped at himself as the blue and yellow flames spread over him. Vince felt a twinge of pity. Just a twinge.

He shot the guy in the right leg, the shot knocking the gangster off his pins, the fire still spreading. The shrieking, dying man would keep his pals distracted and busy for a while.

A short burst of bullets slashed through the window from some-where in the alley, one of them lightly cutting the left side of his face and spitting dust from bullet holes in the wall. Vince jerked back, thinking the clipped report of the gun and the spread of the burst suggested he'd nearly gotten his face shot off by a MAC-10. He turned to go down the hall toward the front door as more bullets cracked through behind him.

The man burning, lying on the ground with the wrecked leg, was still screaming.

Vince heard no sirens. Which was strange.

Fuentes. The bent cop must have called off the local officers. Might have someone in the dispatch center, dealing with that for him too.

At the end of the little passage he flattened against the wall and looked into the living room.

In the thin, indirect light from the street, Vince could see Hal, crouching with a 12-gauge shotgun in his hands just inside the front door. He had his oxygen bottle beside him in its little wheeled case, the tubes still in his nose. Lupe and Pascual were flattened, apparently unhurt, on the floor by the fireplace; the boy clutching his yapping, frightened dog.

Lupe was shouting into her cell phone. "I don't care what the local police say—send the county sheriff deputies! Hello! Oh, *Madre de Dios* she hung up again!"

Diego crouched by a short hallway leading to the back door, watching the alley. There was broken glass on the floor in front of the door.

Hal was wheezing as he reached for the front door knob.

"Better not open that yet, Hal," Vince said. "Anyone hit?"

"No, we're just scared to death, Vincent!" Lupe snapped. "I trusted you to find us a safe place!"

"Yes ma'am. I'm sorry." There was no time for anything else.

He heard gangbangers out back, talking in Spanish, back and forth, muttering about how to get into the house.

"Vince," Diego said, "I think they're about to make their move."

"Yeah, sounds like it." Vince turned to Hal. "Listen Hal, can you ride behind me on the bike if I was to—"

"I'm not abandoning my house!" Hal interrupted. He coughed and added, "My house, my truck, my trailer—I'm willing it all to my grandson. It could help him and I'm not going to let them fuck my property up any more than they have!"

Vince was stymied. How could he save Hal if the old marine wouldn't leave? "Your grandson won't want you to die, Hal. I've got a plan to get us all out of here. I could take you in a fireman's carry—"

"The hell you will!"

"Vince, *they're coming!*" Diego shouted.

"Check your fire, then hit 'em square, Diego!" Vince shouted, hurriedly slapping a fresh clip into his Desert Eagle. He set himself, readying to rush to the window on the street and pick a target.

Diego fired the Glock; bullets cracked through the front door from across the street, one of them clanging off a hinge, knocking the door akilter in the frame.

"You sons of bitches!" Hal shouted. He pulled the tubes from his nose, jerked the door open—

"Hal, no!" Vince shouted.

"Come on, you shit eating cowards!" Hal shouted as he ran out on the porch, shotgun butt tucked into the hollow of his shoulder. *"Deal with a leatherneck!"*

Vince got into the doorway in time to see a hooded gunman pop up behind the Ford pickup truck, pointing a MAC-10 machine pistol at Hal—and the old Marine fired, the shotgun blast catching the gangbanger in the breastbone, blowing a bone-shattering hole through him where the sternum met the clavicle, knocking him backwards. *"Stay away from my truck you shit-heads!"* Hal yelled hoarsely.

A muzzle flash, across the street between houses, gave Vince a target, and he squeezed off a round from the Desert Eagle that brought a scream from the shadows. A rattle of a small submachine gun, the bullets smashing out the windows of parked cars, and thwacking into the adobe wall to Vince's left. Hal was staggering across the street, coughing, pumping the shotgun and firing at another muzzle flash. He stumbled then, hit by a burst from a MAC-10, but the man he'd shot fell thrashing across the sidewalk.

Hal straightened up and kept going, pumping another shell into the shotgun's chamber. *"Come on you cowards! Attack women and children and scared of an old man! Come on!"*

"Hal!" Vince shouted, sprinting across the street. "Good kill, sergeant, now get down—let me deal with this—"

But the shotgun roared again, another man yelled, and then two muzzle flashes from between the houses strobed red, and Hal torqued, jerking with the bullets, and fell on his side between the ragtop jeep and the Toyota SUV. Vince caught a pretty good glimpse of the two gunmen from the flash as one of them fired at him and missed. Vince didn't miss.

Hal lay twitching, his feet against the curb, as Vince reached him and ducked low by the SUV. "Hal...buddy..."

"This is better, man," Hal rasped. "I was dying by inches... this... is..." The last word was swallowed up by the susurration of his dying breath.

Vince had to work on backing off his emotions—and the inner switch was thrown. He moved completely, then, into what his instructor in the Rangers had called the "zone of decision in combat".

Without emotion taking up space, he worked faster, with more focus and accuracy, with more perception. He heard more, saw more. There was a rage that fired his focus and energy in a controlled way; the way fuel burned, locked away in a powerful engine.

Now Vince stood up, looked around—he aimed and fired twice, all in half a second, at two more gunmen stepping out from the shadows at the corner of Hal's house. They were silhouettes—and one was firing at him, but sloppily, the burst kicking up bits of asphalt to his right.

The shooter went down, spinning to fall across the other man who lost the upper half of his head to the big bullet from the Desert Eagle.

Stepping carefully to avoid treading on Hal, Vincent took cover, hunched between the jeep and the SUV, listening and watching.

His peripheral vision caught taillights on his right; his hearing brought him the distinct engine sound of Dutch's truck backing up in the weedy vacant lot, on the other side of the dead-end barrier.

No one else stirred.

No sirens yet. Just silence.

Until a series of gunshots echoed from the back of the house. An AR15 and a Glock, cross-firing.

Vince sprinted across the street and bounded up the three steps into Hal's place.

"Oh my God—is Hal…?" Lupe said, looking up at him from the hall to his left, her eyes glistening. She and Pascual, Superro in his arms, had moved to the hallway, where they crouched, both looking tautly tense.

"He's dead," Vince said, stepping out of the doorway line of fire. "He killed some of them first. I took out some others. I think for a minute we're good out front."

At the back door Diego fired again, then hissed, "Vince, I'm out of bullets!"

"Come out this way, the front's clear for now!" Vince called. "I'll cover you!"

Vince stepped close to where Lupe and Pascual crouched.

"There's blood on your face!" Lupe whispered. "You hit?"

"Scratched," he murmured to her, leaning out around the corner of the wall. He looked into the living room—seeing Diego hunched-over, hurrying toward him.

"I saw one moving toward the side of the house where your bike is," Diego said, coming up to him, breathing hard.

A figure was framed in the back door—in the semi-darkness it was just a silhouette. Vince's hand automatically trained his Desert Eagle on the silhouette's center of mass, but he hesitated to fire. He couldn't see a gun. Maybe the guy had one, maybe not.

What if it was some confused neighbor? What if it was some sort of hostage?

Acting on instinct, Vince dropped flat on the floor, swinging his gun to fire from the new angle, at the same moment shouting "Get down!" to Diego.

Vince's timing was good—the dark figure's gun was lit by a muzzle flash that sent a short burst from a MAC-10 over Vince's head.

The Desert Eagle's reply was thunderous in the living room space, and the gangster was thrown back, yelping as the heavy load rammed through his belly.

Superro yapped hysterically.

Vince quickly got up and said, "Everyone get close to the front door but keep low!"

Then he stepped out of the line of fire from the back door, and in three long strides got to the wall close beside it.

Vince waited, listening. He heard voices, and the mumbling of a dying man.

He looked around the edge of the door, showing as little of himself as he could. No one in sight in the alley.

Gun at ready he edged through the door and looked left—saw two figures standing by a dumpster, craning their heads toward him. He aimed carefully, fired, and one of the heads exploded into a dark burst of fluid, not enough light to see its bloody colors. The other man turned and sprinted back up the alley.

Not wanting to shoot a man in the back if he didn't have to, Vince let him go, then stepped out, looked around, saw no one else. He turned toward the place he'd left the Harley, was there in four strides—and in the oblique street-light gleam he saw, two yards away, a Caidos in a hoody digging around through the bike's saddle bags. The guy had set his MAC-10 down on the seat of the bike. The bike was facing the alley.

Vince dug out his keys with his left hand and jangled them, as he stepped up to the cartel thug. "Looking for these?"

The Caidos looked at the keys, his hands fumbled for the compact submachine gun—and Vince cracked him just hard enough across the top of his head with the barrel of the Desert Eagle.

"In Wyatt Earp's time," Vince said, as the guy crumpled, "that was called 'buffaloing'."

He scooped the MAC-10 from the bike seat and stuck it in the open saddle bag. Then he looked around for other cartel gunmen; didn't see any.

Moving quickly, Vince searched the stunned gangster's pockets. He came up with a combat knife, and two full clips for the MAC-10. He dropped all the items in his saddle bag, then kicked the groaning man's foot.

"*Habla usted Ingles?*" Vince growled, as the man got blearily to his hands and knees.

"Yeah, man, I speak it! Just don't fucking kill me!"

"Get up!"

Moaning, clutching his head, the guy got to his feet, as Vince went on. "I'm letting you go partly so your blood doesn't splash all over my bike, but mainly so you can carry a message for me. Tell Angel I saw what he did in the Yucatan. Tell him he killed friends of mine. Tell him I'm coming to get him—whether he's right here in town, or in Tucson. Tell him I said it'll be very little inconvenience for me to kill him."

"Yeah, whatever, man—"

"Repeat the message back!"

Panting, the guy repeated it. Vince corrected him once. He repeated it again correctly.

"Now go—down the alley! Better yell at your friends not to kill you!"

The guy stumbled into the alley, yelling in Spanish.

Vince nodded to himself. It just might work.

His threat to Angel hadn't been bravado. It was an attempt to get Angel to run. To get out of town. With any luck, he would go to Rancho de los Santos, which was set well away from innocent bystanders. Vince still wasn't sure no non-combatant had been hit by a stray bullet in this fight.

He looked across the alley, saw an open, unfenced place between two houses. That could come in handy. He looked over the back fence and saw Dutch's truck and trailer had backed up into the weedy lot, one of the trailer's doors open, as planned. Vince could see him sitting in the cab of the truck, reflected in a side view mirror, intently watching behind the truck. No one else was visible around the Kenworth.

Vince moved to the front of the house, hunkered down and peered through a space in the stand of cactus. He could see four men a block down, at the corner, who seemed to be arguing. Could be trying to decide if they wanted to try to finish the job or cut their losses; get out before the neighbors' calls to the sheriff's department finally triggered a response. One of the men was on a cell phone—probably to Angel Lopez. Vince guessed that Lopez would tell them to finish it. The reputation of the Caidos cartel was at stake. For the same reason, the cartelito boss probably wouldn't leave Arizona unless there was an APB out for him. But maybe Lopez would get to a safer part of it.

Trying to make his voice only as loud as necessary, Vincent called out, "Diego!"

There was a pause. Then he heard Diego call out from the front door. "Yo!"

"If you and Lupe and Pascual want to stay here and hope the sheriff's department comes, you can do that. But the enemy's still in range—they'll probably rush the house again before help comes."

"Any ideas, Captain?"

"I've got Dutch to bring his truck up into that lot over there on the other side of the barrier. He's waiting to take you guys in back—but it's your choice!"

A longer pause. One of the men at the end of the block was talking urgently to the others. Vince raised his gun—and hesitated. With any luck he could hit a couple of them from here; he was sure they were Caidos, but if he missed, the rounds might go into someone's house.

"Vince—we want to go with Dutch!" Diego called.

"Okay, he's going to take you to a certain place out of town! I'll meet you there. Now listen carefully." He took a breath and spoke as clearly as he could without shouting. "Go out the door, get close to the wall, crouch down and move toward the end of the street. There's just enough space between the cactus and the wall there to get by—then run to the barrier, duck under it, and run like hell to the back of the truck and yell at Dutch, tell him you're there. Get in the trailer and move behind the closed door. He'll transfer you three to the front the first chance he has!"

"Roger that, Captain!"

Another pause. Then a rustling, muttering from the door, and they were coming: Diego, then Pascual carrying the dog, and Lupe, all three crouching, hurrying along the side of the house. They darted past Vince and, his heart thumping, he watched as they ran to the barrier at the end of the street, crept under it, ran to the back of the truck.

A burst of gunfire.

It rattled on the metal of the truck-trailer…

Then they were all in the back. None of them had stumbled. They'd got there safely.

Letting out a long breath he hadn't noticed he'd been holding, Vince shook his head. A good plan and a bad plan, at once. They could have gotten shot running for that truck.

But now the truck was roaring away, one of the trailer's rear doors flapping, clacking.

The freeway was just two blocks away. With any luck Dutch would reach the freeway, get a good piece down the road, and then find a place to pull over, transfer the passengers to the front of the truck and fully close the back of the trailer.

It could still go sour.

Vince walked to the back corner of the house and peered down the alley. He could see men coming his way, guns in hand.

Good. They were focused on him.

He went to his bike, started it up, revved it once, put it in gear and rode it fast and hard out from behind the house, across the alley. Bullets slashed by him. One spanged off his front fender. Then he was between the houses on the farther side of the alley, riding over a strip of lawn, into a driveway and out into the street.

Now all he had to do was get out of Dodge without getting shot off his bike.

Chapter Five

It was an hour past midnight, chilly out but not cold, at the rest stop just off the 17 freeway a hundred miles north of Phoenix. The place smelled of diesel exhaust mixed with resiny desert plants.

Vince sat at a picnic table under one of the pine trees dotting the parklike swathe of land. With him at the table were Lupe and Pascual. The boy was dozing off; Lupe was silent with exhaustion. Semitrucks were pulled up at the curb of the rest stop; drivers stood around by their rigs talking, drinking coffee from vending machine cups. One camper van was pulled up, too, about sixty feet from Vince; the driver, an old white-haired gent, was in the restroom. His Golden Retriever was up on the front seat of the camper van, paws on the dash, staring fixedly toward the bathroom outbuildings.

On the freeway, a hundred yards away, came the irregular roaring of trucks and the humming of cars going by. Dutch's truck was parked nearby, nosed in toward the rest stop. Vince's Harley was on its kick-stand beside the table. Leaning against the bench beside him was his large backpack, which Dutch had brought in the truck.

Waiting for Dutch and Diego to get back, Vince watched the

entry road. He had used the truck's first aid kit and cleaned the slight wounds on his face, after pulling out a few splinters, and he could feel the night air on the cuts.

Pascual was twitching in his sleep, head on his arms. Lupe, a little disheveled, was glumly nursing a cup of hot chocolate, with one arm draped across the boy's shoulders. Superro was asleep at the boy's feet. Beside Pascual's hands several candy bar wrappers rustled in the slight breeze. Dutch and Diego were coming back from the vending machines, talking in low voices.

Vince was watching for a light blue Camry. Dierdre had rented one in Phoenix. She was meeting him here. Maybe soon; maybe in an hour or so.

Might be good if she met Lupe and Diego and heard their story. But she'd naturally try to persuade them to come with her to the FBI office in Phoenix, where they'd be asked a lot of questions; maybe even held for a while. The boy had some connection to the Caidos and Lupe would be afraid to tell the feds everything. What would they do with her and the kid, while they were setting them up to testify? They'd want to hear their story on the attack on Hal's place. She'd have to tell them about Vince or lie to the US Government. They would videotape those lies. She could end up in prison.

Hal. Vince hadn't even had time to move Hal's body to the house. He felt sick, thinking of the old marine dead in the gutter. Least he could do was make some calls, later. Make sure Hal's nephew got his inheritance—and Hal got a decent burial.

The county sheriff deputies and the ambulances had started to show up about ten minutes after the truck took off, or so Dutch had inferred from a news report on the truck's radio.

There had been no arrests. Everyone involved in the fight who was still there, was dead. The other Caidos had already bugged out.

One of the ambulances would have taken Hal to the city morgue. His grandson, maybe, would identify his body.

Vince grimaced. Was Hal collateral damage?

But... no. He'd gone out like a warrior. In Vince's mind, Hal deserved a posthumous medal. But he'd never get it.

Diego and Dutch sat down across from Vince at the picnic table. Diego had an immense candy bar in one hand, half eaten; he was chewing on one side of his mouth, industriously using his remaining teeth. In his other hand was a large plastic bottle of Coca-Cola. Dutch had two cups of coffee and Vince knew he'd drink them both. They planned to go as far as they could tonight, to get far away from Santo Virgil. It was the only plan they had.

Except that Vince had just now made up his mind about his own plan for them. If they wanted to go along with it.

"I'm still thinking about Hal," Diego said. "Man, I was getting to like that damn old jarhead. Barely got to know him. Then—*boom.*"

"Maybe he saved our lives," Lupe said softly.

Vince nodded. "He gave us the edge we needed." He felt a wave of fatigue roll through him, carrying self-disgust with it. Should have protected the old Marine.

Diego said, "Didn't seem like he had long to live. And those bastards shot up his house. They were attacking all he had left."

Because they followed me there, Vince thought.

He took a deep breath. He knew these feelings of old. Sometimes in combat, necessary combat, some of the men under his command had been killed. He had felt every one of those deaths, wondering what he should have done differently.

"It wasn't your fault, Vincent," said Lupe softly. She was looking at him. She'd seen in his face what he was feeling. "Those men are to blame. Not you. They're... I won't say *evil*. Who knows what their lives were like? Bad, mostly. But they were so damaged, they were not good for much but selling poison, and murder. And recruiting boys like my Pascual. It is on those men, what happened. Not on you."

"I'll say one thing," Diego said, his voice hoarse with emotion. "That son of a gun died like a hero. That's the way he'd want to go, Vince. And it was fast, too. Not the slow death from his lungs quittin' on him. I'd like to go that way myself."

Vince snorted softly to himself. If Diego stuck with him, he might get the chance to go that way. But Vince had other ideas.

"Mama... *la fuega*..." Pascual muttered. Then he sat bolt upright, staring around him, his eyes round with fear and disorientation. *"El mundo está muerto!"*

Vince looked away, his eyes stinging. Pascual thought the world was dead.

Lupe threw her arms around her son. "No. We are all here. You see the freeway! So many people!"

Pascual shook himself, licked his lips, and his eyes came into focus. "I had a dream... that everyone in the world was dead."

Lupe looked at Vince. "He heard that man screaming out back. He asked why he screamed, and Diego told him the man was on fire, and then he saw all the dead men out front..."

Dutch grunted. "Natural enough. Was I his age, seeing all that... There'd be nightmares."

"Pascual is tough," Diego said. "Maybe he was going to be the wrong tough. Now he knows better."

"Those men," Pascual said. The dog was awake now, trying to climb up on Pascual's lap.

"Those men were trying to kill you, boy," Pascual said.

"They were trying to burn down the house you were in. Vince and Hal—we all did what we had to."

"You killed some, Diego?" Pascual asked him.

"Me? Wounded a couple, I think. One of 'em pretty badly."

Pascual picked up a half-eaten piece of granola bar and fed it to Superro, saying, "We don't have any place to go!"

"You can always go to the state police, or the FBI," Vince said. "I have a friend in the FBI. If you go to them, you should tell them what happened."

"But then your name comes out," Lupe said. "And they'll blame you."

Vince gave her a smile of resignation. "Oh, I'm getting used to it. But there's another plan. Pascual—you know Diego was in the Army. But did you know he spent a lot of his time as a boy on boats?"

Pascual shook his head mutely.

The old man from the camper van was walking his Golden Retriever now. Superro growled at them as they passed. When they'd gone out of earshot, Vince went on, "Yep, Diego was a fisherman's son. Grew up catching lobster and tuna over in Florida."

Diego nodded. "It's true! I was sick of boats for a *long* time, man! So," he shrugged. "I joined the Army! Then I got sick of sand, and desert and solid ground."

"You ever miss those boats, Diego?" Vincent asked.

Diego nodded, and snapped his fingers. "Been wanting to mess around on boats for a while now! Living in the wrong place for it."

Vince took a breath and took the plunge. "I've got a place on Harstine Island, in Washington, at the southern part of Puget Sound. I've got a house there, and a dock on the Sound."

"What you mean, on the sound?" Pascual asked.

71

"Puget Sound. It's like a *really* big bay. Almost a sea to itself. It's connected to the Pacific Ocean up in Washington State. There are two boats on my dock. One is a small cabin cruiser, the other is a launch with a little engine on the back, and oars too. Oh, and there's a canoe in the boat shed."

"Diego has *bueno* skills," Lupe said. "He built a deck for me, he fixed a door, lots of things. He can do some plumbing too."

Diego rubbed his head. "I was a general maintenance man when I got taking..." He made a dismissive wave. "That's all over."

Vince nodded. "My house is livable but it has only three finished bedrooms—there's one that's partly finished, a deck that's half-finished, some walls that need painting. A long list of work needs doing. If you're willing, Diego, I'd like to hire you to do that work. And I need someone to assist you, and help you take care of the place. Maybe collaborate with me on another project, if you're interested." He looked earnestly at Lupe. "I have some money." He cleared his throat again, strangely embarrassed.

Vince sipped a little coffee and went on, "I feel like I got you in deeper with the Caidos than you should've been. Now you're running. You're in firefights. I feel... that's on me. So... you're *all* invited to live in the house, for starts. Indefinitely. You wanted to move out, you can do that. I won't be there for a long time so you'd have to do without me, but I'll arrange some money for you."

"Live there?" Lupe gawked at him. "In your house?"

"Yes. On Harstine Island."

"What is it like there?" Pascual asked, his eyes glittering. "Does it have palm trees and the hula girls?"

Vince chuckled. "Sorry, doesn't have either one. Not that sort of island. It's rainy up there, and shady, and it has a nice summer but doesn't get crazy hot like in Arizona."

"That would be a relief," Diego said.

"It's covered in big old trees mostly, redwoods, and pines and a lot of underbrush—but there are roads and some nice houses tucked away in it. There are docks there too. Oyster beds, fishing… And it's not a remote island—it's right across the estuary from the mainland."

"Vincent," Lupe shook her head. "That is crazy."

"Maybe. It's just an offer. But see, this money I have, from some work I did in Mexico, and some money I inherited… I want to invest it. And I want to invest it right there, where I live. I want to build something. Like my dad did." He cleared his throat. Was this in fact crazy? Maybe. But he had wanted to do something of the kind. Have a chance for a more normal life. "Now, there's pretty much no really good restaurant in the area. Harstine is connected to the mainland there by a bridge, and there are a couple nice little towns within a few miles. There are some well-to-do people on that island, and people in town, who would love a Latin Cuisine restaurant. Something… you know, like you were talking about."

"Oh, I was just dreaming!" she protested.

"Doesn't have to be just a dream. I feel like I owe you—but this is something I want, too. You could be the manager and co-owner and chef. Great Mexican food, sure, but anything you wanted. Gourmet, like your father's cuisine. What I'm thinking is, we fix up the house and build an extension for a small restaurant. We buy the ovens, the whole shebang, with my money. I'll be investing in the restaurant—I'll be a partner. You'll be part owner and chef, Lupe, and you can hire whoever you need. Diego is maintenance man for the whole property. I'll arrange the licensing. Everyone gets a salary—"

"How much do I get?" Pascual demanded, pulling Superro on his lap.

This time they all laughed—except Pascual, who seemed deadly serious.

Vince shrugged. "What would you contribute, Pascual?"

"Me? Um…" The boy blinked. "I can be a waiter."

"You're not quite old enough for that," Lupe said. "You need to be in school."

"School? Pah! I can learn about the business and stuff. And boats!"

Vince grinned. "Yeah. But you'd need to go to school, in the town there. There is… there's stuff you can do in the restaurant. We'll figure it out. And you can assist Diego around the house. I'll give you a little money for work you do. You'd be paid per job you get done. Diego will have an account he can draw on for that and for supplies, lumber, whatever he needs." He turned to Lupe. "I'll set up the salaries as a trust. I have a banker in Seattle, I'll talk to him about it."

"It sounds wonderful, but…" Lupe shook her head, overwhelmed and maybe a little suspicious. "Too good to be true. There are sayings about that, Vincent."

Vince nodded gravely. "I understand that. You'd be taking a risk on me. But the money will be there when you arrive. In fact… I stopped in Phoenix and cashed some Traveler's Cheques…"

He took two envelopes from his inside coat pocket and slid one across the table to Lupe and one to Diego. Diego took his immediately—but Lupe didn't touch her envelope.

"These are just gifts," Vince went on. Because of all you've been through, and it'll take care of you till I get back home. It's three thousand-five hundred for each of you, for initial expenses on the road and clothes and food and so on. Motels. And if you go to Harstine—well, Dutch is going to Seattle… yeah, Dutch?"

"Yep," Dutch said, grinning. "Picking up a load of fancy Seattle coffee. I can stop at Harstine on the way. Take you folks right to Vince's house."

"I'll give you the address and the keys, Lupe," Vince said gently. "These people, the Caidos, don't know who I am. And if they did, they wouldn't know about my place on Harstine. You should be safe there. It's a long, long way northwest of here."

"I've never seen the ocean," Pascual said.

"No?" Vince smiled. "Diego can take you out on the Sound, and then to the Pacific, sometime, if it's okay with Lupe. He can take both of you and Superro too on my cabin cruiser. We'll see Diego gets his licensing for that. He can show you how to do some fishing…"

"But I don't really know you, Vince," Lupe said, somewhat reluctantly. As if she wanted to accept but had reasons to doubt him. "I can't move into some strange man's house."

"Look—" Vince rubbed his hands together, thinking. "If you were offered a job by a man you didn't know, and it was working in his house, at a good rate of pay, you'd probably take it, wouldn't you? And a chance to be partner in a restaurant? I mean, as long as you had your own room and he behaved himself?"

"Ye-es, probably…" Her eyes lit up. "To put it like that… *probablemente!*"

"I know there's still trust involved. It's a leap of faith. But I really want to help you. I feel bad you and Pascual got tangled up with me, this way, losing your home. I want to give you another one and—I need something better to look forward to, someday. Some other way to live. So I'd be honored if you and Pascual and Diego were to stay, rent-free of course, at my place…"

"And Superro," Pascual prompted.

"Well of course, you have to have some protection!" Vince said.

Lupe laughed. "I don't know, Pascual… You want to earn some money and go on a boat with Diego?"

"Yes," he said flatly. "Hella *Si*!"

"But you won't see your friends at school again."

"My only friends are Jerry and Miguel." Pascual shrugged. "Maybe I see them again sometime." He made a face. "But not Jerry. He's trying to join the Caidos. I don't want nothing more to do with them. And Miguel smokes that vaper and I don't like it, he looks *estupido*—I tried it. Made me sick—"

"He got you to *smoke*?" Lupe asked, outraged. "He's not old enough to smoke!"

"He stole it from his sister."

"*Madre*—!" She slapped her hands on the table. "I don't want you to see him again anyway!" She turned to Diego. "Are *you* going?"

Diego looked at her in surprise. "Not much doubt of that. I'm trying to live by collecting cans! I'm all over this!"

She seemed pleased but still skeptical "It all seems like… too much. I don't like to owe a man so much."

"You won't!" Vince said. "First off, you're bringing the skills. I sure don't have those skills. Second, you'll be working your—ah, working really hard, there! You'll contribute more than your share!"

"Then—" Lupe took a deep breath and picked up the envelope. "I accept!" After a moment her smile melted away. "But Vincent—you have never tasted my cooking. You don't know—maybe it's not so good. Suppose you invest all this money and it's not… not up to… you know."

Vince glanced at Pascual. He wanted to make the boy laugh. "If that happens, well—" He spread his hands, pulled a comically rueful face, and shrugged expansively. "Then I'm screwed!"

Pascual laughed.

76

Vince was sitting alone at the picnic table, now, at one-ten in the morning. He watched as Dutch drove away, the big semitruck taking Diego, Lupe, Pascual, and Superro on a journey far to the north and west. It was a long way to Washington State. The boy, his mother and the Chihuahua were tucked in the sleeping nook in the back of the cab; Diego was in the passenger seat beside Dutch. They'd be stopping at motels, from time to time, but only after they got well away from Arizona. Vince had given the other helmet to the boy as a parting gift.

As the truck swung onto the access road to the freeway, the white, blue and black SUV of an Arizona State Trooper pulled up across from Vince.

Okay, so maybe this rest-stop wasn't the best place for Vince's meetups. Naturally the troopers would stop here, if they didn't have anything else going on.

The trooper parked, lights flashing, and got out of the SUV. Vince picked his cellphone from the picnic table and looked into the little screen, mostly to seem unconcerned about the trooper. The guy strode up to the table and Vince glanced up, raising his eyebrows. "Officer."

He was a fairly young white trooper, maybe not long out of the academy, in the classic long-sleeved khaki uniform with a matching flat-brimmed, forward-tilted campaign hat. Not a tall man. The trooper's name was on a little tab on his shirt pocket flap: *E. Pennyman.* Holstered on Pennyman's right hip was what Vince judged to be a Glock 17 Gen5, probably chambered in 9mm.

"I got a call about some people here for a couple hours," Pennyman said, in a voice that sounded almost teenage to Vince. "Someone thought some folks might be camping here."

"Trucker friends of mine, remembering old times," Vince said. "They gave me a call so I swung by. They don't get through here much. They left, and I'm going too, in a minute." He nodded toward his motorcycle. "No one was going to camp here."

"I heard there was a Mexican woman and her kid," the trooper said. "You're saying they're truckers?"

"Ol' Dutch likes to bring his wife and son along on short trips."

The trooper was looking at Vince, his head tilted to once side, as if trying to remember something. Maybe the beard wasn't working.

Another car was pulling up at a parking slot near the trooper's SUV. Vince glanced at it, but the lights from the cop car made it hard to see what color it was.

"Someone cut your face there?" the trooper asked.

"Just a minor accident at work."

The trooper nodded. "I'll just run your license and the bike's plates. Let's see some I.D."

Vince hesitated. An I.D. check would show him wanted for questioning in the Lincoln Memorial incident. He'd be arrested.

If he refused to show it, or said he didn't have identification on him, the trooper would call for backup and likely it would end up with Vince arrested. His fingerprints would be taken. Would the FBI get him out? Probably not. He'd be shipped back, in cuffs, to D.C. to deal with things he didn't have time for. But did he have a choice?

There was another consideration. He had the Desert Eagle on him, which was not registered to him, and the MAC-10, loaded, in the bike bag. He'd figured he needed the extra firepower—but maybe he should have ditched it. The MAC-10 could connect him to the shooting in Santo Virgil.

That was a lot to explain. And he would be arrested for the illegal weapons.

He'd probably have to let himself be arrested. This wasn't a bent cop. Just some young guy trying to be a swinging dick of a trooper. Vince couldn't bring himself to hit him, and he sure couldn't shoot him.

"You going to show me that I.D., fella?" the man growled, putting a hand on his gun butt.

Vince nodded. "Okay I stand up so I can get my wallet out?"

"Slowly."

Vince stood up, took his wallet out—and Dierdre Corlin walked up. "Officer, I don't mean to get in your way."

He turned toward her frowning—and then stared at the FBI badge she held out for him to see in the streetlamp light.

"FBI?"

"Agent Corlin. You can run my information, if you want."

Vince looked at her with a mixture of relief and mild surprise at her timeliness. He noticed she had let her hair go honey-brown again. It was gathered back in a bun behind her head. She wore a woman's business suit, in gray and blue, shiny low-heel shoes.

"This man. You know him?" the trooper asked.

"I do. He's an undercover asset. I'd rather not release his name."

"He said he was here meeting some old trucker friends. And their family."

Vince shrugged. "They were about sentiment—the agent here is business. Just mixing business and pleasure."

The trooper looked back and forth between them, frowning. Then he looked for a long moment at Vince. "I might know this man's name. But I'm not certain."

"Again—I'd rather not release that," Dierdre said, coolly. "How about if I sit here with my associate, you look me up in the system. They'll show you my face. I can give you personal I.D. too… It's got my Bureau number on it…"

She opened her purse, fished out the I.D. and handed it over. He nodded. "Have a seat ma'am, please." He pointed at Vince. "You too. Hands on the table."

"Sure," Vince said.

The state trooper backed away, then turned his back, a little reluctantly, to walk to his car. Dierdre sat down by Vince.

They watched as he got into his car and called in Dierdre's information, asking for an official photo of the agent.

"He was worried about turning his back on us," Dierdre said.

Vince nodded. "That was good timing, Dierdre. I was about to let him take me in."

She smiled quirkily. "Tempting for me to let him do that too. Get you out of the mess you're in here. Get you transported to D.C. to wait for that pardon."

"You wouldn't do that to me, would you?"

She made a *tsk* sound and said, brightly, "Maybe!"

"I have two unregistered weapons with me. One used in a firefight yesterday."

"Oh great," she sighed. "Man, I'm tired. Jet lagged. Driving half the day." She let out a long breath. "You know what, up north about ten miles there's a Howard Johnsons, a Wyndham they call it now. Restaurant and bar open there till two-thirty. If you don't get arrested, how about we get a drink and something to eat. I'm starved."

"And if I do get arrested?"

"I'll raise a toast to you, in your absence."

Vince laughed softly. "Deal."

The trooper got out of his car, came striding back to them, Dierdre's I.D. in his hand—the hand he'd have used to draw his weapon. That was a good sign.

He walked up to her and handed her the I.D. "Agent—my lieutenant says not to insist on I.D.ing your asset here. He says to leave you to it." He looked at Vince and shook his head. "I hope the lieutenant knows what he's doing."

He turned and walked back to his SUV, got in, turned off his lights and drove toward the freeway.

Vince let out a long breath. "Good thing his lieutenant's impressed by the FBI."

She nodded. "Not everyone is. That could have gotten ugly."

"I might have underestimated that kid."

"That was you, in Santo Virgil? The firefight?"

"Yeah." There was a question he was almost afraid ask. But he had to ask it. "Listen—you hear an up-to-date report on it?"

"I did. Actually, it was on the car radio—nothing official."

"Any non-combatants hurt? Stray bullets, whatever?"

"My understanding is no. Just known cartel enforcers. And a man who apparently took the fight to them."

Vince nodded. "Hal Robbins. Ex-Marine. Vietnam vet. He figured he had maybe two years to live. And he didn't like people shooting out his windows."

"Some balls on that Marine."

"You got that right. He turned it around for us."

"Those illegal guns—past time you should get rid of them."

"Since I'm wanted for questioning, I don't think I can get hold of a weapon legally. My own legal hardware is way back in Washington state. And there's a heavily-armed gang hunting me."

She nodded thoughtfully. Then added matter-of-factly, "It occurs to me that I'm insane to hang around with you."

Vince nodded solemnly. "I didn't want to say anything—wouldn't want to make fun of someone's psychological problems."

Dierdre chuckled.

Vince put his phone in his coat. "So—anything in the news about the firefight? About the people who *didn't* die?"

She shrugged. "News said it was cartel. Sinaloa was mentioned."

"Except it wasn't them."

"Funny that."

"Any mention of Lupe and Pascual and Diego? Or me?"

"A bearded shooter someone on the street said was known only as 'El Gran Extrano'."

Vince frowned "The 'Big Stranger'?"

"I think that's you, Vince. But no one's got a really good description of you. Your real name wasn't mentioned. The report didn't describe anyone else."

Realizing the implications, Vince slapped a hand onto the table. "Fuentes' people are keeping it on the down-low. And Angel's hoping to deal with it himself. Just call it a 'gang fight' and spread rumors about which gang."

"Sounds right. I got a call from Agent Chang, in the car. One of the dead gangbangers was shot in the head at close range with a small caliber pistol. It looked like he'd been wounded by one of you guys, and executed. That wasn't you, or your friends?"

"Hell no. Diego wounded some guys…"

"Maybe one of them had to be shut up completely."

Vince nodded. "That's Angel Lopez's style."

They were quiet for almost a full minute. The freeway was quiet, then roared; was quiet again… and roared again.

Diedre rubbed her eyes and said, "How about that late meal?"

"It's a…" He almost said, *It's a date.* Instead, he went with, "…a good idea. Meet you there."

"Okay. I'll book a couple rooms with the bureau's app for that stuff.

It'll be on the expense account. You won't have to give anyone your name that way. You'll have yourself a room. I'll get myself a room. We'll get some food, a drink, and some rest. That's my advice as a federal agent who once thought about being a lawyer."

He grinned. "Good advice."

"One more thing."

"What?"

"That beard isn't working as a disguise. Or any other way."

He stood up, nodding, and put on his backpack, then got his helmet from the motorcycle's handlebars. "I do have a shaving kit in the bags here..."

An hour and ten minutes later, shaven and showered, changed into the one clean change of clothes he had in the backpack, Vince found Dierdre in the bar of the Wyndham. He was wearing blue jeans and an old Ramones t-shirt and moccasins without socks.

"Bar's closing in three minutes, folks," said the yawning, Asian-American guy behind the bar.

"Okay, we'll head out and fend for ourselves," Vince said.

"Kitchen's still open for another forty-five minutes," Dierdre said, tapping a menu. "I've got something to drink in my luggage. Suppose we have a couple of omelets sent up to my room, and you tell me what your next lunatic plan is."

"Works for me," he said, as she ordered the food from the bartender. Vince didn't drink hard liquor much, but he needed one tonight. And he liked being alone with Dierdre. Nothing truly intimate was likely to happen but still, just being alone with her would make him feel like a regular human being again.

That's all it should be. He knew the odds against him making it through another intense off-the-books mission, outnumbered and outgunned, wasn't good. Especially since the cartel was arguably more dangerous than the Germanic Brethren had been. They were far more experienced. Stupid to get Dierdre personally involved in his life.

He berated himself inwardly for that thought. The stupidity, he told himself, was thinking she'd be interested in that level of involvement. Oh, they'd had a moment or two. But why would she want to get snarled up in a relationship that would ruin her career?

"Come along, Mr. Culaine." Dierdre said, sounding like a tour guide. "The elevator's this way."

As the elevator doors closed, he asked, "'Mr. Culaine'?"

"I didn't want to call you Vince, in public, or Bellator. And I didn't want to seem like I was a hooker with 'come on, big fella.' So I picked my great grandfather's actual last name. I'm three quarters Irish, see. They couldn't understand his brogue at Ellis Island, so they wrote it down as Corlin. He went with that, thinking it was expected of him."

"I may keep it."

Fuentes didn't want to answer the phone. He knew who it was. But he made himself pick it up. "*Hola.*"

"Fuentes? "Yes, Angel?" Fuentes said in Spanish. He shifted the phone to his other ear.

"What went wrong?"

"We underestimated them. Especially 'The Big Stranger'."

"How did they get away?"

"In the back of a semitruck driven by we don't know who. And the big guy, he rode off on a motorcycle. He rode it through somebody's yard, between houses, and across a railroad track and got away."

"You get license plates on the truck and the motorcycle?"

Fuentes winced. He'd been afraid Angel would ask him that. "No. Both had mud smeared on them. They did it on purpose, before they left the trailer park."

"Obviously. You haven't found out anything about this man?"

"Which man, Angel?"

Angel sighed. "Idiot! The Big Stranger!"

"No." Fuentes hesitated. "Have you?"

"Only that he threatened me. He said he knew me from Mexico. Said he was coming after me here—or in Tucson."

"Why stick around? You have men to deal with such a person."

"Do I? You mean—like you?"

Fuentes licked his lips. "Yes. But… what I mean is, why stay where he can make a target of you? He's obviously a man of… of skills. Military background."

"That much we have guessed, yes. I want you to find out who he is. Did he leave fingerprints in the house?"

"Maybe. We have men looking."

"I'm going to the ranch. He knows nothing about that place. No one does. I want you and Renaldo to find him and kill him. And the others with him."

"The boy?"

"The boy too. Does that make you cry sad tears, Fuentes?"

Fuentes closed his eyes. "No, Angel. All of them. It's them or you."

"Them—or you, Fuentes."

Angel hung up, and Fuentes, alone in his home office while his wife and children slept in the quiet house, reached for the bottle of tequila in the cabinet…

Dierdre's hotel room was standard, mid-level hotel fare. Peach colored walls. A double bed, a flat-screen wall mounted TV. Dark yellow curtains. A garish painting on the wall of a desert sunset, like hack artists turn out by the dozen for hotel rooms. Beige carpeting. The room smelled of the salsa omelets they'd eaten, the remains on a tray over by the door.

Vince sat on the desk chair. Diedre had hung her coat up in a closet and kicked off her shoes and now she sat cross-legged in the center of the bed, staring into a laptop. They each had a glass of Jameson Irish whiskey within reach, three fingers poured from the bottle she'd brought in her luggage. She'd only taken one sip from hers. Her glass was waiting on the lamp table by the bed. Vince had drunk about a shot, and stopped there, for now. Last time he'd drunk hard liquor was more than two years before, at the little bar near Harstine—on his last date. He'd only had three shots and a beer, but when Vince came back from the men's room and saw a burly guy grab his date's arm, he lost it. Tore into the guy.

Only the fact that the town police chief was a friend of his had kept Vince from being arrested, after he broke the guy's jaw. His jaw and a couple of ribs. His date had been furious—she was used to fending off drunks, she'd have been fine, and she'd once dated the guy. Still liked him. And Vince had come within a hair of killing him.

PTSD and hard liquor make a bad cocktail. He'd forgotten his meditative training, in that moment.

He'd redoubled his work on himself, after that; on the skills he was trying to teach Diego. But he still had to be careful. He'd go easy on the whiskey tonight.

Vince tried not to stare at her. There was nothing sexy about the pose or her clothing. But to Vince, Dierdre would've been sexy wearing anything. One of the golden-brown curls over her forehead had come loose and was hanging like an upside-down question mark. He gazed at it with fascination.

She frowned at the laptop screen and shook her head. "Nothing new about your gunfight in Santo Virgil. Maybe that's for the best." She looked at him curiously, closing the laptop without looking at it. "Vince—what you did for Lupe Vasquez and her boy, and Diego, giving them a new life."

"Don't forget Superro."

"And Superro..." She grinned. "Well, it was amazing."

"When I told you about it, I thought maybe you'd figure I was being a sap."

"No. Not at all. You helped people who needed help."

He shrugged. "Anyway, I do need someone to look after my place for me. And I needed someone to finish the carpentry on it. That's Diego. And I needed to invest my cash, so... It was really for my benefit."

"Sure it was."

"It *was*. And..." But then he decided not to tell her the underlying reason: He just didn't think he was going to live very long, considering the course he'd set for himself. *Make a difference in the world with the skills you've got.* He figured he was right on course for dying young. He simply wanted to leave his house and property to someone who'd be significantly helped by it. He'd be contacting his lawyer as well as his banker.

Finally, he said, "Oh—it's a lot of things."

She looked at him with narrowed eyes and sighed. "Anyway, I have a friend in the Seattle office of the Bureau. I'll see if I can get her to look in on them. See everything's all right."

"And do it without being a scary federal agent?"

"And that, yes."

"Then I'd be grateful."

Dierdre looked at him appraisingly. "You *know* how many men you killed yesterday?"

He nodded. "I do." After a moment he added, "I had some help."

"Right now, you just look a little tired—like you've played football with some friends instead of getting in a firefight. How do you keep from letting it shake you up?"

"I could ask you the same. You've been through a lot yourself. Undercover for almost two years with a bunch of domestic terrorists. They figure it out and torture you. When we got out of their base, we were both under fire. Then you flew the heli and you were under fire in D.C.."

"The torture…" She quirked her mouth to one side and closed her eyes for a long moment. "I'm still working through it. A lot of people have had a lot worse. But if it hadn't been for you, they probably would have killed me… and I owe you, Vince."

"Uh-uh, you do not."

"I do." She put the laptop on the little table, leaning against the lamp, and picked up her drink. "And I think we have a weird… bond."

"How weird? Freaky?"

"You wish."

He smiled, glad she understood that he was kidding. But something serious came to mind. "They injured you, during the torture. Were you ever wounded? Like—gunfire?"

"A little shrapnel when I was flying helis in Iraq. And once with the Bureau I was wounded, a .38 round in the hip." Her hand went unconsciously to her left hip. "We were about to serve a warrant, I knocked, and someone shot right through the door. The impact kicked me off my feet. My partner returned fire. I managed to get off one shot. He got away but we snagged him at the airport. But what happened to me—it's nothing compared to what you've been through, overseas, and in the Yucatan, and then fighting your way through the Brethren's headquarters. How do you keep a lid on it, inside?"

Should he tell her? Maybe she'd think he was odd. Well—wasn't he? He shrugged. "I met a man when we were guarding a mosque in Northern Iraq. Naq'shbandi sufi. When I was on leave, he taught me the meditation I use... I lost track of it for a while and picked it up again when things got rough."

"What's it like?"

"Sort of like the mindfulness meditation people do now. But more so. With some special techniques added..." He shrugged. "All I know is, it works. In combat I go into a special mindset—it's afterwards I need the meditation."

"Meditation is better than medication. Unless medication is all that works."

"I've heard that."

"No mention of studying meditation in your file."

"I didn't tell anyone about it except Diego and Chris."

"Could you teach me, sometime?"

"If you want." Vince liked the sound of that. It was an excuse for more time with Dierdre, even if it was platonic. But that, once more, brought up the big question—should he be with her at all? Maybe it would be good for him. But probably—not for her.

"You going to tell me what your plans are?"

"Will you put them in a report?"

"Now you've got me on the spot."

He didn't say anything.

After a moment she said, "Not immediately. Not till you've had a

89

chance to set them in motion." Dierdre rolled her eyes. "I do hope I don't go to jail for covering up for you."

"Why are you doing it?" he asked impulsively.

"Because… you…" She sipped a little whiskey and then she said. "You saved my life. At the compound. You stopped them from…"

He wanted to ask, *Is that the only reason?* But he didn't.

"I'll tell you this much, Dierdre—I'm hoping Angel Lopez is retreating to Rancho de los Santos. He'll be away from non-combatants and maybe I can find a way to take him down. And the whole place. They have a drug processing station there. A big one. Does the Bureau know about it?"

"The place in the Sedona area? Near—what was the town… Stapp?"

"Yep. Near Stapp."

She nodded. "I saw one report on it. It wasn't conclusive. One guy tried to turn evidence. He was so stoned, so crazy, no one took him seriously. Then he hung himself in his cell."

"If he really did hang himself."

She made a *hmm* noise deep in her throat. "There was a report from the DEA saying that the Caidos were planning to move operations that were normally in South America up to the USA. It seems to be Lopez's big plan to establish all his drug factories right here in the continental USA."

"From what Diego says, that's Rancho de los Santos."

"An ironic name for the place."

"Are there satellite photos of it?"

"Not that I know of. If there are, I can't give them to you—unless you meet with the Arizona Bureau chief, get his approval which would probably mean…" She snorted. "First, he'd have to arrest you."

Vince grunted. "Let's not ask for the satellite photos."

"Your friend Diego tell you anything about the set up in Santo Virgil?"

"Grocery store owner named Renaldo Silvano works for Lopez. Angel Lopez's boss in Santo Virgil."

"That clicks with some of our intel too. Vince—why go after Angel alone at the 'rancho'? If it's a big drug operation, why not work with us? And the Drug Enforcement Agency? Let us do the grunt work. Let us take the risks."

"How long would it take?" he asked.

"How long?" She blinked. "Um—a while. To make sure we had the goods. A year maybe."

He snorted. "He'll be gone from there then. And he's the heart of my mission."

"Your self-appointed mission!"

"I don't expect you to understand. I'm heading out there, and I'm going to see what's possible. I'll give you information when I can. But I can't wait a year."

"I'll go with you."

"I don't think you should. Put you and your career in jeopardy."

"I don't know…" She rubbed her eyes. "Jet lag catching up.

She yawned—and Vince stood up. He took a sip of whiskey and put the glass down. "I should get out of your hair. I'm going to leave early in the morning for Stapp. Talk to your people… but tell them to stay out of my way."

She got off of the bed, moving with slow deliberation, and walked up to him. She hesitated, then put a hand on his chest. Not a hand to push him away—it was a touch looking for contact. It wasn't an outright invitation—but it was an opening. "Vince. Stick around tonight. We can… relax. Talk this out."

His heart was thudding—and he stepped back so she wouldn't feel it with her hand. "I don't think... I'd be your friend... if I did that. I care about what happens to you, Dierdre. I'd better..."

He felt a strong pull to stay where he was. To step closer and take her in his arms and see how she responded. On some level he knew that if he kissed her, she'd kiss him back.

But he'd sworn to himself, and before God, to do the right thing for the people around him. It was the only way he could fulfill his mission and not end up hurting more people than he'd helped.

"I'd better say good night."

Don't go near her. If you do, you'll kiss her.

Vince turned away, walked to the door and opened it.

"Vince..."

He turned back to her, part of him hoping she'd talk him out of leaving.

Dierdre reached under the bed and pulled out a box. She carried it within a few feet of him, stopped—looked at him, chewing her lower lip as she did it. Then she put the package on the floor. "I got you a present. So, if you go after them—you can see them coming. Take it with you."

He picked up the package. It was a substantial rectangular box, fairly heavy. "Whatever it is... thanks." He smiled, and nodded, and hurriedly left the room.

It's for the best, Vince told himself. He needed to put everything behind him but the mission.

He carried the box back to his room, set the box on the mattress and opened the package. It was a BT-100XL-SD Oberwerk binocular telescope. It was big, twelve and a half pounds of metal, with a tripod folded up beside it. Vince knew this was one of the most powerful binoculars in the world—and it cost almost three thousand dollars. Had she maxed out a credit card? Had she been saving her money?

She'd given this to him so he could "see them coming" she'd said. To keep him safe.

He'd take it with him, in his backpack. He'd need it. Tomorrow morning, he was going to pick up Angel's trail.

Chapter Six

In a gray cloudless dawn, Dutch's rig was barreling down a freeway that ran straight north through an arid scrubland, fifteen miles south of Las Vegas. Up ahead the neon lights of Las Vegas were glowing on the horizon—they never stopped glowing. You couldn't see the town yet—it was just the shine of the place: a multicolored shimmer with an electrical vibrancy to it.

"We going into Vegas, Dutch?" Diego asked.

"Not planning to. Going past it."

"Suits me. Place makes me think of them bug-zapper lights. They get attracted to the light and then—*zap*. Except people are the 'bugs' in Vegas."

As he changed lanes to go around a slow RV, Dutch said, "I had a friend, spent a little too much time there. Lost everything. Killed himself."

Diego grunted. "Lotta stories like that." They rumbled on, the cab vibrating softly on the freeway, and Diego added, "You must be tired, man. Wish I could help you drive, but…"

"You got to be trained to drive these rigs," Dutch said. "I'm fine. I'm used to all-nighters. But this afternoon, we'll stop for gas and something to eat. And we'll lay over a little in a park on the way. I'll take a nap for an hour or so in back and you folks can sit outside, walk the dog, whatever you want."

"I have to say, sometimes Vince frightens me, Diego," Lupe said, in Spanish. Her voice came like a ghost from up in the sleeper behind him and Dutch.

Pascual was asleep beside her. Lupe had slept for a while, then awakened. Maybe troubled by some bad dreams herself.

"Why does he scare you?" Diego asked, in English.

"Killing… comes easy to him."

"I wouldn't put it that way," said Dutch. "He's pretty careful about who he takes down."

"He was worried about stray bullets hitting the neighbors, back in town," Diego pointed out.

"Oh, I feel that Vincent is a good man," she went on sleepily. "I am trying to trust him. But… to be able to kill so many, so easily. I looked him up on my phone, on the internet, and he… he is *that* Vincent Bellator. He killed all those men. Hundreds. With a machine gun!"

"Some of them, earlier in that mission, he killed up close and personal," Dutch said. "But those men were armed domestic terrorists. They were in the middle of trying to massacre a lot of people. They were murderers—Neo-Nazis trying to kill U.S. senators for being black, and planning to kill everyone else there too, all that big crowd come to hear the senators speak. Vince saved the lives of almost everyone in that crowd. He tried telling the police, the FBI—but he wasn't believed. Then it was too late to wait for them to do something about it."

"If anyone ever deserved to die, it was those guys he killed," Diego muttered.

"Yes," Lupe said. "I'm sure that's so. But still… to be able to do such a thing…"

"He has always saved a lot more people than he's killed," Diego said. "I fought beside the captain in Iraq. Green Berets detachment sent in to help his Rangers. One time my platoon was cut off from the rest, and the ISIS sons of… well, they were closing in on us—they had us in their sights from two sides. Shot two of us and then Vince came looking for us, and he sizes up the sitch, started running along the ridge and cut down on them. He just kept on, running down a trail, firing, taking them down. He caught an AK47 round in his left shoulder and another in his side but he kept coming—kept on shooting. He had their attention, so we were able to back his play and we ran up a trail, caught 'em between two fires. Vince got a Silver Star and a Purple Heart for that—I think it was his seventh Purple Heart—and we thought he was robbed. He deserved the Medal of Honor, the way we saw it. He was never much interested in medals. Used to give them away to the kids in town."

"Sounds like he saved your platoon."

"All twenty of us. Two men wounded, but everyone got out of there alive. Except the terrorists."

"But in that fight at the Lincoln Memorial," Lupe said, "he was not part of the Army anymore. He was not under anyone's… you know, their control."

"He *was* under control," Dutch said. "His own." He drove in silence for a minute and then went on, "You know what he told me about killing those guys? He said, 'When it comes to Nazis, as far as I'm concerned it's still World War Two'."

"*Hell* yeah," Diego said.

"When he shot those Nazis in D.C., he knew he was risking going to prison, but he had to take care of people who needed protecting. I know for a fact killing people *does* bother him—even the Nazis. He knows they're just people who were lied to, who had lost their way in life. But—the way Vince sees it, some people are so dangerous you can't take a chance on them. The Caidos are poisoning Americans with drugs—they're murdering people straight out too. I've seen Vince be merciful, when he could be. But sometimes the cops can't handle what has to be done, and you have to go to war—even if it's your own private war."

The Harley roared through the breezy afternoon, down the two-lane desert highway, southeast into the Red Rock State Park. Behind Vince was the New-Age redolent, touristy town of Sedona. Vince was riding with his visor open, and ahead was rugged countryside, much of it tinged red by sandstone and iron in the dusty soil. Orange-red rock formations rose on the horizon, like rusty chimneys huddled together; red dust billowed around their bases. In the distance he saw Cathedral Rock, and felt he was riding his Harley into an old John Ford movie.

Easterly, he knew, four miles beyond the farther edge of the state park, was the small town of Stapp, within the Santos Basin.

Diego's friend in Stapp, if he was still there, was named Soren Lenger. *"Hangs at a bar called One Percenters…"*

Vince passed a truck pulling a long horse trailer and glimpsed the black-crystal eyes of horses watching him through the slats; then the bike rushed past a squat, red-dusted Dodge truck, before swinging back onto the right lane and accelerating down the ramrod-straight road, picking up his speed to ninety miles an hour. Vince knew if he hit a pothole at that speed, it'd probably be the end of him. He tried to care about that and couldn't. His hands started to go numb from the increased vibration in the handlebars.

The vast state park unfolded to either side of him, as if he were revealing it by unzipping the road as he rocketed along, and he was suddenly among massively layered looming red rocks, their edges smoothed by sand-laden desert winds. Saguaros reared to either side; gulleys opened their scarlet throats and then vanished behind him.

The road was beginning to curve around rock formations, and he had to slow. It was just as well, he figured. He was about a hair away from losing control of the Harley.

What's up with pushing it this far?

Dierdre. He had let her go… and she was behind him.

Vince slowed down, trying to look like a biker out for a leisurely ride. He passed out of the state park, and into a broad basin opening between him and the low buildings of a town, about a half-mile ahead. Some miles beyond the town rose a line of distant red-and-gray stone hills. The basin was desert scrubland, sporadically thatched with stands of cacti and Arizona sycamore; mostly flat except for a few washes and the occasional outcropping.

Another minute, then he slowed as he got near a sign announcing the Stapp town-limits.

The town's sign claimed eleven-hundred and ten people were living there. But it was hard to see where they'd put them all. The highway ran right through the middle of the little town; stop signs and lights forcing a slow-down, and on both sides were boxy 1940s vintage store fronts and cafes and inns. Vince could see a dozen side streets but they didn't extend for long.

Almost running on fumes, Vince rode up to a gas station, pulling up at a pump.

As he filled the Harley's tank with gas, he glanced down the main drag. Though his visor was up, his face was in shadow.

To the left, Christmas wreaths, with plastic greenery and blood-red synthetic poinsettias, were hung on the old-west-style lamp posts. Most of the windows along the highway were strung with dully-glowing chains of Christmas lights, lit up in broad daylight. A nearby shop sold "Authentic Native American Jewelry and Crafts". There was a bar, The Silver Spurs, made up to look like an old west saloon. But that seemed to be the extent of the town's tourist lures.

The town's economy was not booming. There were a good many empty shop windows; failed businesses. A small grocery store still functioned—it was also a liquor store. He noticed a large false-fronted building with a sign declaring Stapp Hardware and Sporting Goods.

The buildings all carried wind deposits of desert dust, red and dull yellow, collected in the corners of signs and along the tops of eaves. At the end of the block was a small red brick building with "Stapp Police Department" in raised stainless-steel letters across the face. One old-school black-and-white police sedan was parked in front.

Vince looked to the right; a little way down stood a three-story hotel, the *Desert Peace Inn,* claiming to be a bed and breakfast. It looked like it might tip over without the other two businesses snugged on either side to hold it up: a storefront that offered guided tours of the state park, and a closed gift shop. Beside the gifts shop was another storefront, its windows boarded over. Then came a graveled driveway leading to a lot at the back of the One Percent Bar & Grill—Vince could see Harleys and "rice burners" parked back there. Farther down the road there was a scattering of fast-food drive-ups, an espresso kiosk, a bank—a branch of his own bank, in fact—and a Wal-Mart.

In the gas station's convenience store Vince paid a chunky Native American woman in cash for the gas, a handful of energy bars and two bottles of water.

He rode the trail bike down the street, parked it in front of the Hardware and Sporting Goods Store.

Vince thought about keeping his motorcycle helmet on to hide his face in the Hardware/Sporting Goods store, but he decided that would only make him more conspicuous—he'd look like he was going to rob the place. He took the helmet off, hung it on the end of a handlebar, put on a pair of sunglasses, and went in, hoping the shopkeepers would have forgotten his face if they'd seen it on the news. Right now, he had red dust on that face and a day's growth of beard too.

Vince took off the backpack just inside the door, leaned it against the door frame out of the way, and went immediately to camping supplies. He selected a well-made waterproof sleeping bag, a one-man tent, a pack of dried food, a canteen and a small camping shovel. He carried it to the glass counter, where a stolid older woman wearing khaki pants and a green Stapp Sporting Goods shop-apron was standing in front of a rack of shotguns, hunting rifles, and carbines made to look like AR15s. Her name was sewn in cursive over her heart: *Velma*.

He looked wistfully at a Weatherby Vanguard Select hunting rifle, already fitted with a scope. But even in Arizona you'd need I.D. to buy a rifle and he didn't want anyone running his through the system.

She glanced at him, and he could see her size him up, probably thinking him another motorcycle bum just passing through. "What can I do you for?" she asked, in a twangy southwest accent.

"I'll take these things and three boxes of the Samson there," he said, pointing at the .50 caliber handgun ammo.

She raised her eyebrows at that. "What you hunting with that kinda load, a brahma bull?"

"You never know, ma'am. I hear there's fossils out in that desert. Might be some dinosaurs still around."

"Only livin' fossil out there is my husband, and he can just stay out there," she said.

He laughed, to put her at her ease, and paid for the goods in cash.

"Watch out for those dinosaurs now," she said, as he carried his packages to the door.

I'm the dinosaur, here, Vince thought, putting the ammo and food in his backpack. *Became that when I left the Army. Some reptilian killer that doesn't belong in the world, anymore. Out on an endless mission to savage his enemies.*

It wasn't what his parents had envisioned for him.

Something Dierdre had said over dinner came back, as he put his backpack on, and went out to his Harley.

"You know, Vince, if you get that presidential pardon you can restart your life. But not if you keep getting in gunfights. With luck no one will find out it was you at Hal's place. But if you keep going after Lopez, it'll come out. If I don't tell them someone will. They'll find out, Vince, that you're on a vigilante mission. No one likes the cartelitos, but you're not allowed to execute them."

"They always fire the first shot."

"Do they? Always?"

He took a deep breath. "I guess it would depend on ground tactics."

"That's right. You can't fight all those people and expect to live long—and you sure can't get far always letting them have the first shot. Even if you survive, you'll end up in prison for taking the law into your own hands. The president might take a risk on pardoning you once but she can't pardon you twice. Vince, if you let it go—or just work with us in some way that doesn't involve going off alone on your personal mission—Lopez will go down. In time."

"Do you know where Lopez is now?"

"Not exactly."

He wondered if he should tell her everything he knew.

But if he played the FBI's game it would mean a long surveillance period—and Lopez probably leaving the country.

He'd made a promise to Chris Destry. And to himself. How could he explain to her, about guys like him and Chris and Diego, out there in the field? She'd flown missions, but the fanatical camaraderie of a Black Op team in the field was impossible to understand unless you'd been steeped in it.

Steeped in blood. In living day after day with almost no sleep, with death always an inch away...

A vow meant something huge, to a man like that. It was part of his soul.

Still, she was right. His life would be longer and happier if he let it go. He could let the Bureau do it their way. He could have another life on the island. With new friends. With a new business.

Maybe even with Dierdre. Who was so painfully right about everything. What she said was so true, it hurt.

Except...

Vince Bellator had made a vow.

The juke box in *the* One Percenters was playing "The Golden Age of Leather" by the Blue Oyster Cult.

One Percenters, Vince knew, was a sardonic reference to an old-time claim from some motorcycle club that "Ninety-nine percent of bikers are sober law-abiding people." Hardcore bikers had laughed, hearing that, and took up wearing breast-pocket patches that had *1%* sewn on them.

This afternoon there were five motorcycle club bikers in the over-warm, cave-like One Percenters Bar and Grill. And then there was Soren Lenger.

Diego had described Soren: Long silver-blond hair flowing over his narrow shoulders; a scraggly silver-blond beard. "Big nose, small eyes," Diego had said. Scar on his upper right cheek, not acquired in a fight—got from trying to smash through a plate glass window while very, very stoned. Usually wearing a sleeveless denim jacket, cut roughly down to little more than a vest. A flying dragon tattoo along his right forearm. Diego's description fitted the man sitting alone, nursing a beer in a booth along the left-side wall.

A wannabe biker, never quite made it into the club, Vince judged. He could come in this biker bar here because it wasn't the MC's private club, which was probably somewhere out in the boonies.

The others, sitting at the bar with a girl, had cut-down denim jackets too. But the backs of their jackets sported the club colors: *Sonora Scorpions MC* curved under a red image of a striking scorpion. They looked as rough as any bikers Vince had ever seen. Arizona was an open carry state and three of the men had pistols holstered on their hips. A shotgun awaited on hooks over the bottles at the bar, and the woman serving drinks looked like she'd be comfortable using it.

In a booth on the right, near the juke box, was a mustachioed dark man, maybe half Native American, half Mexican, wearing a sweat-stained ivory-colored cowboy hat, a silver eagle on its band. He had a double shot of tequila in one hand and was talking in Spanish into a cell phone.

Vince walked over to the wannabe biker sulking over his beer. He leaned his backpack against the booth divider as the man squinted suspiciously up at him.

Vince gave him a friendly nod. "Soren Lenger, isn't it?"

"You don't look like a cop," Soren said, leaning back to look him over. "But you could be a bill collector."

"Really? Me? Come on."

"Maybe not. You got all that red dust on your face. Looks like a bike helmet thing."

"I came here on an old Harley trail bike."

"Bill collectors don't ride Harleys. Unless…" He glanced toward the men at the bar. "Might depend on who you're collecting for."

"I'm neither cop nor bill collector. Just a friend of Diego Fernandez."

"Diego?" Soren looked away, a sullen sadness in his eyes. "What about him?"

"He told me where to find you. Said we might be able to help each other. Can I buy you a drink?"

"Well, shit. I guess so, if you're a friend of Diego's. What's your damn name?"

"Culaine."

"Cool Aim? That's a corny moniker, man."

"Cul-*aine*."

"Cool Brain? Whatever. I'll take a Jack Daniels with a Coors back."

Vince nodded and went to the bar, just as the Wi-Fi juke box started a Kid Rock song that always got on his nerves. The talk at the bar went quiet as five tanned, battered faces turned silently toward him. Vince didn't meet their eyes. This was their hang-out in town, and he was an outsider. No reason to challenge the pecking order if he didn't have to. Sometimes meeting the eyes of men like this was enough to constitute a challenge.

Vince smiled at the bartender, a woman in her mid-thirties, darkly tanned skin fetchingly contrasting with her crystal-blue eyes.

Her lipstick was pink gloss. Her plunging gathered Mexican blouse displayed copious, surgically-enhanced cleavage; she had brunette hair, shaved on the side, spiky on top, and tattoos on her right shoulder and forearm of videogame and anime characters. He recognized one of them—AstroBoy. On her left inside forearm was a tattoo of the Sonora Scorpions colors. She wore very tight silver lame pants. Vince admired the completeness of it: the monumental cleavage, the pants, the pink lip gloss—everything necessary to maximize tips from a mostly male clientele.

"What'll you have?" she asked, in a smoke-roughened voice.

"I'll have a draft, IPA, and we'll need a double Jack and a Coors back."

"You got it." But she put the tip of her right index finger to her tongue, reached out, ran it down his face. She showed him the result on her fingertip. Red dust. "I got a nice clean damp bar towel for that."

"Thank you." He'd rather not, but what could he say? He'd rather have red desert soil on his face?

She brought him the towel and went to get his drinks as he looked in the mirror to wipe his face. He used the opportunity to indirectly look at the men at the bar. They'd gone back to talking—except one, who had a thick white beard, braided down to his breastbone, eagle eyes glinting under thick white eyebrows. Gaunt, lined cheeks. An old timer, still looking Vince over.

Vince had the uneasy feeling the aging biker had recognized him. A lot of outlaw MCs were involved in drug dealing. Would these guys have a deal with the Caidos?

At the end of the bar was a sylphic young woman with long, straight blond hair; she wore a red jean jacket over a tight Kyuss t-shirt, and red jeans. She was peering toward him, open-mouthed; a face and a look in her big brown eyes that made him think of a deer caught in the headlights. Or a frightened child.

Vince gave the bartender the towel back. "Thanks."

"You clean up pretty good, mister," she said looking at him appreciatively. "I'm Doris."

"My name's… Carl. Carl Culaine." Smiling as winningly as he knew how, Vince laid down enough cash to more than cover the drinks and a tip and returned to Soren with the drinks.

"Thanks!" Soren said, licking his lips. "Is that a double?"

"It is," Vince said sitting across from him.

Suddenly the music stopped—and didn't restart. Vince wanted to talk to Soren without being overheard. He went to the juke box, and selected, 'Eat the Rich' by Motorhead. That, he knew, would be loud enough to cover their conversation.

As he returned to his seat, the older biker with the braided beard seemed to recognize the song—he spun on his stool to Vince and gave him a thumb's up.

Vince grinned, gave the thumbs up back, and returned to Soren, who'd already downed half his whiskey. "Soren—I understand you know something about…" He leaned closer. "…Rancho de los Santos."

"Whoa, man…" Soren shook his head. "When I told Diego about that, I was high. I didn't know what I was saying."

Vince chuckled. "You worked there. I can pay for the information, Soren. Five hundred. But I'll need you to go out there, in the area, with me. Partly for confirmation—two hundred fifty when we head out, two hundred fifty when I locate the place."

"It's not that hard to find. There's a road."

"I don't want to approach it from the road. We'll find another route. I'll need you to answer questions about what we see out there."

106

"They'll see me, man. They'll kill me! I'm lucky they've left me alone this long."

"I'll protect you. A thousand dollars, Soren. Final offer."

Soren grimaced. "I don't know. I mean—sure, I'm broke. I need about four hundred to get my wheels out of hock." The song ended, but someone put on another Motorhead number, 'Ace of Spades' and Soren swilled down half of his beer. Then he shrugged. "Let me think about all this for a minute, dude. How's Diego?"

"He's good. He's got two years clean and one year sober. He's just headed up to a western Washington State for a new job."

"Doing what?"

"Construction."

"Yeah? Good for my man Diego. Me—I got nothing going on. I want to leave Stapp, for good—but I need my bike back. Yeah, let's do this thing. How we going to get out there?"

"I'll give you enough to get your bike back, and six hundred besides, later on. But you got to show me this place."

"How I know I can trust you?"

"You can trust the color of my money, Soren."

"What you going to do with the Caidos out there? You fuck with them they'll cut you to pieces."

"My business."

"Yeah, whatever. At this point I don't give a fuck. Except—one more requirement. You got to buy me a double cheeseburger at Marilyn's Café. And a beer… two beers… to go with it."

"Done deal. I'm hungry too."

They shook hands on it and agreed to meet at the café in an hour. Vince got up, picked up his backpack, and went out through the back door to the dusty parking lot. On his way he noticed that two of the bikers and the slender blond were no longer at the bar.

A brisk wind was driving red dust through the sky, tingeing a herd of racing clouds as Vince went to his Harley. He started to put on the backpack but a cry of pain swerved his attention to a little utility shed against the back of the bar. The woodshed doors were open and inside, with the mops and buckets, were two Scorpions bikers crowding against the thin blond girl from the bar. The shorter man had a hand raised as if he'd just backhanded her. She was pressed against the back wall, with her long hands held up to block the next blow.

"Don't, Willard!" she whimpered, looking at the shorter of the two; a fireplug of a man with long matted brown hair and a procession of scorpions tattooed up his left arm. His right hand was gripping her crotch.

The bigger man—with droopy mandarin mustaches, purple sunglasses, and a hooked nose festooned with little silver rings—had hold of her hair. He had a pot joint stuck in the corner of his mouth; it drooped like his mustache, drooling smoke.

"You said if we gave you a line you'd put out," said Mandarin Mustache. "You had your blow."

"I'm not doing you both, and not here," she said, her voice breaking. "I meant—I'd do Arty! Just him!" Vince figured Arty must be the mustachioed one.

"Keep your damn voice down, Nilla!" Arty growled.

Vince shook his head. He didn't want to get sidetracked with these thugs and probably the local cops into the bargain. But it just wasn't in him to let them have their way with her.

Nilla tried to rush past them and Arty grabbed her by the throat and slammed her back against the wall. "Pull her trousers down, there, Willard," he said. "I'll get through her panties myself."

"Who says you go first?" Willard complained.

"I'll get her one way and you t'other."

108

"Let me go, it's outdoors and you stink and you're hurting me!" Nilla cried.

"Oh Hell," Vince muttered. He drew his Desert Eagle from under his coat and said loudly *"Gentlemen! A word!"*

Chapter Seven

The two Sonora Scorpions swiveled toward Vince. Willard had his pants undone and one hand in the fly.

"Willard," Vince said, pointing the Desert Eagle, "you've got your hand on the wrong weapon." He started slowly toward them, both hands on his gun, moving the sights slowly back and forth between Willard and Arty, as he went on, "This automatic fires a .50 round. It'll blow your ass right in two, one shot. Now, I don't want to fire it. I might hit the girl. I'm trying to help her, not kill her. And I don't want trouble with the Scorpions. I don't want trouble with the cops either. But I'm not going to let you have her."

Willard slowly pulled his hand from his pants, and glanced over at Arty, who seemed frozen with surprise.

"Now," Vince went on, "you might be thinking of pulling the girl in front of you and drawing your guns. But then I'll just shoot Arty there through the head. I can't miss from here, and then I'll get Willard even if he gets me too."

"What the fuck you want, you fucking psycho?" Willard asked, shaking his head in dull amazement. His face was mostly beard and snub nose, red now in angry mortification. He had tattooed tears of blue ink coming out of the corners of his eyes. His right hand was now creeping toward his holstered pistol.

"I want you to let the girl go," Vince said, stopping within arm's reach of Willard. "Don't touch that gun, Willard, or I'll splash your brains all over that shed."

Willard froze.

"Gentlemen—what do you want to do?" Vince smiled at them like a tourist agent offering them a choice of travel arrangements. "You want to dance with Mr. D—or live to fuck again?"

"What you give us for her?" Arty demanded, trying to save face.

"I've got a hundred-eighty dollars in my pocket, right now," said Vince. "All I have on me. I'll give you that. And I won't kill you. In return, you leave her alone for good."

"Fuck that!" Willard said—his voice halfway between a snarl and a whine. "She's gonna be our whore and we're gonna break her in!" He sounded like a man angry at being cheated out of his life's dream.

Then Willard reached for his revolver—and Vince cracked Willard on the noggin with the butt of the Desert Eagle. Hard.

Willard's eyes crossed and down he went—as Vince swung the gun to Arty.

"Reach for a weapon and I pull the trigger," Vince said.

Arty said, "Chill!" He slowly put out his right hand. "Let's see the money."

Vince reached into his left-hand jeans pocket, tugged out the small roll of bills and tossed it to Arty, who caught it, flipped through it with a greasy thumb, and nodded. "Good enough. But the brotherhood's not gonna be happy you pulled a gun on us."

His pistol still leveled, Vince stepped back and said, "I went easy out of respect for your MC. If I'd wanted to, I could have crippled you two and taken her out of here, before you could touch your guns."

"Oh, is that right? You going to play commando?"

"Rangers and Delta Force. I'm not playing."

"Oh, sure buddy, right!"

"Tell you what. Drop your gun, and I'll put mine away—and you can step out here. I'll let you take a swing at me. And then, Arty, *I'll unscrew your head from your shoulders like a twist-off bottlecap.*" Arty looked into Vince's eyes, and then he shivered. "Well, fuck—a deal's a deal, I guess."

"Drop your gun. You can come back for it, soon as I ride off. Just drag your little compadre there into the bar and put a cold compress on his head. He'll be all right."

Arty blew out his mustache ends then dropped his pistol on the ground. Vince stepped back and watched him drag Willard through the back door and into the bar.

He looked at Nilla. The deer in the headlights look was back. So was the gaping mouth. One of her front teeth was noticeably longer than the other.

"What you gonna *do* with me?" she asked breathlessly, her eyes growing even bigger.

"Drop you off any place you want, long as it's not too far away," Vince said. "Come on, let's get on the bike. It'll be tricky with the backpack… you'll have to sit on my lap for a ways."

Nilla was wearing the overcoat and knit cap he'd bought her as they left the Walmart, where he'd cashed his last thousand-dollar traveler's check. They were out in the cold wind now—it was one reason he'd bought her the overcoat and hat. Vince was carrying the backpack. They'd made him check it at the door when he came in.

He'd had to show I.D. to cash the traveler's check—they didn't run his I.D. through anything, they just checked it against the name. He had plenty of money in the bank but he was reluctant to use an ATM until he really had to. He didn't want to leave tracks in the system.

"What ya gonna do with me now that ya own me, Vince?" Nilla asked suddenly, as they reached his Harley. She seemed more interested than scared.

"I told you, I didn't buy you, I just sort of… bailed you out. You need to leave town because those two pricks might start looking for you." He shrugged into the backpack. "One reason I got that hat and coat for you was so they wouldn't spot you quite so easily. You should put your hair up inside the hat."

"How'm I going to leave town if you don't give me a ride? Hitchhike?"

"I noticed a Greyhound bus stop. Sign said next bus to Sedona was…" He looked at his military-issue watch. "About fifteen minutes from now. I'll buy a ticket from the driver for you to pretty much anywhere it's going. Maybe you can join a cult in Sedona or something."

"Join a what?"

"I was joking."

"Oh! I don't get it."

"Where are your parents?"

"I'm not a kid! I'm twenty-one! For two months now!"

"Yeah but—where are they?"

"My mom's in Red Rock Correctional. For another eight months. My dad, I don't know where he is. Not for ten years."

Vince grunted. "I see."

"But *you* can take care of me, right?" She stepped closer, gently caressing the line of his jaw and gazing up at him with her big doe eyes. She lowered her voice. "I can make you feel good, Vince. And I need someone like you. I'm scared. The Scorpions think they own me."

"They run girls?"

"Um—some do. Like them two at the bar—anyhow they want to. It's not the club doing it."

"Who was that old guy with the braided beard, in the One Percenters?"

"That's Orville Ortega. Club President. He's like half Mex and half Indian and half German—"

"That's too many halves. But I get the idea. He's not running girls?"

"No, he don't like it, but he don't like to butt into what his guys do, most the time."

"Yeah, okay. Orville. How's he make his money? Drugs?"

"Not no more. He got so he's down on it. Too many people he liked died, that's what he says. Makes his living from a 'cycle repair place. And he sells guns. The kind he's not supposed ta sell."

"Interesting. You have any other relatives you can go to?"

"I got an Aunt Suzie in Phoenix. She don't want to see me."

"Are you addicted to anything?" She opened her mouth to answer, her face screwed up in outrage—and he put a hand over her mouth. "Nilla? Don't lie."

She kissed his hand and he hastily removed it. "I done some drugs. I just did a line with Willard and Arty. But I'm not *addicted*-addicted, you know. I don't even like 'em much. But it's like, I try to feel better sometimes. It kinda works and it kinda don't. We going somewhere?"

"I'm trying to decide if I can trust you with some cash when I send you on your way."

She squirmed in place and wrung her hands. "You don't like me? I'm really, *really* good in bed—"

"Girl, it's not that, you're not… um… I'm sure any guy would be lucky. But I've got some really dangerous business to take care of."

"I can help ya! Just stay with me tonight and we'll see how you feel tomorrow and if you—"

"Nilla!"

"What?"

Vince noticed they were being stared at by an elderly couple loading bags into their station wagon. He lowered his voice to a whisper. "You're too young for me."

Also too damaged, too uneducated, too needy, and that was just for starters. But he left it with too young.

"I told ya I'm—"

"I know, I know. Let me think."

Vince knew that if he left Nilla alone in this town, the scummier Scorpions would come looking for her. They would force her into a human-trafficking prostitution deeper than she'd ever imagined—it would be a form of slavery. She might end up seriously addicted to drugs. She might end up dead.

Just as he'd ended up feeling responsible for Lupe and Pascual, he felt he had to take care of Nilla because he'd gotten entangled in her life. He knew her mother had likely modeled the ugliest side of street life, for her. Nilla didn't know a better way.

Then, there was the feeling he sometimes got. A feeling—almost *a voice,* from some high, lonely place within him, telling him he had to help some particular person. He felt it now.

It felt like he had been there for Nilla, today—because something higher wanted him to be there.

But still. He couldn't take care of everyone. He had another mission. How was he supposed to help her? " He turned and looked her in the eyes. "Listen—you ever held a job?"

"'Course I did! I was a cashier at Gulley Wash Ice Cream and Soda. Then I was a waitress at Marilyn's. She fired me because I spent too much time talking and I added up some of the checks wrong. But I was a good waitress, I never stole nothing, I never spilled nothing."

"Uh huh. A diamond in the rough." Should he do this? Another crazy move. But it felt right to him. "Okay… I might have a job for you. It'll require some training and you'll have to take a long trip… I'll give you some money. God help Diego and Lupe."

"Who's that?"

"I'll tell you about them later. They're good people." How would Lupe take this? He'd have to call her, talk to her about it. She might not want Nilla round Lupe. His instinct, though, was that Nilla genuinely wanted something better. That she'd jump at a real chance. Lupe might well understand that. She'd needed something better herself. "Nilla—You want to work in a new restaurant way up north?"

"Will you be there?"

"Sometimes."

"Then… Okay."

"It'll be a long trip but I'll give you money to take along. You can take a bus, get to a train, or maybe hop a short flight. I'll give you all the information you need and a phone number to call Lupe and Diego. I'll tell them you're coming. Before I head on… this job I have to do… I'll call them up. If you change your mind about going, you can keep the money."

"I could keep it? But ya don't own me?"

"I don't, no."

She pouted, looking close to tears. Vince wondered how much damage the girl's family had done to her.

"Vince?" "Yeah?"

"What's ya last name?"

"It's… I'll tell you some other time. Not right now. Less you know about me the better right now. But if you go to the address I give you up north, they'll know who I am. Ask for Lupe. She's expecting you. She'll train you."

"Is this one of those things where they say ya gonna be a waitress but it's a whore and they won't let you leave and stuff?"

"Jesus! No!" But then, he didn't blame her for asking. Those things happened. "No, I swear to you, they're good people. You don't have to stay with them, either. If you don't get along, you can leave."

Nilla stared off over the parking lot for a moment and then said, wistfully, "I'll see ya for sure, for real, up there, sometime?"

"Yeah." *If I don't get killed.* "We'll... work that out later. You'll see me—we'll hang out with everyone else." He had no intention of ever getting into an intimate relationship with Nilla. "If it doesn't work out, we'll find something else for you." He let go a soft groan. "How do I get myself into these things?"

"What things?"

"Never mind again. Come on, let's get you a sandwich to take on the bus..."

"Wouldya give me a hug before I get on the bus?"

"A hug? Sure."

"Okay."

"Now, let's climb on the bike, in the same awkward way, and hope to hell we don't get stopped by the cops for it, because it's an illegal way to ride."

"Okay. I like riding with you."

"How'd you come to find this place, Soren?" Vince asked, as Soren brought them both tin cups of coffee from the rusted iron woodstove.

"That's a story, man..."

It was an hour after dawn, miles out in the desert northwest of Stapp. They were sitting in the ruins of an old wood and adobe house, with enough walls and roof left to provide a little shelter. The weather was turning cold—at an average fifty-five degrees Fahrenheit, it had been warm for December in the high desert. Now a cutting wind was soughing in through the fractured walls of the abandoned house, driving the temperature down and slapping at the small fire they'd built in the old fireplace. Vince was wondering if Nilla had kept going past Sedona. Was she cogent enough to get all the way to Harstine Island? Or would she wander off and spend his money on drugs somewhere? At least she was away from Stapp—away from the likes of Willard and Arty.

He took a protein bar from his coat pocket and ate it with his coffee, looking around, thinking this was a strange place to end up just before Christmas.

The previous night, soon as it was dark out, Soren got his beat-up 1987 Harley out of hock and, after sticking some extra cans of gas on the bike's saddle bags, he led the way here on a disused gravel road across the basin. The two bikes were parked in the house, near what remained of the door. According to Soren, the abandoned house was six miles from the rancho.

They'd made camp on the bare, dusty floor inside, Vince building a small fire in the old fireplace. They'd eaten take-out sandwiches they'd brought along, Soren nursing a pint of Jack. In the spare light from the fire Soren had used a pencil stub to scrawl a rough layout of the Rancho de los Santos, which Vince committed to memory.

Now, looking around at the ruined house, in the roseate and blue tinged morning light, Vince noticed bullet holes in the walls. And he noticed Soren, standing by the stove, coffee cup in hand, staring at the backpack.

"You're wondering what's in the backpack," Vince said.

"It's a big pack. I mean—your underwear? Granola? Trail mix? Or..."

"There's some food, and a change of clothes. There's a Kevlar vest. Also, a MAC-10 with a couple of clips. And some more ammo for my handgun. A high-end set of binoculars. A few small tools that might be useful, like wire clippers. A camping shovel, too. Stuff like that. No money or drugs, if that's what you're thinking."

"You don't seem like you're into getting high. What's the camping shovel for? A latrine?"

"For one thing." After a moment he added, with a shrug, "And graves, when needed."

Soren stared at him—then laughed, mistakenly thinking that Vince was kidding. "But I've been wondering if you're gonna tell me who you are. Culaine? Bullshit."

"I don't think it's going to matter long, so—my name is Vince Bellator."

"Like—*Captain* Bellator? Who Diego talked about every time anybody mentioned the Army?"

"The same."

"Was he really in the Green Berets?"

"He was. Saved my life once."

"He said you saved his!"

"We tried to get each other's backs out there."

"You going to tell me what you're after out here?"

"I paid you to answer my questions, Soren—not to ask me questions."

"Okay, man, fair enough." Soren slurped coffee and wiped his mouth with the back of his hand. Then he put it on the floor, took out the makings and started rolling a cigarette.

"That is just tobacco, right?" Vince asked. Knowing some people mixed pot in with their tobacco.

"Yeah. Bugler. Cheapest they had for sale."

119

"That's good. We need to keep a clear head today."

"You ever smoke pot?"

"I have, of course. You think I'm a dweeb? But it makes me either paranoid or stupid, so I didn't get into it."

"I know what you mean." Soren lit the rolled cigarette with a zippo lighter and took a puff. "You ever take acid?"

"No. Psilocybin mushrooms, though. It was instructive. Not something I'd do often."

"Heroin?"

"Government issue morphine, when I got shot. Didn't care for it. But I put up with it for a while." Vince nodded toward the bullet holes across from them. "You shoot those holes in the wall?"

"Nope." He gave a sigh that had a particularly miserable plangency to it. "I was here when it happened…" He moved to the wall, put his back against it, slid down it till he was sitting on his sleeping bag. He sat there sipping his coffee and gazing thoughtfully at the bullet holes. "Yeah see, I had a girl. Her name was Rosa. She lived in this house with her folks. They had all the land by the creek there, for a quarter mile either way, added up to a lot. They had sheep and goats out there. Selling goat milk to those fancy organics people, and making Indian jewelry. Bred Indian ponies too, or that's what they called 'em. They were actually a Norwegian breed. They got by."

"Native Americans?"

"Not that many pure-blood Natives around here. Those are mostly on the Res. But she was half Southern Paiute. We went to high school together, and we were close. She kept an eye on me and then we did some X and fell in love and…"

"You took MDMA and fell in love? If that's what you want to call that."

"We *stayed* in love, man. After."

"Oh okay. A rarity. What became of her?"

"Rosa wanted to go to college in Phoenix and her dad didn't like the idea. She decided to raise money for it working at the Rancho. You'd be surprised how many people work for these dope dealers just to get college money. That's how fucked up it is now with colleges."

Vince nodded. True, that.

Soren went on, "This was like three years ago, when they started up making the shit there, and bringing in the Chinese garbage."

"The meth and the fentanyl."

"Yeah. We'd started doing the meth, see. Her and me. She knew where Manny got it…"

"Who's that?"

"Oh, he's dead. Another dead guy. I knew three or… yeah, four people died from opiate ODs. Anyway, yeah, the Caidos were paying a lot of money to put on the gas masks and work in those tin roof buildings cutting the Fentanyl and packing up the meth from their lab and shit, and I followed her out there and they started paying us in dope as much as money and…" He gave out a dry sobbing sound. "And… we couldn't deal. A little fentanyl, a lot of meth. We were going insane. She wanted to kill herself. I said, Baby we got to get out of here. We slipped away, we left, and we came back here, to this house you're sitting in, thinking we were gonna go to Phoenix the next day. But Jorge—we called him The Man Without a Soul, when we worked at the ranch—he got the idea we were gonna go to the feds or something. Not our plan. Then Jorge and the cartel fuckers came here, looking for us and they shot Rosa's dad, and they shot her brother, and they set fire to the house, and Rosa and her mother and I ran off and I heard Rosa yell. She caught a bullet, Rosa did I mean. Only managed to get away because we rode the horses out, rode 'em into a place it was hard for them to follow. Real narrow

121

gulley, see. They couldn't get their Humvee through the rocks there. So, we got away and…" He cleared his throat. "Rosa was dead the next day. Her Ma wouldn't eat and she died pretty soon after that and… I tried to join the Scorpions, thinking they'd protect me from the Caidos—Orville doesn't like cartelitos—and that didn't work out and I started drinking and didn't quite stop… and I guess I don't wanta say no more about it."

"And all that happened here?"

"Yeah. I come back here sometimes to talk to Rosa. She still walks here, man. She's *here*. She's a ghost and walks around the house calling for her folks. I talk to her but she don't answer me."

Vince nodded. He wasn't going to tell Soren that he was imagining the ghost of Rosa. "So's that part of the reason you're out here helping me? It's not just the money?"

"Oh, I don't even know why I do half the shit I do, man. Let's not talk about that anymore. Let's get something done."

"Okay. Let's saddle up."

Angel Lopez never admitted it when he was mistaken about something. Not out loud. He regarded it as a bad policy, to admit a mistake.

But as he watched Pavel Krupin and Boris Lorvec get out of the limousine, in front of the compound's main house, Angel was feeling increasingly sure that his association with the Russians was a mistake. These KGB men—no, not KGB anymore, they'd changed it to SVR. These SVR agents were beginning to remind him of loan sharks who'd preyed on his family, in Veracruz.

The loan sharks had started out offering hope, saying don't worry about the payment schedule, and then they moved in and took everything his parents owned. Soon after that, Angel and his brother and two others in his small gang of boys, none older than fourteen, had killed the three loan sharks, stabbed them to death as they slept. And later Angel had started his own loan shark business. It really bugged him to be the one preyed on. Better to be the shark than the shark's meat.

But Angel couldn't kill these Russians—as much as he'd love to see the expression on this smug Krupin's face as his throat was cut. He knew the SVR would find him and kill him if he did that.

Krupin had advanced him the money to buy into major narcotics. And then he'd hovered in the background ever since, telling him what to do. Keeping fifty per cent of the profits in a "special account", claiming he'd get it later. Involving him in the smuggling of goods to the big ship that was going to spread propaganda in the USA.

Angel didn't give a goddamn about politics. As far as he was concerned, he himself was going for King of the World. A monarchy, with Angel Lopez as monarch. That was his idea of politics. But he was nervous about giving the FBI another reason to come after him.

"They won't find out who's supplying the ship," Krupin had assured him.

But Angel knew very well that if the CIA and the FBI did find out about his connection to that ship, they would come after him, and Krupin would shrug and vanish.

Thinking all of this, he forced a smile on his face, and stepped off the porch, extending his hand to Pavel Krupin. They shook hands, Krupin's feeling clammy.

Angel didn't extend his hand to the looming, watchful Lorvec. Both he and Krupin wore off-the-rack suits today; long dark overcoats, shiny Moscow-issue faux-leather shoes. Angel had a quiet contempt for their clothing.

"It's cold and dusty out here," Pavel said, looking around the compound. They spoke in English. "I thought it would be hot and sandy."

"Even Arizona has winter," Angel said, shrugging. "And no one can tell the wind what to do. Come in, and have a drink, then we give you the tour."

"The tour first, then the drink," Krupin said.

There it was again: the Russian was telling, not asking.

Curly Estrada was standing, arms crossed, beside them, and he gave a snort at what the Russian had said. Angel gave him a warning glance and Curly, sometimes too vociferous, didn't say what he was thinking.

"Bueno, Pavel," Angel said, nodding, just as if he didn't care. "Let's have our tour. Right this way."

I will kill this man, someday, Angel promised himself.

They walked around the back of the wide ranch-house, past a cluster of prickly pear cacti, and to the first of two hangar-like buildings with steel roofs. Beyond them was the new building, a three-story dormitory for workers.

"Of course, you know," Angel said, as the two Russians, and the two hulking, scowling Ukrainian bodyguards, followed him, "if you want to see the product prep rooms in the cutting room, you must wear gas masks, and special coats that cover your clothing. The fentanyl—the Chinese synthetic heroin—the dust from it will make you sick otherwise. It is incredibly powerful, uncut. It might kill you."

There was some muttering amongst the Russians. Then it was decided that one of the Ukrainian bodyguards would go in, with the gas mask and special clothing, and have a quick look, and report.

The meth-lab building was dangerous too, but not so much, so they were all able to have a quick look inside from just inside the door. "So many employees here," said Krupin. "How do you keep them all under control? Some will talk."

"Fear, of course," said Angel, shrugging. "Making examples. And also, we have initiated a special dormitory here. Make them comfortable there when they're not working. Television rooms, a bar. We keep them here a certain amount of time. We have an elaborate system I can explain…"

While the Ukrainian was looking over the fentanyl processing building, they looked over the dormitory building. Cluttered rooms, each with three bunkbeds, baskets of dirty clothes. "Do they not have the… the trace chemicals in here?"

"We haven't yet shown you the shower rooms behind the work buildings," Angel said. "We take precautions."

"Tiresome to have to bury people out in the desert," Lorvec muttered, chuckling to himself.

"You have something to say?" Curly said, glaring at Lorvec.

"Me?" Lorvec feigned surprise. "No. You?"

Krupin spoke sharply to Lorvec in Russian. Lorvec shrugged and stared into the middle distance with a blank look on his face.

Angel took them back outside, and pointed out the fences, the razor wire around the place.

"Doesn't that look suspicious, from the air?" Krupin asked.

"People think it's a toxic-waste processing plant," Angel said placidly. "The police in town, the mayor—they are all my people. Just like Fuentes back in Santo Virgil. All is smoothed over."

Krupin grunted skeptically. He said something more to Lorvec in Russian, who laughed softly to himself. Angel would have given a great deal to understand Russian just then.

Krupin cleared his throat and said, "Let us go in the house, and talk about the shipments to…" He broke off as one of Angel's armed guards rushed up. Like all the guards he wore a private security uniform to give an appearance of business legitimacy, should anyone come around. He had a gas mask hanging down around his neck.

"Boss, there's been a… a problem," the young guard said in Spanish. "The man is dead, he insisted, he…"

"What man?"

Angel demanded. "The man from… he said the Ukraine. He came with this Russian here with you, boss! This Ukraine man insisted he would try some fentanyl. I told him—I said it in English—the drug there is uncut, right now, it is pure! But he said it was nothing to him and he took off his mask and he took a handful up his nose… and he's dead!"

"The imbecile son of a whore!" Angel snarled in Spanish. Then he took a deep breath, finding he was not entirely displeased about this—it might serve as a lesson to Krupin about how serious the work here was. About the risks he ran. He turned to Krupin. In English he said, "Your man is dead. He wanted to try out the fentanyl and he would not listen. Maybe his English was bad…"

Krupin swore softly in Russian. Then he said, "Just as well. I don't want idiots on my staff. We were talking of graves in the desert…"

"We shall take care of it," said Angel. "There is plenty of room out there for the dead."

It was about nine-thirty in the morning and the wind of the desert winter whistled almost musically past the chimneys of rock towering to either side of Vince and Soren. On the basin below, red dust lifted, rippled like silk scarves, and settled back as the wind slackened.

The two men were lying on their bellies, peering north out over the desert basin, at the barely visible buildings of the Rancho de los Santos about a mile away. Vince and Soren were in nearly the only high vantage point in the basin, here: an outcropping of sandstone, hoodoo towers of rusty-red jutting up from shelf atop an escarpment over the desert flatland below.

Their motorcycles were hidden among the boulders behind them, and they were stretched out in the shade of the rocks, trying their best not to be seen. The Caidos drug processing compound was a long way off, but there could be sentries out there with their own binoculars or patrolling nearby. They could have observation drones in the air too. The cartels, in Vince's experience, operated somewhere between an organized gang of thugs and a well-supplied and trained paramilitary outfit. He knew better than to underestimate them.

Vince wriggled back, downslope a little, and picked up the Oberwerk binocular telescope Dierdre had given him. This wasn't the place to use the tripod. He wrestled the heavy instrument up to his observation place beside Soren, and propped them up on a rock, got up on his elbows, looked through the eyepieces, and adjusted them.

A clump of tall saguaro cacti sprang into clear view. Vince slowly moved the instrument's lenses till he found the Caidos narcotics prep compound in an almost entirely barren flatland of sand. Too bad—not much cover around it.

The compound was surrounded by metal hurricane fences topped with razor wire. There was a big metal gate with a guardhouse out front—and on the gate was a sign: *Central Arizona Waste Processing*.

To the west, outside the high compound fence, was a tarmac airstrip. On it was a high-end twin-engine prop plane. If Angel was here, he'd probably come in on that.

Just inside the southern fence was a disused horse paddock, left from the previous owner, and an old weather-grayed barn that looked like it was falling in on itself. Vince tracked the view to the main ranch building, one-story, quite wide. Metal roofed. Adobe-over-wood walls in two wings. Mason stone chimney. Two communications antennae on the rancho's roof.

A black limousine was pulled up in front of the rancho. There were five SUVs and two jeeps parked on one side of the front door; on the other side were two Humvees, and two pickups; parked along the west side of the rancho building was a school bus painted dull green.

As Vince watched, a sentry in a private cop uniform, an AK47 on a strap over his shoulder, strolled around the rancho house and past the Humvees. Vince could see two armed, uniformed men at the gatehouse, and others walking the perimeter. He made out six men on the perimeters and suspected more.

Behind the ranch house—visible from his higher elevation—were two-story buildings, like medium-small hangars, with elaborate ventilation systems up top. One of them had a surprising number of dead birds on the steel roof. Must be where the fentanyl processing happened. Remembering the crude diagram Soren had made, he figured the three-story building in back was employee housing. It was all reminiscent of something Apple computers would have going in China—but without the drugs.

He lowered the eyepieces and said, "Soren—how many sentries are there, total?"

"Been a while since I was there. Last I knew, fourteen men. Might be more now. Lot of them are in those buildings in back, keeping an eye on the dope."

"How many workers?"

"Twenty. Ten in each building. A couple of the meth-lab workers are chemists. Or were, in my time. Most of the lab workers are women, now, I understand. These Caidos, they think women are more manageable. I'm not so sure about that myself."

"Security cameras?"

"For sure. Lots of them. I never counted them. Most buildings have some."

"How does the power come in?"

"There's a power line from the highway. I gotta ask you…"

Vince looked at him. "What? Spit it out, Soren."

"Maybe you ought to tell me what you plan to do. I'm kinda worried about those workers in there. They get offered a shitload of money and they're all from *no* money. They got sucked in. But they don't deserve to die. Or go to jail for half their lives. You going to turn them over to the feds?"

"Not my plan. Why? You think I'm some kind of freelance snitch?"

"I don't know *what* the fuck you are except you killed a lot of people in your time, man."

Vince nodded. "Fair enough. I'm not giving anyone to the feds. I can't tell you everything, but Lopez knows what I plan for him, anyway. So, I'll tell you that much. My plan is to kill Angel Lopez. I owe him for some things he did. I made a vow. Him and his bodyguard."

"How you going to do it without the workers in there getting hurt?"

"Haven't figured that out yet."

"How you figure to do it anyway with all those men down there?"

"That's an open question too. For the most part. I have some ideas. First thing is to destroy that plane over there and as many vehicles as I can so that Lopez can't get away… If he's there. I think I saw him just now but I'm not completely sure."

"Listen, Cool Brain. Bellator. Whoever you are. I don't want to get killed out here. And I don't want anybody killed that shouldn't be. I don't want 'em to get killed because of me."

"I'm not going to hurt the employees, Soren. I'm not going to kill anybody who doesn't need killing. You can take my word for that, or not." Vince looked through the binoculars again, and saw the black limousine pulling away. The men who might well be Lopez and Curly were watching it go. Who was in that limo?

He turned back to Soren. "Why do they call it 'Ranch of the Saints'?"

"You're stretched out in the middle of the reason." Soren turned over on his back and pointed up at the chimneys of rock looming over them. "See those? Some folks call them hoodoos. Now back in the day, there was more grass around here. You could raise cattle. And some Mexican ranchers came in and they saw those things—from down on the basin, them rock towers look like giant people. And they said they were the saints watching over them. Maybe you should say a prayer to those rocks." Soren cackled to himself. "Some people used to come out here and do it."

Vince looked up at the eerie semi-human shapes looming over them. "I'm not praying to those rocks. I'm going to have to hope they're on my side. Either way I'm going to do what I'm going to do."

He looked back at the rancho through the telescope. "Well, well," he murmured.

Walking in a group between one of the outbuildings and the house were five men, heading for the limousine. Vince couldn't be sure, but he thought one of them was Angel Lopez, and beside him was the one they called Curly.

Who were the others? One of them was blond. Could they be the Russians?

"See something?"

"Yeah. Maybe so."

"So, Vince—all those sentries, all those gunmen at the compound… what you going to do about *them?*"

He turned to Soren. "Are any of them legit security guards?"

"Hell naw. They're all cartelitos."

"Then that part of the plan is simple, Soren. If I have to, I'll kill them all. Every one of them."

Chapter Eight

"You really shouldn't be here, Corlin," said Agent Chang, as they drove the Crown Vic into Stapp.

"You tell me this now, Richie?" Dierdre said, as she pulled into the parking lot of the little police station. "We've been driving for hours. You just think to mention that I shouldn't be here?"

"It's just things you said in the last half hour. About Bellator. About Angel Lopez. 'Maybe sometimes you need to let a Vince Bellator do what he does.' I mean—come on."

She turned the engine off and they sat there, the dust settling around the car. "Just thinking from different... points of view. It's just talk. Devil's advocate. You know?"

Chang shook his head. "You're caught up in his slipstream," Chang said.

"Last time, Vince Bellator was right. You said so yourself. If he hadn't done what he did, all those people in that crowd in D.C. would be dead. And those senators would be dead. And Professor Shit Head would have gotten away."

"So Bellator *did* kill that guy?"

"Seems pretty obvious. But the Bureau either didn't find proof or didn't want to. The killing of him and his bodyguards had all Vince's…" She cleared her throat. "Bellator's hallmarks."

She glanced at Chang. Saw him looking at her. Something in his eyes… Anguish.

Dierdre knew Chang desired her, though he'd never made a move. Maybe he was even quietly infatuated. She found him attractive enough, but… She'd long ago made up her mind, *No intimate relationships with other agents.*

Anyway—there was Vince.

To Dierdre, Vince Bellator was like the planet Jupiter to a passing asteroid. That asteroid is going to fall into Jupiter's gravitational well. Vince was gentlemanly, intelligent, roughly good looking, ripped, decisive, dangerous yet kind. He was a protector of the innocent. It was in his nature, maybe in his DNA. He had a sense of humor. He had saved her life twice. He was relentless, he was powerful, but he never boasted, swaggered, or showed off. He had vulnerabilities and he was honest about them. He was effortlessly sexy.

Don't think about that, Dierdre.

It would be stupid to fall in love with Vincent Bellator. Dangerous for her career. For her life. For her peace of mind.

But deep down she knew it was too late.

"What happened at the Lincoln Memorial," Chang said, "was a unique event." He tapped his fingers on his thighs, and then—in a decisive motion—unhooked his seatbelt. "Let's talk to this cop—see if we can find enough cause to take Lopez down without Bellator having to play cowboy again."

"Are you clear about what *not* to say to the Chief here, Richie?"

"Yes, we only went over that about eight times."

"Twice. Okay, three times."

They got out of the car, went through the door to the front desk. A deeply tanned officer, who looked to Diedre like he worked out but still drank too much beer, stood up behind the counter. He appeared to be a police sergeant, with crewcut blond hair, a brilliantly toothy wide smile. His blue and black uniform had an off the rack look to it. His name was under his badge: *M. Hills*. "Folks, how can I help you? Directions?"

"Not exactly," Dierdre said. She took her badge from her purse and showed it to him. Chang moved his coat aside so the cop could see the badge on his belt.

"Officer Hills, I'm agent Corlin," Dierdre said. "This is Agent Chang. We'd like to talk to the Police Chief." She handed him her card; Chang handed over his own.

He blinked at their badges, licked his lips, then flashed his smile again—but it wasn't as confident. "Uh—What can I say your, uh… I mean, you know, the subject of…"

"We'll tell him ourselves," Dierdre said, looking him in the eyes.

Hills wilted a little and then said, "Just a moment, ma'am… agent…"

He went past two empty desks and into a back hallway. There was a murmur of garbled male voices.

"I guess it's not as if we came here with a summons, or a warrant," Chang said.

"Oh, he'll see us," Dierdre replied softly.

Hills came beaming to the hallway door. "Chief Galway will see you. Come on through. Down to your right."

They found the plump, surprisingly pale Chief of Police standing beside his desk. Hands were shaken and names exchanged. A man of about forty-five with receding brown-gray hair, he was wearing the local version of a blue police chief's uniform, with gold braid encircling one shoulder.

"Oh, I should've known who was who from your cards, there," said Galway, with a folksy chuckle, as he sat down. "Take a seat and tell me how I can help the FBI."

They sat down, Dierdre taking a pen and notebook from her purse. She poised pen over notebook as Chang said, "We're looking into the activities of the Caidos Cartel in Arizona. We have sources that suggest that Angel Lopez, the boss of the cartel, is operating in this area. Have you or your officers heard anything to suggest that?"

"No, not at all," Galway said, his eyebrows raised. He laced his fingers in front of him and frowned down at them. "I don't think we've heard anything like that." He unlaced his fingers and laced them again and shifted in his chair. "The cartels are all in Southern Arizona."

"They were," Dierdre said. "They seem to have moved north. Are you familiar with a company called the Central Arizona Waste Processing?"

Galway's face went blank, then puzzled. "Oh sure! It's about twelve, fifteen miles from here. They employ a good number of people out there. I looked in on them once—didn't want to stay long. There's toxic waste out there. The county environmental engineers were out there too."

"Really?" Chang said. "Do you have their names?"

"The engineers? Ah... no. Not... not as such. I could ask around." He frowned down at his laced hands again. Then up at them. "Is there some reason to suspect something's off with that facility?"

"We're not entirely sure," Dierdre said. "Just checking off the boxes." She wrote a few things in her notebook, mostly just to keep the police chief on his toes. Then she added, "They just seem to have a surprising number of armed men out there."

Galway unlaced his hands and rubbed them thoughtfully. "Dangerous stuff, toxic waste. But, uh… I couldn't speak to that. I haven't counted their security guards."

"We need to get a deeper sense of Stapp," Dierdre said.

"What… kind of sense?" Galway asked.

"Every town has some drug dealing," Chang said. "Locally—where is it sourced?"

"As to that," said the chief, seeming relieved, "a lot of the problem here is speed; amphetamines of one sort or another. It comes from meth labs outside of Phoenix—so we understand. We've been exchanging info with Phoenix PD on that."

"How about fentanyl?" Dierdre asked.

That sudden blankness in his face again. "Oh… haven't seen much of that here. Oxycodone shows up. I mean—kids stealing their parents' prescription drugs, mostly. We can show you our narcotics files, if you like. And by the way there's a biker club here I don't care much for, to say the least—the Sonora Scorpions. We've caught a couple of them with drugs. Not dealing quantities but…" He snorted. "Bikers, am I right?"

"I would in fact like to look through your files," Dierdre said.

Galway nodded vigorously. "How's tomorrow morning? We need to get them organized for you. We're a little understaffed today."

Dierdre hesitated. But she didn't have the legal authority to insist on seeing them now. "That'll do. We're over in the High Desert Inn."

A half dozen more questions, none of them productive, and then Dierdre and Chang went back out to the little parking lot and sat in the Crown Vic.

Dierdre looked at her notes. She hadn't written much.

"You think he was covering up?" Chang asked.

"He was nervous. Scared even. I think he's in it up to his neck."

"Didn't tell us anything, really. He seemed relieved when you got onto looking into local drugs."

"Because Lopez doesn't distribute locally. 'Not in your own backyard'. I notice he got a very sort of distant and puzzled look when we talked about the waste-processing plant. So-called."

"It's almost the only local industry here, except an outfit that digs gravel and sand for concrete. Galway knew exactly who we meant. But he acted as if he had to work at remembering the place."

"We've got nothing to go to court on." Chang looked at her. And kept looking at her.

Dierdre looked back at him. "What?"

"Is Bellator out here? In Stapp?"

Dierdre pretended an intense interest in her notes. Then winced, realizing she was acting like Chief Galway. She sighed and put the notebook aside. "I'm not sure."

"But if Lopez is out here—Bellator has an obsession with Lopez. And you suggested we come out here." His look became a stare. "You're out here to find Bellator?"

She snorted. "No!" She wasn't, after all.

"Then you want to take Lopez down... to protect Bellator! Keep him from getting his head shot off!"

That was...

It was quite true.

She took a long breath. "I'm doing my *job* out here."

But she was actually here, she knew, in a bid to try to save Vince Bellator's life—or maybe save him from prison. If she could get enough evidence to call out a raid on the Central Arizona Waste Processing compound, she might be able to have the place raided ahead of Vince. If Lopez happened to be there, onsite, he could go to prison for a long time. Vince would have to let his mission go.

137

And then…

Chang groaned softly. "Jesus, Dierdre, that's it, isn't it?"

"We need to take Angel Lopez down, no matter what. Why not now?"

"We're not the DEA—"

Dierdre's phone rang, then. She answered, relieved to get out of this exchange with

Chang. He was her friend, and a man she respected. She didn't want to lie to him.

The call was from the Washington bureau offices. "Agent Corlin here."

"Agent Corlin, this is Phil Lazlo." A gravelly voice she'd only heard twice before.

Dierdre swallowed. It was the Deputy Director of the FBI.

"Where are you now, Corlin?"

"Stapp, Arizona, sir. Chang and I are looking into the possibility of a Caidos presence here." D.D. Lazlo went implacably on, "We're calling you back in, Agent Corlin. You're to fly out from Phoenix ASAP. Things are coming to a head here. You're suspended from duty, at this time, for your part in the extra-judicial action at the Lincoln Memorial. Personally, I'm sorry about that. I think I'd have done the same thing you did. But—I have to tell you, you are likely to face federal charges. You are hereby required to report within twenty-four hours."

Riding their Harleys side by side, Vince and Soren tooled up the dirt road toward the Sonora Scorpions MC property at the eastern edge of Santos Basin. Outcroppings and boulders humped up close behind the buildings, and the wind blew red dust past the hurricane fences around the front of the acreage. They rode past the bones of mule deer, the skull standing out white in the sickly shine of the pale winter sun; they passed a stand of winter-barren cottonwoods, shivering in the wind; they crossed rattlesnake trails and coyote tracks.

Then they reached the front gate of the club. Wired to the fence beside the gate was a metal sign, with two bullet holes in it, and with the Sonora Scorpions colors on it. Below that, was wired a fierce yellow and red *NO TRESPASSING!* sign.

The gate was open but two bikers lolled on a bench in the shade of a three-sided shack, close beside it. Keeping watch, Vince assumed. Both were red-bearded men with long, gray streaked red-brown hair and deep-set eyes, their arms blue with old tattoos. A half empty bottle of tequila sat on a little gray wooded table beside them, next to a handful of motorcycle tools and greasy motorcycle parts. There was a tall bong sitting there too, oozing smoke from its glass chimney. A half-deconstructed Indian Motorcycle engine lay in the dirt beside the bench.

As Vince and Soren rode up, the two bikers stared at them as if trying to decide if they were real or hallucinations. Vince noticed a double-barrel shotgun leaning on the wall next to the tequila bottle.

The Harleys pulled up about thirty feet away, Vince and Soren letting the engines idle, straddling the bikes. Soren leaned toward Vince and murmured, "That's the Pierson brothers, on sentry duty. Buzzard Pierson's the one missing an ear there. Clap is the one missing the front tooth."

"Remind 'em who you are, Soren," Vince said softly.

"Hey, Clap! Hey Buzzard! You remember me—Soren Lenger!"

Buzzard stood up, scooped up the shotgun. Vince's hand slipped into his coat to the butt of his gun but he didn't pull it. Buzzard hadn't leveled the shotgun at him. The biker squinted at Vince and then at Soren—and then back at Vince. "Who the fuck?"

"It's *me*, Buzzard," Soren said, genially. "I've been out here at least three times, brother!"

"He ain't no club brother!" called Clap. "Ask him what he wants!"

"What you want, Soren-I-been-here-brother?" Buzzard demanded mockingly.

"We come to buy some goods from Orville!" Soren replied.

Vince took a handful of large bills from his pocket and waved them. He had decided not to worry about the government noticing his whereabouts right now, so he'd withdrawn money from a Stapp branch of his bank. By the time the law traced him and sent someone out, he'd have left the area—or he'd be dead.

"I remember that guy!" said Clap, coming out, now carrying a large revolver. He pointed at Vince. "He was in the bar and he jumped Willard and Arty out back!"

"Is that how they tell it?" Vince asked, grinning. "They can talk to me about it. But I do need to talk to Orville."

"Go ahead and call Orville, Clap," Buzzard said, never taking his eyes off Vince.

Clap pulled a small walkie talkie out of his back pocket, thumbed a button and said, "Orville! Two riders out here! They wanta buy from you! It's that big son of a bitch that suckered Willard, and that Soren guy!"

Static from the walkie talkie and then a voice, fuzzed with static. Apparently Clap understood it. "Says let 'em in, but escort 'em," said Clap.

"Get your hand out of the coat with that gun, real slow," Buzzard said. "Put it on the ground."

Vince did as he was told, leaning over to lay the gun carefully down in a tuft of grass; placing it carefully to keep dirt from getting in the barrel.

"Ride slowly inside, I'll follow!"

They rode through the gate, Buzzard following closely, gun in hand. To the right was a building that looked like an old highway roadhouse, with stone outer walls, small windows through which Vince could see Sonora members shooting pool. He could hear a Johnny Cash song playing. 'Ring of Fire'. Something more than ten Harleys, an Indian Scout motorcycle, and one Vincent Black Shadow were parked alongside the roadhouse.

"Hold up right there," Buzzard called out. "Shut off them engines."

Vince and Soren stopped the bikes, shut them down, and climbed off, setting the kickstands. Vince was sorry he didn't have the Desert Eagle. He had the MAC-10 in the trail bike's saddlebags, which Buzzard had been too stoned to check, but Vince had high hopes he wouldn't have to use it.

To the left was a large, well-kept two-story house, painted a sunny yellow with oxblood trim. Clean white lace curtains in the windows. Front yard had a white picket fence and a neatly arranged rock garden, stones alternating with aloe vera plants. The house was something a man builds for his wife, Vince thought. Orville's house, maybe. Parked next to the house was a black Dodge Ram pickup and a 2016 Mercedes Benz in gold sparkles.

The gravel entry road between the buildings ended about a hundred yards onward in a pile of the familiar red sandstone that replaced the back fence of the compound. Vince noticed what seemed like a narrow path between two of the boulders.

The door of the clubhouse opened, magnifying the last chorus of the Johnny Cash number, and out came four men wearing

Sonora Scorpions togs. One was Arty, another was Willard, his head bandaged up; the other two, Vince didn't know: a smaller biker with a rat-like face and dull blond dreadlocks was muttering to Arty; towering over Willard was a big man, even bigger than Vince. The massive biker wore a Native-American style buffalo fur headdress, complete with horns. He had stoned gray eyes and a Van Dyke beard and mustache. On his arms were inaccurate tattoos of Native American symbols. He didn't look a whit Native American.

"That's the guy, Sig!" Willard said, pointing at Vince.

"You bring your big sister to beat me up, Willard?" Vince asked, nodding toward Sig.

"Oh, Christ, Bellator," Soren muttered.

"What'd you say?" growled the big man.

"Willard pointed me out to you," Vince said. "I thought maybe the idea was to sic you on me."

The big man came to a stop. Vince was literally in his shadow.

"You said—big sister?"

"Oh, sorry. Must be that fake fur on your head. You're his brain-damaged brother, maybe?" "You hear that, Sig?" Willard said, hopping in place in his urgency to prod Sig after Vince.

Vince had speculated that if Willard and Arty were here, he was going to have to prove himself. Speculation borne out.

He looked at Arty. "You spend that cash I gave you already, Arty?" he asked lightly.

Arty looked at the ground. "Oh, I…"

Willard glared at Arty. "What cash?"

"I paid him to let the girl go, Willard," Vince said. "He didn't tell you?" He pretended surprise.

"Never mind that!" Sig roared. He pushed Willard aside and stalked toward Vince—who circled around to Sig's left side. He didn't want the Harleys getting knocked down.

Sig swung around and charged at Vince.

Vince stepped aside at the last possible moment and stuck his boot out to trip the big man.

Sig pitched face-down with a resonant thump.

Vince sighed. "Come on, Sig! Watch your step! Think about your balance, your center of gravity!" Vince thought it best to make Sig as angry as possible. A man caught up in anger usually fights badly. And Vince needed an edge. Sig was… *big*.

"Oh, he's a professional wrestler!" Willard said. "Just you wait!"

"Is he?" Vince said. "But this fight isn't fixed like those are."

Hearing that, Sig growled and got quickly to his feet; he tightened his fists and rushed, swinging a left at Vince.

Ducking easily under the roundhouse, Vince set himself and brought his right knee up in a Muay Thai move that cracked hard into Sig's ribs. He felt bone fracturing, then he spun out of reach.

Yelling with anger and pain, Sig staggered, then got his feet under him—but Vince moved up behind him and he shoved Sig's head dress down over his eyes.

Soren and Arty laughed at that.

Vince spun again and slammed a spinning hook-kick into the big man's belly just under the cracked ribs. Sig gasped and went down on his knees, wheezing and cringing with pain at the motion made by the wheeze. Then wheezing again—and cringing again.

Vince pulled the headdress away and tossed it across the road. "Now you know why those things are a bad idea, unless you're an Indian medicine man, Sig." He reached down and took the only weapon he could see on Sig, a sheathed knife, and tossed it with the headdress. "I cracked a couple of your ribs on purpose, Sig," he went on. "I could have killed you, if I'd wanted to. I'd suggest that you don't want to fight me anymore, 'cause you're at a disadvantage now. Am I right?"

Moaning, clutching his side, Sig nodded.

Vince patted him on the shoulder. "See, you're learning things, that's good. We all have to keep learning, brother."

Turning away, Vince noticed Willard arguing with Arty about the money.

He heard a hearty, rasping laugh from the porch of the house, and saw Orville strolling to him, a can of Coors in one hand, the other outstretched. "You did good, Culaine," Orville said. "What you told Arty might just be true. You were Delta Force?"

Vince shook his hand. "I was."

"I was in the Navy. My brother, he was a Marine Corps badass. Got himself KIA though."

"Sorry to hear that."

"You got my respect! Sig's needed a little education for a while now. I told him today he looked like a bitch in that headdress. He give me some big-ass fantasy story about Indian spirits from when he took peyote once."

Vince nodded. "Psychedelic warrior."

"That your trail bike there?" Orville asked. "What is that model?"

"Rebuilt 1966 Harley SX 250 Aermacchi MX," Vince said.

"You rebuild it yourself?"

"No, a close buddy of mine rebuilt it with his old man. My buddy died in a firefight, and I did a favor for his family so—they gave it to me."

"Nice piece of iron man, but isn't it a little small for you?"

"Sometimes does feel that way," Vince admitted. "But believe

144

it or not I ran it to the top of the speedometer on the road to Stapp. Ninety!"

"That right? You're lucky you didn't blow out a cylinder or something."

Vince nodded. "Whose Black Shadow is that over there?"

Orville grinned and slapped his chest. "That baby is mine!"

"Beautiful. An old piece of machinery though—early 1950s. How's it run?"

"Oh, it runs like a top, man. It's totally rebuilt! I had to have some of the parts machined. You know what a pain in the—hold on a second. *Arty, Willard, Slim, get that bullheaded dumbass into town, get his ribs bandaged up! Now! Put him in the back of my truck and take him in that! Keys are under the front seat!*"

Moaning, Sig let Willard and Arty help him up. He tottered with the three men over to the Ram.

"Yeah, so that Black Shadow," Orville went on, "you know how much those fuckers are worth—even rebuilt?"

"I've seen them go for more than two hundred grand."

"I was offered *four* hundred grand for it!"

"Wow." Vince looked at the Black Shadow with real envy. "Orville—I am in need of some ordnance. A good military grade rifle with a scope, ammo, and maybe some explosives. C-4, say. I'm not saying you've got that stuff…"

"Who says I do?"

"No one specifically. Just… hints."

Orville snorted. "And who says I *don't!*"

Vince laughed. "Listen—I should tell you something. We need to trust each other, so I should be straight with you. My name isn't actually Culaine. It's—"

"Vince Bellator," interrupted Orville. "I knowed who you were.

I figured it out at the One Percenters. I tell you what, my ancestor tree's gotta apples, oranges, pears on it. I'm all kinda stuff. But I got black and red in me and I don't put up with no fucking Nazis. We don't allow that stuff in this club. What you did in D.C.—man that took motherfucking *balls*. I thought you might be him but I wasn't sure you were the guy till I saw you playing with Sig there. I figured if you wanted an alias, that's your business. But I tell you something, a man like you—I could use you in this club. In fact..." He lowered his voice almost to a whisper. "I got no one to take over. None of these guys measure up. And I'm gettin' long in the tooth. If you ever needed something to belong to with fewer rules than the fucking Army, who knows, you could be the man..."

"That's flattering, Orville," Vince said. "I'll keep it in mind."

"Now, the goods you want, the best stuff, Vince, it's kind of expensive."

"I took more than three grand from the bank."

"I'm inclined to give you a discount for teaching Sig some humility, Vince. It's in them rocks back there. Let's have a beer in the club. Then we can go see what I've got to sell..."

Vince looked at the boulders, and the little path between two of them. "You have an armory in the rocks?"

"It's an old silver mine. Played out. But I've got a use for it."

Dierdre used the little hotel's guest-office computer to write the letters and printed them out. She glanced at the door of the little cubicle, beyond which was the hotel lobby. No sign of Richie Chang yet. He was still on the phone up in his room, arranging their rather sudden flight to D.C. from Phoenix. He'd have to cancel her ticket, but he didn't know that yet. Chang had several calls to

146

make so she was pretty sure she could get out of the hotel before he came downstairs.

She proofread the first letter. After an address and date, it read:

To: Mr. Philip Lazlo, Deputy Director
    Federal Bureau of Investigation
    Washington D.C.

Dear Deputy Director Lazlo:

This letter is to convey to you my immediate resignation from the Federal Bureau of Investigation. I have decided that my part in willingly piloting the helicopter during Vincent Bellator's intervention at the Lincoln Memorial has made me a possible source of disruption to the good order of the Bureau. As I acted without authorization, the Justice Department should not be held responsible for my actions. For those reasons I choose today to resign. I will give my badge, business cards and special identification to Agent Richard Chang, to turn over to the Bureau for me.

While I cannot return to Washington D.C. immediately, I will return soon to submit myself for any federal charges which may be laid against me.

I am honored to have been able to serve my country in the Federal Bureau of Investigation.

A hard copy of this letter will follow the email attachment.

Yours sincerely,

Dierdre Corlin

"'Return soon'… in a relative kind of way," she muttered to herself, as she got a pen from her purse.

She choked back tears as she signed the letter. She scanned it and sent the scan through the hotel's guest computer to the Bureau. Then she read through the note to Chang.

Dear Richie:

I have submitted my resignation to the Deputy Director at the FBI. Enclosed is a copy of the letter I've sent them. I'm going to scan the letter, and send it via email attachment, and I'll be sending a hard copy too. I will have gotten this done by the time you read this letter. I will be very selective for a while in answering my phone. I *do* intend to turn myself in fairly soon, but I have some things to do first.

Please cancel my plane reservation. I'll be staying in this area for the time being. Please do not seek me out. I ask you that, as a friend. I'll be in touch eventually. I am enclosing my badge and Bureau I D. card, please take them to the Deputy Director for me. I also enclose the Visa expenses card. I will have to turn in my gun later. I'm sorry to have taken off like this but I'll be back around.

It has been an honor serving with you. Please take care of yourself.

Dierdre

The tears came then, silent but unstoppable, as Dierdre signed the letter. She took a deep breath, wiped her eyes, put the letter to Richie in a manilla envelope, along with a badge and the ID and the Visa card and a copy of the letter to the Bureau, sealed it, and wrote *R. Chang* on it. She filled out an express-mail form, using the Bureau's payment code and put the letter to the Deputy Director in the express envelope.

Dierdre took all this to the front desk, where the blue-haired elderly lady with the arthritis-gnarled hands took charge of the envelopes. "Now let me see—this one for your friend, I'll hold here for him," she said. "I can get that express mail out for you today, ma'am, but it won't be overnight from here."

"That's alright. Is there a place I can rent a car?"

"Only place in town for car rental is down at the gas station, they have four or five they rent out."

"I'll just walk down there then. Agent Chang will be settling up for us."

Dierdre picked up her luggage, all packed and ready by the front desk. Going out the front door, she felt the reality of her resignation. And what she was getting herself into.

Down the rabbit hole, Alice, she thought.

Dierdre really did feel as if she were in freefall.

The gas station was just a block away. Using her personal credit card, she rented a Ford van of the "soccer mom" variety and drove quickly away. Just as she turned up a side street, she saw Richie Chang driving down the main street in the Crown Vic, probably looking for her.

She wasn't a fugitive officially, yet. Maybe it wouldn't go that way at all. But she felt like one.

Richie didn't spot her, and she turned up another street and headed for the stores at the other end of town. She'd buy a sleeping bag and a few other things. She was planning to sleep in the van, that night. It might be dangerous for her to stay in town. If the Chief of Police was dirty, he'd probably told the Caidos that she and Chang were here.

And there was no telling what Angel Lopez might do about it.

"I can't believe Clap thought you were going to leave without that Desert Eagle," Soren said, as they got off the bikes behind the ruined house.

"Said he was just 'taking care of it for me'," Vince said. "He's totally full of shit, of course."

Vince had the bolt-action Tango 51 Tactical Operations Inc rifle, complete with scope, strapped across his back. He had a box of 7.62X51mm NATO .308 ammo to go with it. He bent over to take his other purchases from his saddle bags: Three sets of C-4 explosive, with blasting caps, detonation cords and triggers, four M67 grenades, three battlefield flares, and two additional clips of ammo for the MAC-10.

With arms full of gear, Vince started toward the house—and stopped when Soren said, "I think I'm gonna get my stuff and take off, Cool Brain."

Vince turned to see Soren staring at the explosives. "You a bit spooked by my shopping?"

"Last time I saw a guy with stuff like that, he was joining one of those domestic terrorist militias—the kind you mowed down back in D.C."

"They mis-use the stuff. I won't."

Soren nodded. "Probably true. But... I don't know how much good I'd be, out there. It's not my thing, bro. I can do a bar fight. Protect myself with a shiv. But firefights, bombs... I want to try to restart my life somewhere, man. Not end it real quick. Maybe that makes me a chickenshit."

"No," said Vince. "It makes you rational. Come on in, I'll pay you off and send you on your way."

"You really going to hit those Caidos tonight?"

"Orville says he heard Lopez is still out there. I'm worried he might fly off in that plane before I get to him. I need to make sure it's no good to fly, for one thing."

"You ever think that if you were to put a bomb in the plane and he and that prick Curly were in there, you could deal with 'em both

150

that way? While they were in the air, you know? Christ, listen to me, you got me planning on blowing up planes."

Vince smiled ruefully. "I did think of it, sure. But who'd be flying the plane? Maybe some pilot they hire for the job. Could be the guy knows almost nothing about what goes on out there."

"Doubtful. But yeah—there's a chance of that."

"I check my fire carefully." In truth, Vince figured, the pilot could still get caught in the crossfire. But Vince would never deliberately kill him, unless he knew the guy for a cartelito.

He turned away, went around the corner of the ruined house. Just before going in, Vince stepped by one of the holes in the wall and looked through—and saw no one waiting in ambush.

Half an hour later, Vince watched Soren ride away on the Harley. He had gotten to like the guy but he was glad Soren was bugging out. One less responsibility.

He looked at the sky. It was getting toward dusk. Filtered through a thin membrane of clouds, the sun was a bloodless disk hurrying to the horizon.

Vince scanned the basin, didn't see anything out there except the lengthening shadows of cacti and scrub trees. He turned and went into the house to get something to eat and think about tactics.

He had eaten some dried food bars, was just loading the rifle, when he heard a clatter of rock falling nearby. It had sounded like something sliding down the hillock on one side of the ruins.

Maybe just an animal passing by, dislodging some rock as it went. Or maybe a man. Could be coyotes—or Caidos.

Vince put the rifle down, picked up the MAC-10, and went silently to a hole in the back wall, crouching to look left and right through the gap. He saw no one, but it was dark on that side of the house. He slipped through and stopped. Listening. Nothing.

He started toward the hummock…

And then someone stepped up behind him, stuck a gun in his back and said, "Freeze right there, big man."

Chapter Nine

Vince was impressed. He couldn't remember the last time anyone had successfully snuck up on him. "You are one sneaky son of a bitch," Vince said, hoping to get the guy talking. As opposed to shooting. "How'd you do that?"

"I tossed some rock down that little hill over there," said the man behind him. "Draw you out there. Circled 'round."

"Usually, I'd have heard you anyway…"

"Oh, making no noise is a skill I got from my ancestors. My dad taught me how to sharpen it up. Granddad taught him. Drop that weapon and put your hands up."

Vince thought about spinning around, maybe do it fast enough to get out of the way of that barrel and fire his MAC-10. He must have tensed, because the guy said, "Don't try it. Won't work."

Vince snorted. "Mind-reader too?"

"Body language reader. You have till three to drop that weapon. One, two…"

Vince dropped the MAC-10 and raised his hands.

He heard the man behind him take a couple steps back. "Now

turn slowly around. I'm going to back toward the corner of the house. You're going ahead of me inside."

"Sure thing."

Vince turned around. He couldn't see the man clearly in the dim light. He was able to make out that his captor was of medium height, trim, and he had a Winchester rifle in his hands.

The stranger backed up, into the weak light of the sundown, and stopped, and Vince saw he was Native American, full blood or close to it. Which made sense, because of that native indefinable-something in the accent. Fairly young guy, not more than thirty. Black-brown eyes, short black hair, neatly parted, wide cheekbones, a beak of a nose, a look of wry amusement on his clean-shaven features. He was wearing a red-plaid long sleeve flannel shirt, blue jeans, and hiking boots.

"Anybody ever tell you that you dress like a grunge-rocker from 1990?" Vince said, trying to stir the guy into more talk.

"You dress like a guy who thinks he's passing as civilian. But you're not fooling anybody."

"I've been a civilian for some years now."

"Only technically." He waved the muzzle of the Winchester toward the house. "Go on ahead of me."

"That where you plan to shoot me?" Vince asked, as if making casual conversation.

"Whether I shoot you depends."

"On what?"

"Right now, it depends on if you go where I goddamn tell you."

Vince nodded, once, and walked into the ruined house. An evening wind was pushing through the big holes in the wall, making his clothes flap. He stopped in the middle of the room. "I've got a knife in my boot. You want me to take it out?" He was hoping to earn this man's trust.

154

"No—take off the boots—without touching the knife. Once you have a knife in your hand, a guy like you…"

"How do you know what kind of guy I am?" Vince asked, sitting on the floor to pull off his boots. He tossed the one with the knife well out of reach. He still had his back to the man with the gun.

"I've been watching you for quite a while. Spotted you over at the Santos rocks, while you were spying on the Lopez compound. I got a look at your face. You're Vince Bellator."

Vince sighed. Maybe he should go back to the beard. "Someone hire you to kill me?"

"You'd already be dead if they had. I'm a good shot with this Winchester. No. I'm worried about my sister."

"Whatever was done to her, it wasn't done by me."

"She's working in that compound. Trying to get the money for medical school. She started having second thoughts about it when some of our people in Maricopa Res died from fentanyl overdoses."

"She had no concern for anyone else dying from that crap?"

"She's pretty angry at the world. At the white establishment. She thought alcohol was the big danger to the Res—and stuff like meth and opiates were used by spoiled white kids in the 'burbs. Then the narcotics started spreading everywhere. Meth.Oxy. Fentanyl."

"What were you doing out in the desert when you spotted me?"

"Same thing you were, scoping out the compound. I want to get my sister out of there."

"They won't let her leave?"

"Nope. The Caidos think anyone walking out on them is gonna rat them out. They keep promising to let them leave—but they don't."

"What's that got to do with me?"

"I thought you were maybe working for the FBI. And if the place gets raided, my sister spends the next twenty years in jail. I read in a chatroom you were like a shadow agent for the FBI."

"Don't believe everything on the internet. I did share a little info with the Bureau but…" Vince shook his head. "I'm no federal agent."

"How about the other guy you were out there with?"

"Soren? Just an itinerant biker. I hired him as a guide, is all. And to help me make some weapons connections. He's harmless—and he's leaving the area."

"If you're not a fed, what's the surveillance all about?"

"Reconnaissance. Reconning the enemy. My enemy is Angel Lopez. I have nothing against your sister. I figure people processing the narco garbage are desperate for work. I am not holding them responsible. In fact…" He was beginning to have enough of talking to someone over his shoulder. "You mind if I turn around? You can aim that gun right at my heart, if you want. I'll just stay on the floor, and you'll be way out of my reach."

"Yeah, I guess so."

Vince turned around and sat cross-legged. "I don't suppose you'd take the word of an Army Ranger—and just trust me?"

"Hell no. I don't care who you worked with. It's about the man you are. I'm gonna sit down. I want to get out of this wind." He sat across from Vince, legs crossed, gun laid on the floor facing Vince. He kept his right hand on the gun.

Vince had no plans to jump him. "How'd you get out here?" he asked.

"I got a cousin sells electric quad bikes. Real quiet. He loaned me one. It's… a little ways from here. Hidden."

"You know my name. Fair is fair."

"There's no fairness involved." But he looked Vince in the eyes for a long moment. Then he said, "I see you."

"Good to know your eyes are functional."

"The guys with the medicine in my tribe—it's what they'd say: I can *see you*—who you are."

Vince had been developing his own ability to judge character since becoming an officer in the Army. The sensory keenness of combat had sharpened that ability even more. He nodded. "I know what you mean."

"My name's Harris Ahakhela." After a moment he added, "Harris because my old man said I made him think of a Harris Hawk. Something to do with how shiny my black hair was. Shape of my nose."

"What tribe?"

"Yavapai."

"Yavapai. 'People of the Sun'."

"Look at that, you read a book sometime."

Vince grinned. "A few. Your people have some connection to the Apache."

"Old alliances. Nowadays the Apache are more interested in their casino money."

"Your sister wants to be a doctor?"

Harris nodded. "That's Bianca's dream. We don't have enough access to good medical treatment on the reservation."

"Ironic to help make poisons and want to be a doctor."

"She's figured that out."

"You have ambitions of your own?"

"I'd like to teach ethnology—and Yavapai culture. I've …" Harris broke off. "Fuck all this. Tell me what your plan is. How does it affect my sister?"

Vince hesitated. Could he really trust this kid that far? But he needed a way to get the factory workers out safely. Harris would be motivated to help him do that. And he had a feeling Harris would know if he lied to him, or tried to mislead him.

"I saw Angel Lopez execute a family, in Mexico. I wasn't able to stop him. I tried… He killed my best friend. I took a vow: I'm going to kill him. I'm going to have to get through a lot of Caidos thugs to get to Lopez. I'm determined to protect people like your sister. I've been trying to figure out how to do that. If you're willing to work with me, I think we can get her out safely, along with the others…"

Harris sat back a little, raising an eyebrow. Then he said, "Let's build a fire. Getting cold in here. And we'll talk."

The big metal column of the outdoor heater ticked to itself. Somewhere a coyote warbled eerily. The wind sighed and whispered.

Sitting in a padded deck chair on the patio behind the ranch house, Angel decided he needed more information before he made up his mind about leaving. He took out his cell phone and called Sergeant Fuentes. He used the phone number that no one knew about but him and the Fuentes. They spoke in Spanish.

"You find out where the Big Stranger is yet?"

"No," Fuentes said. "But we're close, Angel."

Even over the phone, Angel could tell Fuentes was scared. Maybe more scared of the feds than he was scared of Angel Lopez. That was something Angel did not approve of. He wanted all of his people to fear him--to fear Angel Lopez first and foremost. He was jealous of their fear. "What's going on, Fuentes? Don't lie to me. Don't assume I don't already know."

"Angel… let me close the door." There was a pause, and then Fuentes came back on the line. "What is going on… the FBI has been coming around. They came to my office. An agent named Butterfield and another man. They asked some questions that made me think they know about our… our deal."

Angel was stunned to hear the feds knew about Fuentes' connection to the Caidos. But then he'd heard the FBI was asking questions in

Stapp, too. He'd given Hills his marching orders about that. "What did you tell these federal bitches, Fuentes?"

"Me? Just that I had no special knowledge of the Caidos."

"Yeah, they're onto you. You'd better make yourself useful to me and fast, my friend."

"Angel… believe me—"

"You said you were getting that Big Stranger's fingerprints run for me?"

"We just found a good print, today, across from that house, Angel. He touched that old man's arm in the street—got blood on his hand. Touched a car bumper. But we ran into a problem—he is very… his files are high-security. Classified. We don't know why. We can't get the information released. Not even his name."

"I might know someone who can help. I'll call you back. See you keep your mouth shut."

Angel hung up, and immediately called Pavel Krupin. The Russian came on the line immediately. "Yes, Lopez? What is it, I am in…" Some of it was lost. Fading signal.

"Can you hear me, Pavel?" "Yes, I'm on a plane. It's not such good Wi-Fi."

"I hope to be on a plane tonight, as soon as I settle a couple matters. Listen—Fuentes has a fingerprint for my enemy. I have a suspicion he will be your enemy too. Because all his information is classified. We can't get his name from the fingerprint, or anything else."

"I think I heard most of… said. I… my man inside, still. I will see if he can get the file released to you, Fuentes. I will ask him to copy me. I do wish to have… myself… If you…" Then his voice fuzzed out entirely.

Angel hung up. Krupin had understood him, that was enough. He called Fuentes back.

"Yes, Angel?"

"My associate believes he can get the file to you. As soon as that's done you will get it to me. Send it as an attachment to the company email, to my attention, yes?"

"Yes. And don't worry—"

"I won't," Angel interrupted. "You're the one who should worry."

Angel hung up—just as Hendershot came walking up to the deck, hands in his pockets against the cold of the desert in December. The pilot was a tall, pale man in a sheepskin coat, khakis, cowboy boots; he had a drawn face, a wide jaw, smile lines around eyes that weren't smiling now. "Mr. Lopez, I'm overdue to head back. We were contracted for a short stay and a return." He glanced back toward the big hangar-like buildings with the armed guards in front of them. "I don't like to be at a place where they process toxic waste too long, either, to be honest."

Angel smiled. The man was entirely taken in by the cover story. Too bad he couldn't be trusted to know the truth.

In Mexico, Angel had his own pilot, a man who was deep in the cartel. But that pilot wasn't licensed for the USA. The FAA and Homeland Security looked closely at pilots. "Don't worry, Captain Hendershot, we're leaving tonight!"

"Really? I would've thought in the morning." Hendershot looked at the sky. "Heavy winds up there. Less turbulence tomorrow morning."

"Tonight, Captain Hendershot! Just see the plane is ready. I'll let you know when I am ready too."

Angel watched the pilot walk away, hunched against the wind, and began thinking again of Sergeant Fuentes.

Jorge stepped out onto the porch from inside. "The dinner's almost ready." Jorge was a chunky man with a pitted face and dead eyes. His voice was usually a monotone. But he was very efficient. Angel appreciated the fact that Jorge could cook too. It amused Angel to think that Jorge liked only three things: good food, money, and virginal girls who were too scared to scream.

"Jorge," Angel said, looking musingly up at the red electric glow of the heater post. "The FBI is sniffing around Fuentes. I expect some information from him, today. I need that information. Once that comes through, it would be well if Sergeant Fuentes had a convenient car accident."

The clouds are working with us, Harris thought, walking as silently as he could through the cold dark desert. *The clouds give us shadow tonight. They blind the stars and moon. The sky is on our side.*

The lights around the compound didn't reach far into the Santos Basin and didn't touch Harris as he glided soundlessly between small outcroppings and thickets of prickly pear and Joshua trees. He was approaching the airstrip on foot from the desert side, after having stashed his ATV—the electric quad bike—a quarter mile off in the basin.

As Harris moved toward the plane, crouched and stepping with exquisite care, he felt his pulse thudding, his mouth going dry. Maybe this would all end up with him shot, or in prison. Maybe it wouldn't help Bianca. But she'd gotten word to him that she felt trapped. There was a passel of bodies buried out in the desert; people who'd tried to wriggle free of the Caidos.

He had to try to get her out. He was certain he couldn't get past all the guards without Bellator on his side. He had to do this.

Harris imagined his father visiting him in some prison hospital, telling him, *"You were the one I could trust not to be stupid. But this time... you were stupid. Out of your damn head..."*

Maybe so, Pop. But I had to do it—the other guy was big, and doesn't have my mad skills for silent approaches...

Harris reached the plane, slipped up its shadow to the wings. *"That plane's an old Beechcraft Super King Air,"* Bellator had said. *"Maybe 1982, or so. Turboprop. Fuel tanks are in the wings... My dad had one from that era..."*

He took the tools from his small backpack, stood up under the wings, found the panel Vince had told him about. He had the penlight, held it with his left hand, pried open the panel with the tire iron. It was harder work than he thought. He had to pry one side, then the other, then back to the first. It took five minutes, six... and then it popped open. He spotted the fuel line and set to work. It took all his strength to dislodge it—but it opened enough to begin to pour a thin stream of aviation kerosene out. The smell of the fuel was powerful.

Don't make any sparks with the tool, he told himself, stepping back.

Harris ducked under the plane's fuselage and went to the other wing—this one was on the side toward the compound. He was able to stay in its shadow but he still stood a good chance of being spotted. He was in a hurry now. Too much hurry; he cut the side of his hand on a pried-open panel, this time. Blood ran down his hand and wrist. He ignored it and went to work on the fuel line. There—but ouch, that hurt, the fuel splashing the cut on his hand. He ignored that too.

Harris stepped back, put the tire iron in his pack, got the wire clippers out, went to the engine casing and opened it. Engines weren't mysterious to him—he saw the wires that needed clipping. He had to disable the engine too in case the kerosene fuel flow let them down, but it didn't. He went to the starboard fuel tank, found a good spot to light the kerosene inside the wing. The blue flames licked out and swished up to the tank; he ran to the port tank and repeated the operation.

Then he sprinted with every ounce of speed he had, into the desert... as the flames gushed inside the wings, pressure built, and the fuel tanks blew.

Chapter Ten

The *whump* of an explosion drew them all to stare toward the desert.

"What the fuck!" Hendershot burst out, stopping to point at the burning plane. Blue and yellow flames surrounded the burning Beechcraft with a Halloween glow. "The Beechcraft's on fire!"

Angel put his suitcase down beside the SUV. They'd been about to drive the SUV out the main gate and around to the plane but now he stared at the fire, startled. "*Que...*"

But he knew how. Someone was coming after him. Not the style of the American authorities. It would be the Sinaloa or...

It was Curly who said it, after stepping up beside him to stare at the fire. "*El Gran Extrano!*"

Yes. That's who it was. The Big Stranger. He'd threatened Angel; said he would kill him.

"We'll drive out of here," he said, in English so that Hendershot could understand. "Some of us will go in the Humvee."

"Here's Jorge."

The Columbian came running breathlessly up to them, with the three Caidos guards who'd been with him escorting the workers into the dorms. "Jefe! Who—"

But then the big mustached guard beside Jorge lurched, and fell twisting onto his left side. Dead before he hit the crack.

There came the distant crack of a rifle.

Much of the guard's head was shot away.

Before they could quite react, another guard fell; shot through the heart. The third one ran, got four steps, and went down, shot through the side of the head.

El Gran Extrano…

Angel threw himself flat. "Snipers!" he shouted. Curly threw himself flat beside him.

Jorge ducked behind the front of the SUV parked up against the ranch house, as a bullet cracked by, hitting the wall where Jorge had been a split second before.

"No no no *no!*" Hendershot was yelling, running to the door of the house.

Angel rolled over once to get closer to the SUV, then crawled under it.

"Angel!" Curly hissed, crawling under beside him. "What do we do!"

"I'm thinking…" He looked between the wheels of the SUV, out at the desert… it was all darkness beyond the compound's lights.

There was another distant *thump* sound—and all the lights went out.

Vince was flat on his belly behind a thick, five-foot-high stand of prickly pears, Tango 51 propped in his hands. He wasn't looking through the scope just now—he was eyeing the road, about a hundred yards from him, where blue sparks jumped and spat from a severed power cable on the ground. The fallen wooden power-pole burned close by.

Good quality detonator, he thought, looking at the fallen wooden power pole, about a shattered and burning beside the road. *Transmitter worked fine.*

The plastic explosives he'd planted under the power-pole had gone up promptly, when he pressed the transmitter button. He had another C-4 package set up, down the approach road; the third one he was saving for something special.

He had left the power on long enough so the light would make it easier to take out some of the guards. He'd hoped to target Angel, but the Caidos boss had been standing half behind a man Vince thought was probably the hired pilot. He was reluctant to kill the pilot. And Angel was now under the SUV. No good shot.

There—two Caidos guards came out of the ranch house. The beam of a flashlight made a wriggling glow around their feet.

Vince brought the rifle to his shoulder, aimed through the scope—and fired. One man went down—just went limp and collapsed.

The other ran back inside as Vince was using the bolt action to chamber the next round. He fired that round through the front window. Chambered another round, fired again; loaded and fired over and over, sending the last of his clip through the windows. He knew the ranch house had a back door—he hoped that with the fusillade of shots, the guards in the house would retreat to the other buildings. He wanted them to take shelter away from the bus. Force them into one area where he could target them more effectively.

Vince looked up from the scope, glimpsed flashlight beams at the back of the house, moving toward the rear buildings. The scare tactic was working.

The Tango was fitted with a flash-suppressor, and from where he was shooting, the copse of cacti blocked his muzzle flash from most of the men hiding at the cars out front. But someone over there was firing—he could see the muzzle flash from behind one of the cars. They were firing out into the desert, nowhere near him and nowhere Harris would be; probably panic-firing at some tree blowing in the wind.

Good. The plane burning up, the nearest power pole blowing up, four men shot down and the power going out—all that was going to spur panic. And their panic worked in his favor. The fence worked in his favor now too. It was intended to keep intruders out—but for now it was keeping the men at the house contained.

The wind swirled the dust thickly past and Vince had to squint to keep it from blinding him.

He heard the Caidos shouting at one another. Voices ringing with authority came from the group of vehicles in front of the house. With the power shut, the gate was shut. Eventually they'd get it open manually so they could escape in cars.

Vince took the MAC-10 from his backpack. It had extra clips taped to it. He had his Desert Eagle in the holster and the loaded sniper rifle across his back. He had changed into his cammie tactical pants with two big cargo pockets. The pockets were heavy with ammo. His combat knife was back in his boot sheath; three grenades bulked in his side pockets. He wore a dark Kevlar vest over a black t-shirt. It was chilly out, but being in action would keep him warm.

He took the heavy wire-cutters from the backpack last, then jogged rapidly northeast, angling away from the compound through the deep shadows across the road, till he was parallel with the upper northeast corner of the fence but still about fifty yards away. He sprinted to the corner of the fence, counting on the darkness and the distraction of the Caidos to hide him. He had gone deep into the specialized state of mind, the combat mind; the *zone of decision* that made him who he was in battle.

Breathing hard, he reached the corner fence post. There was a camera on it, but it was dead since he'd cut the power. He noticed flashlight beams bobbling near the ranch building, and out of the space between the two processing buildings. He was in near darkness; the light from the burning plane on the other side of the compound was just enough to light the work he needed to do.

Vince busied himself cutting the hurricane fence, making a fairly big hole so if he had to retreat this way he could get through quickly.

He kicked the cut piece of fence out of the way, tossed the cutters aside, took his rifle off and left it against the fence—it would be too awkward to move quickly with it, inside. He might hit some of his enemies with it from here, but the muzzle flash would expose his position and there was little cover here.

Vince wormed through the hole and got quickly to his feet, moving low and fast, keeping to the blackest shadows till he got to the nearest building. Its aluminum walls, held by steel posts, resonated with sounds from inside. Blurred voices.

He heard someone shouting in Spanish from the ranch house, "Get that gate open, idiot!"

A uniformed man came running across the compound's open area, between the buildings, a MAC-10 in one hand and keys jangling in the other. The Caidos guard wasn't looking Vince's way; he was heading toward the closed gate to the road, presumably planning to open it manually now that the power was out. There was another, smaller gate that led out to the airstrip, but it wasn't big enough to drive through.

Breathing hard, the Caidos guard came loping within twenty feet of Vince—who drew his combat knife and ran up behind the guy, fast as he could. The Caidos guard heard him, started to turn, eyes and mouth wide with fear—but Vince was in reach now, slamming the knife down overhand to punch through the cartelito's left temple, and into his brain. The man went limp, and Vince jerked the knife loose.

The gate for now was staying closed and locked.

Vince took the keys from the dead man's hand. Then he headed back to the fentanyl processing building—just as a door opened and a man stepped out. The man shone a flashlight around—and then right on Vince, who ran up to him and used an upthrust with the combat knife to cut hard through the guard's vocal cords, the blade slashing deep into his throat. Reflexively the man dropped his flashlight and clutched at his throat. Vince pulled the knife loose then drove his shoulder into the man's chest, knocking him back through the open door. The dead man fell inside.

Vince took a second to look through the door. He saw an emergency lantern set up on a table beside at least thirty bricks of white powder. Around it stood several Caidos in security guard uniforms staring aghast at the blood-spurting guard: a dying man they'd probably had dinner with. There were no factory workers in sight.

One of the guards looked up at Vince and had the presence of mind to aim his gun.

Vince ducked to the side before the man squeezed off his shot. A burst from a MAC-10 whined out through the doorway.

The dying man should keep them amused, inside, for a minute, Vince thought, as he slipped around the nearest corner of the building. He'd take care of the other guards in his own time.

By now, he hoped, all the workers would be in the dormitory. They would be under close guard but should be reasonably safe. And Harris should be coming through the fence...

169

Harris saw the hole cut in the fence exactly where Vince Bellator had said it would be. The wire cutters lay beside it. Vince's rifle was there too, leaning against the fence.

Once he'd gotten back to his electric quad bike, Harris had ridden in a wide circle around the back of the compound. He'd left the quad bike about a hundred yards away. How was he going to get it back to Cuz Looey? Have to come back for it, probably.

Right now, he focused on pushing the Winchester rifle through the gap in the fence and crawled through after it.

Harris slithered through—and froze, hearing a gunshot. Sounded like the gun had been fired from the ranch house out into the desert. He could hear the bullet hitting a rock somewhere out on the Basin.

He chuckled to himself. They thought the attackers were still out there.

The ranch building, his destination, was outlined in the light from the fire still licking up from the wrecked twin-engine plane. Flashlight beams wavered around the east side of the house. He heard an engine starting up. A big one, maybe the Humvee.

Harris slipped through the deepest shadows up to an outbuilding, some kind of well house, between the processing buildings and the ranch house.

The repainted school bus they used to transport workers was on the far side of the house from him. He hesitated. Should he just sprint for it?

He peered around, saw no one looking his way, and ran for the bus, his Winchester cocked and ready in his hands. He was almost there when a large man in a badly-fitting security guard uniform came out from the shadows between the bus and the house with some kind of submachine gun in his right hand, a flashlight in his left.

The guard and Harris fired simultaneously.

Angel and Curly were hunched low inside the idling Humvee, Curly Estrada at the wheel. Just outside guards crouched to both sides of the vehicle, guns in hand, watching the desert.

Angel fingered the hefty .45 automatic S&M pistol in his right hand. They were waiting for word about the gate. Alvera and Cortes, trusted lieutenants, were ducked down in the seats behind.

"You hear that?" Curly said. "Gunfire from behind the house!"

"I heard it," Angel growled, lifting up to peak over the dashboard of the Humvee. Where was Jorge? "Could have come from anywhere. I want to know—why isn't the gate opened?"

"No power," Curly said, stating the obvious.

"I told him to open it by hand, stupid!"

Jorge came up to Curly on the driver's side window. Angel snapped at him, "Where've you been, Jorge!"

"I was… I sent…"

"Never mind—is the gate open?"

"I sent Valdano to open it. He hasn't come back! I think that Big Stranger is back there!"

"We could go in the ranch house," Curly suggested. "Use it as a base, fight it out with the bastard, boss!"

Angel shook his head. "We're staying in this vehicle. You men," he turned to Alvera and Cortes, "Take Pedro and Matias out there, go in the house, wait your chance—that bastard is back there! Look for him—shoot him from the back windows! Make them think I'm in the house!"

"Boss," Cortes said, "I don't think we should—"

Angel ground his teeth in frustration and shot Cortes through the head with the .45. Blood and fragments of bone splashed on the back window. The reek of gun smoke spread in the Humvee.

Then Angel pointed the .45 into Alvera's terrified face. "Go!"

Alvera went, scrambling to get out of the Humvee.

"Jorge, you go and see what happened to Valdano."

"You're leaving me here, *jefe*?" Jorge asked. His pitted face seemed almost inhuman with anger.

"No, no, we'll wait for you! Why are you still here? Do what I say!"

"Okay, jefe." He hurried off.

Curly said, "There's a lot of dope in those buildings, a million-dollars' worth, boss. We can't leave it to this son of a whore!"

"I got a call from Fuentes, just before we stepped out front. He has the report on this Big Stranger. His name is Vincent Bellator. He's former Delta Force…"

"What is that, 'Delta Force'?"

"CIA elite team—special forces. The best, most experienced Special Forces, Curly. He was top operator for them in Iraq, Afghanistan, Syria. The best of the best. He killed more than two hundred men, alone, last year, in D.C. All those Nazi idiots…"

"That was *him?*"

"He killed a lot of our people in Santo Virgil. He's deadly, man. We know who he is now, we'll get him from a safe distance, next time. But this time he has the drop on us, Curly. He has the edge. He could have help, too. Maybe he's working with the feds. Maybe they're coming. No, I'm not staying here."

Jorge came running back. "Jefe! Valdano, he's dead! Gate still closed!"

Angel was about to demand why Jorge hadn't gone on to open it—but he knew why. There was too much open space in front of the gate. Bellator had gotten him.

Instead, he said, "Just get in the Humvee! I will handle this!"

* * *

Vince had heard two gunshots from over by the rancho house, but when he glanced that way, he couldn't see anyone over there—and he had to focus elsewhere.

He was between the two processing buildings, now, pressed against the wall by the corner. Looking around the corner he could see someone's shadow cast by the light from inside the door.

Drawing out one of the grenades with his left hand, Vince pulled the pin with the thumb of his right hand and stepped out enough to fire through the door with the MAC-10. The guard was in view and the burst from the hand-gun-style submachine gun caught the uniformed Caidos in the chest and mouth as he shouted.

The man went over backwards, gargling his last words in his blood. Vince stepped back out of the doorway. Holding the grenade's lever down, Vince stuck the MAC-10 in his belt, took the grenade in his right hand, released the lever, leaned over and with a sideways pitch, tossed the M67 through the door.

Someone shouted; someone else screamed. Vince risked a look through the door from the nearer edge and saw the Caidos running toward a back entrance—but the grenade had gone right where he'd meant it to go: Under the table with the stack of pure fentanyl. Only one of the men had thought to put on a gas mask.

Vince grabbed the door, pulled it closed just as the grenade blew. Frags rattled hard against the inner walls. There were confused shouts, men coughing inside…

Then silence.

He held his breath, opened the door enough to see the guards sprawled on the floor. None had made it out the back. They were dead or dying from inhaling a cloud of pure fentanyl.

Then he saw that the guard with the gas mask was frantically tugging at the back doorknob. Vince hesitated, disliking shooting people in the back when it wasn't absolutely called for. But he saw blood running between the man's shoulder blades. The grenade had wounded him. Critically.

The guard didn't quite get the door open… he sank to his knees and sagged against the doorknob, still clutching it as he died.

The cloud of fentanyl was drifting Vince's way. He shut the door firmly.

He heard scuffing sounds to his left, turned in time to bring the MAC-10 to bear on two guards rushing up from the meth processing building; Vince finished out his Mac clip on the guard coming on his right as the one on his left aimed his submachine pistol—just as Vince turned on his heel, turning sideways to the remaining guard; most of the burst flashing past on Vince's left; a couple of rounds closer skipped off his Kevlar vest as he dropped the MAC-10 and pulled his Desert Eagle. He fired the big .50, and the second guard went down in a welter of blood. It had all happened in under two seconds.

Close one, Vince thought, as three more guards came rushing out of the dorm building, raising their weapons.

Before they could fire, Vince squeezed the trigger on the Desert Eagle three times, his hand tracking in perfect coordination with his eye; one man spun and fell as the second one staggered, the third fell backward like a lopped tree. The staggering man stared, went glassy-eyed, and collapsed.

A low-pitched chattering of gunfire from across the compound. Bullets cut past Vince and he saw a jittering muzzle flash from the back window of the ranch building.

He scooped up the MAC-10 with his left hand and rushed to the deeper shadow between the two buildings; two rounds whined past his right ear, then he reached the rear of the meth processing building and dodged quickly around the corner.

A gun in each hand he ran along the rear of the building, passing a back door; kept going to the furthest back-corner of the dorm house. There he paused and looked down the dark alley between the two buildings. He holstered the Desert Eagle, reloaded the MAC-10, and took it in his left hand, drew the Desert Eagle with his right. He leaned out, saw another muzzle flash at the back window of the ranch house. He raised the MAC-10 and aimed, emptied the clip toward the window, more interested in effecting suppressive fire than deadly aim. The window was dark; he thought he saw someone moving inside, but it was too far off to be sure. He noticed something else—a dead man lying on the ground, near the bus, barely visible in indirect light from the burning plane. A big corpse, in a security guard outfit. Looked like Harris had some trouble. Good that there was only one body there.

Vince ejected the empty clip, removed the last taped-on magazine, inserted it, and fired once again at the window. Then he ran across the alley to the back of the meth building, kept going to the back door. He tried the door—it was locked.

He pounded on it with the butt of his pistol, shouted in gruff Spanish, *"Open up! Angel is here! Open you sons of whores!"* The door, he hoped, would muffle his imperfect accent.

Then Vince stepped to the right—and waited.

He heard an angry exchange in Spanish from inside.

The back door of the meth building opened a little and a Caidos guard looked out, the silhouette whispering, "Angel?"

Vince fired at the door to drive the man back. There was a yelp and confused Spanish voices from inside as Vince sidestepped rapidly past the door, scanning the interior of the building as he went. He glimpsed four guards near the lab equipment, a man in a white lab coat—no one else. None were line workers. A bullet from inside sang by, just behind him, as he flattened on the other side.

Vince pulled a grenade, tossed it inside.

Men howled in fear. He heard running footsteps and the thud of the explosion; the rattle of metal fragments. A man screaming in pain.

Vince took the second C-4 package out of his pocket. The blasting caps were wired into the C-4, their cords wrapped around the explosive. For this one he used the timer. The timer was set for three seconds.

He pressed the button and tossed the C-4 into the building, threw it so it'd skid under the lab equipment. Then he sprinted to the back corner of the dorms—as the thunderous explosion went off inside the meth building, igniting the corrosives used to purify the amphetamines.

The ground shook, ventilators blew off the roof of the processing building, and red fire thrust out like a roaring demon's tongue from the mouth of the doorway. Several metal panels burst from the outer wall, spewing fire and smoke.

Vince hurried up the alley between the dorm and the meth building; acrid chemical-reeking smoke curled past him. He got to the end, went to a crouch close to the burning building, and fired at the ranch house—another long burst. More suppressive fire; still trying to give Harris cover.

Then he heard an engine rev, saw the bus driving across the compound to the dorm. He glimpsed Harris behind the wheel. It seemed he'd had no trouble hot-wiring the engine. Vince had coached Harris to do it the direct way: use the tool to break open the ignition lock, smash the key mechanism to expose the rotation switch, turn it by hand to start the engine.

Vince fired again at the ranch house. There was some spotty return fire. He ducked back, then stepped out and fired another short burst at the ranch house back window—and at the same time two rounds from his Desert Eagle. He used his last clip from the MAC and he tossed it away.

He glanced toward the dorm to see Harris getting off the bus, running to the open door of the dormitory. "Come on, everyone out!"

"Are they gone?" a woman's voice called, from inside.

"He shot the dorm guards—come on, everybody, get in the bus!"

"Who shot them? Harris what are you—"

"Never mind, just get in! *We're leaving! Move!*"

Vince had figured he was going to have to get to that gate in the fence, use the key he'd picked up to open it so he could manually slide it out of the way to let the bus out. But now he saw a Humvee roaring at the gate, full speed, coming from the front of the ranch house.

The Humvee was big, its front was armored—and it rammed the gate hard.

With a squeal of tortured metal, the gate stopped the Humvee—bending outward, not quite breaking. The Humvee spun its wheels, then changed gears, backed up about fifty feet and accelerated hard toward the gate. Vince had planned for the contingency of Angel Lopez getting away in one of the vehicles. He'd have to—

Bullets from the ranch house cracked close by. Right now, he had to do something about those shooters. In another burst of fire, the muzzle flash lit up several shooters in the window centered in the back of the rancho.

It was pretty far for a throw, Vince thought, as he tugged his last grenade out. But the ranch house shooters were firing toward the bus now. Couldn't let that go on.

He stepped out to the right to get a good throwing angle—

A bullet struck his Kevlar vest, making him stumble back and slamming the air out of him. He flattened against the wall, gasping. The flames from the meth building made him more visible to the Caidos.

Vince glanced toward the gate—the Humvee had crashed through. But the wrecked gate had torn free from the fence and stuck under the Humvee's chassis, keeping it from getting up to speed.

Bullets from the ranch house spat up dirt close to his right leg; wincing at the deep bruise from a rifle round hitting the Kevlar, Vince pulled the pin on the grenade. Holding the lever down, he dodged around the front of the building, then cut to the right, looking for a good throwing angle…

It was a long way off….

The average strong man can toss a grenade maybe 45 yards. Hardly anyone can throw it that far accurately. So his instructor had told him in Rangers school.

But there were competitions. And one man held the record for distance and accuracy with an M67 grenade. His name was Vincent Bellator.

Bullets cracked by as Vince ran three long strides toward the rancho building—and then he pitched the grenade overhand, giving it everything he had.

As he let the grenade go, a bullet struck his Kevlar vest on the right side; the impact half spun him around so he lost his footing and fell on his left side. Bullets sizzled close overhead.

Then the grenade exploded in the back bedroom of the ranch house—a flash of red light from the ranch house window, a yell of despair. And the firing stopped.

Vince got up, thinking he'd broken his own record. Wishing

Sergeant Wardwell could've seen that throw. He glanced at the bus—the last of the line workers were getting in. The headlights were on. It was gunning its engines. He saw the Beechcraft pilot moving back with the others, inside.

He looked toward the gate, and the road back to the highway—the Humvee had gotten free of the gate, was accelerating toward the place in the road where it would pass between two boulders.

Vince reached into his back pocket, took out the transmitter, a small instrument half the size of a cell phone. He looked toward the Humvee, made a guess—and thumbed the ignition square on the screen.

Maybe a second too soon. The Humvee was not quite between the boulders when the C-4—hidden in the road there—exploded. The Humvee's front end lifted up and tilted, in one motion, the vehicle coming down with a clang on its passenger side. Flames licked up from the front of the totaled engine.

But the driver's side door popped open and Curly scrambled out. He turned to help Angel climb up…

Vince pulled his Desert Eagle and fired—but the range wasn't good, and smoke from the explosion was obscuring the men now. Two rounds finished off his clip. He needed the sniper rifle.

He ran toward the fence, where he'd cut his way through. Breathing hard, he reached the hurricane wire, dived through the hole, picked up the sniper rifle, got to his feet—and saw three men, running from the wreckage, and into the desert's darkness.

He raised the gun to his shoulder and looked through the scope.

There was no one to shoot at. They'd run off into the desert, toward the rocky hills a mile or so away.

I blew my chance, Vince thought.

He took a deep breath and stepped back, within himself, shifting his attention to center in a place above the surging frustration; above the anger, and self-condemnation. He wasn't going to waste energy on that.

He had to think it through. Where would Lopez and his men go now?

Maybe they'd circle back to the ranch, past the burning Humvee. Follow the road on foot to the highway and then to Stapp.

Vince shook his head. They knew he was here. Knew he had the sniper rifle. Knew he had some kind of transportation. They were experienced killers. Angel must know by now that his enemy could spot them on that open road and shoot them down from cover. They'd seen him use that rifle on several of their friends, very efficiently.

All those now-powerless antennas on the roof of the ranch house had been for boosting satellite communication. Because out here in the basin, regular cell phone communication was non-existent. But Vince had cut the power to the satellite antenna. So Angel would want to go somewhere he could raise a signal.

Up in those hills. Up there they could call for help from the cartel. Maybe a helicopter to take them out of here.

He was going to have to track them on foot. He had no idea exactly where the quad bike was. And his motorcycle was noisy. It would forewarn them.

Vince hurried off to find his backpack. It held his extra ammo. He reckoned he'd pick it up, reload his weapons, put the pack on and follow those tracks.

Behind him, flames still crackled from the drug buildings.

He seemed to hear Chris Destry's voice, then. *Vince, I wish I could go with you, and back you up. Three armed, experienced killers who have the high ground—sounds like fun.*

180

Vince smiled. That's just what Chris would say.

And he'd say, *Wish you could go instead of me. I'd stay back at camp and put my feet up.*

He could almost hear Chris laughing.

Chapter Eleven

Dierdre sat behind the wheel of a rented Chevrolet van, across the street from Chief Galway's house. It was eleven-ten p.m. There was a light on in his split-level tract home. She could see the shifting blue glow of a television though the white cotton curtains. At that position in the back corner of the house, she guessed it was a bedroom.

That afternoon she'd driven out close to Central Arizona waste processing, and had a look through binoculars. She'd seen some heavily armed guards—far too many of them. What she didn't see was drums of toxic waste, anywhere. No sense of a back-log of waste waiting to be processed. Nor did she see the kind of heavy trucks she'd expect of such a business. Toxic waste processing seemed like a blatantly phony cover. But that alone wasn't enough to get real interest from her contacts in the DEA.

If she could pressure Galway to talk—that could be a breakthrough. Maybe suggest he could make a deal with the Bureau. He didn't know she was no longer an FBI agent. Though in fact she might still be an agent for a short time. It could take twenty-four hours for her resignation to be official.

Her phone buzzed. Dierdre looked at it. It was Richie. She'd call him back later. Right now there was Galway to think about.

She had a vague plan to confront him—and she'd almost made up her mind to march to the front door and hammer on it, when a police car turned onto the street.

Uh-oh. Someone had noticed her out here. Called the cops.

Dierdre shrugged. She wasn't doing anything illegal. She still had a license for the gun.

But as she watched, the police car parked a half block down the street, on the opposite side. A man in a raincoat got out. Why a raincoat?

She thought it was Officer Hills, but she wasn't sure. He started up the sidewalk, never even glancing at her, and went to Chief Galway's house. But he didn't go to the front door…

He went around back.

Chief Galway was tired but he couldn't get to sleep. He was sitting up in bed, in his pajamas, drinking beer, sometimes watching an old Burt Reynolds movie on TV. Now and then he would ponder his gun, holstered in the belt hanging from the desk chair under the curtained window. He wasn't sure why he was staring at the gun. Nor why he couldn't sleep. Usually, he was out like a light by now.

Maybe it was those FBI agents coming into the office; that scary combination of attentiveness and expressionlessness as they'd asked him questions; the unspoken suspicions in the air.

And a little while after that, Sergeant Hills had started acting strange. Distant and scowling.

Galway had sensed something when he'd been looking for a file in the records room—turned to catch Hills in the doorway, staring.

"*What*, Hills?" he'd asked.

"Hm?" Hills had looked back at the paperwork on his desk. "Nothing."

I'm worrying for nothing, Galway thought, finishing off the beer. He just might have to get another beer. This was only his third… Maybe the divorce had been a mistake. It got mighty lonely in this big house. Maybe…

He heard a cracking sound from the back of the house. Like wood snapping. What the hell was that?

Galway muted the TV and listened. Was that the creak of a footstep on the boards?

He looked at his gun, then shook his head, and laughed at himself for jumping at shadows. The laugh cut short when Hills came to the open door of his bedroom, wearing a raincoat for some reason, though it wasn't raining. Hills had jeans and rainboots on under that. What the hell?

"Did I leave the front door open or something?" Galway asked, staring.

"No, chief, I came in through the back door. Sorry—had to bust the lock on it."

He took a .38 revolver from his pocket. Not his usual gun. He held it loosely at his side.

"We got trouble?" Galway asked, hoping this wasn't what he suspected it was. "You trying to cover my back?"

"Not exactly chief. Angel's man Jorge called me. They're doing some housecleaning. And I was listening to you talking to those feds. Sounding scared. When I told Angel about the FBI coming around, well, I told him what I thought. So—they gave me the job."

Galway's mouth was suddenly paper dry. "That's a piddly little gun," he said, looking sidelong at his pistol belt on the chair. He licked his lips. *Stall,* he told himself, "But I guess you didn't want to use department issue. And the raincoat and boots are disposable. In case you get blood on them."

"Smart thinking, chief," Hills said cheerfully.

"And you want to be chief, so…"

Hills nodded. "There is that."

"But see, once you've done me—they'll get rid of you too."

Hills gave his head a skeptical shake. "I don't think so. They got a big operation here. I'm the one who brought you into the deal."

Casually as he could, Galway put one foot on the floor, on the side of the bed where his gun was. "The feds were here for a reason. They're going to close down that compound, Hills. And the Caidos will think you're a liability. Just a door to close behind them when they leave."

Hills raised the gun. "Freeze right there, chief. I want you to be comfortable."

"You figuring on making it look like a suicide?"

Hills gave him that beaming grin—and Galway dived for his gun.

Dierdre saw the strobing flashes in Galway's window; heard the gunshots. She caught the momentary outline of a man with a gun in his hand.

She instinctively took her gun from the glove compartment, got out of the car, her phone in her left hand—and wondered who she'd call with it. Not the local police.

Then the front door burst open and Hills was there, with blood—his own—streaming down his raincoat. He'd been shot in the belly, right side; he was clutching the wound with his left hand and waving a .38 as Dierdre approached him, her gun raised. His tanned face had gone white, his eyes were wide, and he was staring around in fear, muttering, "He shot me…"

"Hills—drop that gun!" Dierdre ordered.

185

He turned the gun toward her and said, "This is your fault, agent!" And he fired.

His round missed—she reacted instinctively, firing at his center mass. The shot knocked him off his feet, and he fell sloppily on the front porch steps, moaning.

Dierdre checked behind her to see if the bullet had hit anyone's house—she saw a new dent in the van, and a flattened bullet lying on the street.

"Oh Christ," she muttered. She called 911 and asked for an ambulance and the County Sheriff's department…

Then she went to Hills. Saw him limply staring; he seemed startled at how everything had turned out, as he gazed into onrushing death. He gasped once, and died.

"Fuck," she muttered.

She had killed a cop. A bad cop, but even so…

She went into the house, found Galway's body, shot just beneath the heart. Chief Galway had just managed to get a shot off before he died.

Dierdre shook her head, and went back to the van, laying her automatic on the driver's seat.

This is what happens when you get drawn into Vince Bellator's world, she thought.

She leaned up against the van, as people came out on their front porches to investigate the ruckus. Dierdre crossed her arms and just waited there, ignoring questions from the neighbors.

Then her phone chimed for a text. She looked at it. Didn't recognize the number. The text said,

VB pretty much razed the Arizona Central compound.

My name's Harris Ahakhela. VB is out of cell range.

I saw a car get away from the Humvee, think Angel was in it.

It got blown up but whoever was in it got away.

VB probably pursuing. Got my people out of the compound.

I owe him. If I can help I will. Please do not show this text to anyone.

Dierdre gawped at the text, as the realization hit her: It hadn't been necessary for her to stake out Chief Galway, to get at the Caidos. Vince had already taken the compound down.

Then, she heard sirens approaching.

Vince Bellator was stalking his prey. He'd put on his balaclava watch cap, and now he pulled its mask over his face.

It was dark, and cold. He'd put on his coat, under the backpack. The clouds had blown away and he was loping along across the basin, following the tracks with starlight and the faint intermittent moonlight and the rare, very careful use of a small flashlight.

Vince had lost track of the hours he'd been at this. Sometimes he lost their tracks and had to find them again. The three Caidos had a lead on him and he was trying to make it up, but he was aware he could be trotting blithely into a trap.

He was tired. He'd had little sleep, for a couple of days. Right now, his limbs and lungs ached.

What was it Sergeant Wardwell had told the Rangers in training, on their endurance treks—seemingly endless uphill slogs with heavy packs and nightmarish conditions?

"If you think you can't go a step farther, you got to ask yourself a question. If I don't stop this trek right now, will I actually die? If the answer is yes, you'll actually die, then quit! We don't want to lug your body back to camp and it's no shame to wash out of the Rangers. The Army will find a place for you. But if the answer is no—you'd better keep going, if you want to be one of us."

Vince smiled to himself, remembering. Good old "Ward Hell".

He didn't feel like he was going to die. So he kept on going, across the basin, north toward the dark foothills, like broken battlements with rock formations looming not far ahead. Keeping behind what cover he could find as he made his way…

When he came to a place where he could take cover for a moment, an outcropping or a stand of cacti, he knelt and listened.

Once he thought he heard voices. Maybe a word or two in Spanish.

The Caidos might yet decide to double back, cut toward the highway. Maybe get there and hijack a car. But they were miles from the highway and there was mostly flat land in between. And their tracks in the sand told their story. Once he'd found a place where they'd tried to wipe them out with a mesquite branch, for a way. But the mesquite branch left a trail too. He found their tracks again. And the mesquite branch.

He had a bottle of water in his backpack, and a little food. He was putting off taking a break, but he'd get a cupful of water and maybe half a food bar down next time he stopped for a listen…

In the thin light the basin was silver-gray, dun in some places. To the east was the edge of a gulley, cutting toward the hills. To the west was a red-rock outcropping, and a long empty stretch of sandy ground. The horizon was broken up by choppy formations that in the darkness looked like a crooked skyline in some old cartoon. Fading stars glowed a sullen blue-white, between chimneys of rock. It'd be dawn before he got there.

Angel Lopez, Curly Estrada and a third man were up ahead somewhere. The cartel boss's patience was likely to wear thin, soon. He'd be exhausted, himself, and looking for a spot to end it all with an ambush. The foothills of the Rincon mountains, just ahead of Vince, would be ideal. The ground rose now, to a low rise of sand and gravel and a trailing indigo plant. Vince sprinted to it, and lay down gasping in its lee, shrugging off his pack, and listening for anomalous sounds in the desert.

He heard little but the wind and the harsh call of a western screech owl.

Vince scanned his surrounds, first peering at his back trail. The dull light shifted around a cluster of Joshua trees that swayed faintly in the wind, turning them into shadowy enemies. Suppose Lopez and his men were down in the gulley, huddled against the cold under some rocky overhang? Waiting for him to pass them by so they could shoot him in the back?

But the tracks argued against it. Still, the tracks were hard to see, now, and he might have missed something.

Vince shivered as the wind rose. His fingers were cold and stiff on the Tango 51 sniper rifle. He flexed his fingers, trying to increase blood circulation. Once close enough to the enemy, he'd switch to the Desert Eagle. The powerful handgun could kill a man a long way out, but it wasn't as accurate as the rifle, long-range.

Carefully keeping the Tango 51 out of the dirt, Vince turned over and used his elbows and knees to crawl up to the end of the little ridge of sand. He exposed himself just enough to peer past it. He'd left the big Oberwerk binocular telescope with his Harley, because it was so heavy—but he regretted it now. The rifle scope wasn't anywhere near as powerful.

Looking through the scope, scanning the terrain ahead, he could just barely make out the tracks continuing onward into the darkness. The thin light picked out the upthrust arms of some saguaro and little else for a quarter mile. Beyond that the ground gradually sloped up into rocky hills occasionally chimneyed with hoodoo pillars. Thick bands of desert broom and dried saguaro and juniper grew between the knobs of red stone. Stunted Arizona Pines festooned the skyline of the hills; rising beyond the hills, looking dull-blue in this light, were the Rincon Mountains.

Vince noticed a little gray light coming from the east. Pre-dawn. There was a lot of open ground out there… He'd be exposed if he ran across it.

He lowered the scope and glanced toward the brush rimming the gulley. Was it thick enough to conceal him?

Vince decided to cut over that way. He crept backwards, then crawled over to his backpack. He dug out the food, lifted up his mask above his eyes, ate the other half of the fruit and protein bar, and put the wrapper in his backpack—he detested littering. He drank a cup of water, replaced the bottle in its pocket and closed up the pack.

He decided to leave the pack where it was for now. He needed to be harder to see—a big pack on his back didn't help—and he had to move quickly.

Then he adjusted the balaclava mask, got up to a crouch, and moved toward the brush by the gulley. *Too exposed here,* he thought, as he loped along, the rifle in his hands.

Vince was almost to the gulley when a bullet cracked over his head. The report sounded like a round from an AR15.

He threw himself into the brush. It was mostly desert broom and juniper, stiff plants that didn't take his bulk without resistance. They snapped and the broken limbs probably would've cut him if he hadn't had the Velcro vest on. Twice on this trek he'd almost tossed the vest—he didn't like armor, unless he was badly outnumbered. It got in his way.

But thinking about it, as he wormed down in the crunching under-brush, with several more bullets cracking by, he had an idea…

Pushing his rifle ahead of him, one hand over the scope to keep light from glinting off it, Vince squirmed toward the enemy on his

190

belly. He'd spotted a couple of muzzle flashes, and he was pretty sure they were about a hundred yards off, come from a shapeless tumble of red rocks up a hill fringed by cactus pear and scrub.

He kept moving slowly forward. A bullet cut through the juniper to his left, making twigs fall and releasing a spicy evergreen scent. Then he reached the edge of the brush—but didn't quite emerge from it. To his right jutted a juniper about four feet high that just might suit his purposes.

Vince let go of his rifle and rolled over till he was face down behind the juniper. He got to his knees behind it, keeping his head low, and took off his Kevlar vest as fast as he could. He lifted it up, and pulled it down over the bush, tugged it into place, fastened it, and pulled branches out the arm-holes so there was a suggestion of arms. Then he took off the balaclava and pulled it down over the top of the bush, facing the enemy. The bush now wore a vest and a mask. He lay back down, took his pen light from a pants pocket, and stuck it in the dirt, propped there so it aimed up at the top of the bush. He switched on the light and quickly lay down. The thin flashlight beam filtered through the back of the upper part of the brush, adding just a little glow to the eyes and mouth of the mask.

Vince pulled the Tango 51 to him, hoping, at this distance, the Caidos would see eyes and a mouth, in rough face-shape, and a torso in the form of the vest.

He tucked the rifle to his shoulder and looked through the scope in time to see a muzzle flash. He heard a thump close to his right—a bullet had smacked into the vest, making the bush rock back—

He adjusted the rifle's position, eased his finger onto the trigger, watched through the scope. Another bullet crack-thumped into the vest. Then another bullet hummed by as the Caidos tried to bring their target down... He could see the shooter now, through the scope, half a man's silhouette as the shooter leaned out a little more to get the kill-shot.

Vince smiled, aimed, and fired.

He saw the silhouette whip around and vanish. He'd hit him, knocked him down. Killed him? No way to be sure. Maybe not. The target had been skimpy.

He looked at the terrain and decided now was the time to risk a sprint to that small outcropping ahead and left, partway to the enemy position.

He wasn't sorry to be leaving the vest behind. Armor got on his nerves. And maybe the other Caidos would keep their eyes on the "dummy" as he ran across open ground.

Rifle in his hands, Vince got up and ran toward the enemy.

"Is Jorge still alive?" Angel asked distractedly.

"Yes, boss," Curly said, glancing off to where Jorge was still writhing on the ground, about thirty feet away, gut-shot. "He is. Not for long. That's my guess."

Jorge groaned to them, "The pain... I need something..."

"He needs to shut up. The only thing we can give him for the pain is to shoot him in the head."

They were hunkered behind the red boulders, Angel looking east, squinting against the light of the rising sun. He leaned back against the boulder. The wind had dropped, but now and then it still soughed through the rocks. "Fucking mother of God but I'm tired."

"Pretty tired myself, boss," Curly said, peering between the rocks with his binoculars. "Oh son of a whore!"

"What is it?"

"A decoy—a mannequin. No, it's a vest and a mask stuck on a

vest. That's what that idiot Jorge was shooting at! He used it to get Jorge out in the open!"

"Then Jorge deserves what he got. Fuck! We have to get up a little higher. We'll get the signal…"

Curly lowered the binoculars and turned to Angel. "Boss, I think we should wait here and ambush the fucker and then find a road out of here."

"No. We're riding out of here. We'll have a helicopter. You watch and see. There's a company in Sedona takes choppers out to look at the canyons. I've got a man in Sedona who can go over there and make sure they come out whether they want to or not. I just need to be able to call them. Now—you kill this fucker while I go up higher on the hill…"

"Boss… Chief… Angel… We need to do this together. This man—"

A bullet cracked between the rocks and smacked into the boulder two inches over Angel's head. "Mother of God!" Angel swore, throwing himself flat.

Curly fired a burst from his MAC-10 through the gap and dodged to cover. "I'll see if I can flank the bastard, Angel," Curly said.

"Yes! Start doing your fucking job!" Angel grated, clutching his .45.

Angel watched as Curly, bent low, worked his way over to Jorge. Curly pulled Jorge up to a sitting position, back against a rock. Jorge groaned in pain. Curly pushed the AR15 into Jorge's hands. "He's coming. He's killed you. Get your revenge, Jorge. Fire out there. Keep him busy for me. Maybe you can kill him…"

Then, carrying his MAC-10 in his hand, Curly slipped off into the rocks.

Vince had moved from cover to cover—from the outcropping to a copse of cactus to a low shelf of rock near the base of the hill. Then he worked his way along it to an enormous sandstone boulder, the size of a small house. He had worked out where the Caidos were when they'd last fired at him—on the other side of that boulder. It was their blind spot, if they were still there; still, he couldn't see them either. They could be anywhere.

He was pretty sure they'd move on up the hill. But he could hear the man he'd wounded, groaning and cursing in Spanish. Would they leave the man there to die? Probably.

On Vince's left the rocky hillside was too steep for a flanking action, which was likely what Curly would go for. Therefore, the attack would come from the other side.

Vince got down on the ground by the curving edge of the boulder, set up his rifle, laid down in a supine sniper position. He scoped the piled red rocks thirty yards across the open area, an apron of sand reaching to the foot of the hillside. There—a moving shadow cast by the rising sun. In the scope, he could see the rough, warped shadow of a big man with an arm extended; a shadow hand melding with a gun barrel. The gunman—Curly, it looked like—came into view, light catching the MAC-10 in his hand.

Then the wind chose that moment to rise; flinging a cloud of red dust, and some of it found its way into Vince's right eye just as he was squeezing the trigger. His aim was dragged an eighth of an inch out of true—which ended up being a lot more at the impact point. A bullet cracked into rock close by Curly's head. The bodyguard squeezed off a long burst as Vince, blinking from the dust in his eyes, loaded another round and fired, almost blindly. He switched the scope to his left eye, looking awkwardly through. Curly and his shadow were gone. *Missed.*

Vince fired again, reloaded, and fired once more; wanting time to clear his vision, and hoping a ricochet might hit Curly.

Then he squirmed backwards, sat up in the cover of the boulder and wiped dust from his eye with the ball of his thumb. "Curly!" Vince shouted. He leaned the gun against the rock and drew his Desert Eagle. "I'm coming for you and Angel! Right now! Come on out, let's do this, man to man!" He figured he'd have a good chance in a face-to-face gunfight with Curly—at this range he could get a shot into Curly while the Caidos was still trying to get a fix on him with the MAC-10—a weapon that was not as easy to fire accurately.

He repeated the challenge in Spanish.

No response. He heard rocks clattering somewhere above him…

And he smelled smoke. He looked up and saw a thin, curling plume of gray-black. Somewhere up the hill, a fire was burning.

Vince strapped the rifle across his back, drew his Desert Eagle, and started climbing the pile of rocks beside the boulder.

The snapped-off mesquite branch was burning nicely, spitting hot sap, as Angel swept it over the juniper bushes along the thin antelope trail. In Angel's left hand was the platinum cigarette lighter he'd used to start the fire. He rarely used the lighter, but now it was going to kill his enemy for him.

"Angel!" Curly called, coming clumsily up the hillside just below. "What are you doing!"

"What does it look like, idiot, I'm starting a fire!" Several shrubs were burning robustly now, and the hissing blue and yellow flames were spreading eagerly along the strip of brush. The rains had been few, this year, in the era of climate-change; the Arizona desert foliage was extra dry. The wind was higher up here, and lustily spreading the fire. He tossed the burning branch into the bone-dry foliage of the mesquite tree, and stepped back, coughing in the smoke, as the mounting flames spat burning sap at him.

"You were going to let me burn up down there!" Curly said accusingly, loading the MAC-10.

"I expected you back right here and now," Angel lied. "I'm always two jumps ahead of you fools! That's why I'm boss! Now come on, I've gotten hold of Caspar, he's bringing the helicopter! We're getting out of here! Up the hill, quick!"

Curly followed Angel up the thin game trail as the fire spread across the hill. The fire crackled loudly, was already starting to roar as they made their way up the steep slope.

Angel knew the risks. The fire could move faster than he expected. It might follow the brush line to cut him off before he got to the landing place. Already he could feel the heat of the rising flames; already the smoke harried him, making him cough. Curly was so close behind, Angel could feel the bodyguard's breath on the back of his neck.

"Curly you're treading on my heels, damn you!"

"The fire is licking at mine, boss!"

Angel forced himself to move faster up the hill as the heat rose around him. If he slipped, he could tumble into Curly. They could slide down into the flames. It was like Hell had come early and was playing games with him. What was it, that priest, Father Ortiz had said? *The arsonist sets himself on fire, because he's making a place for himself in Hell…*

And was not a demon pursuing him? The Big Stranger…

Gasping for air, Angel began to mutter prayers to Nuestra Señora de la Santa Muerte, and Jesus Malverde. Had the Blessed Mother of the Holy Death not favored him before? Had not Jesus Malverde come to his aid?

It must be this man Bellator who will die, today. Not Angel Lopez, oh great Jesus Malverde… I will burn a thousand candles to you, Nuestra Señora de la Santa Muerte!

He reached the top of the hill, gasping, and turned to look past Curly. Far down the hill, emerging from between two rocks just below where he'd set the fire, was Vincent Bellator. It must be him. The big man had a shining automatic pistol in his hand, a very big one gleaming red in the firelight. Angel could not see Bellator's face—it was obscured by smoke and the rippling, translucent red-blue sheet of flames that rose between them.

Bellator almost looked as if he was *within* the flame. Standing there in it, untouched. Raising the gun to point up at Angel.

Angel gasped and lunged to one side as the bullet cracked between him and Curly.

Curly turned and fired a burst from his weapon down the hillside and then ran for cover beyond the crown of the hill. Angel followed him.

But in his mind's eye he kept seeing the Big Stranger, rippling in the flames, coming for him from the heart of Hell itself.

Chapter Twelve

A wall of fire blocked Vince's way.

He'd lost sight of Angel Lopez and his man. Waves of heat were washing over him from the fire, almost in arm's reach; he could feel the intense heat sucking the moisture from his face and eyes. The gun was growing hot in his hand, threatening to burn him. Smoke billowed; the flames roared. It sounded like a giant roaring triumphantly, at last released from its chains.

Vince stepped back and looked around. There was no way through. He decided to head east, then find a way around the fire and cut Angel off on the other side.

He turned—and three rounds from an AR15 hissed by. He saw the man he'd shot earlier, propped against a rock, about thirty feet away, groaning and waveringly aiming the assault rifle at him.

Vince aimed his handgun. "Sorry about the gut-shot," he said, firing the Desert Eagle. "Not intended." But the man was dead now and couldn't hear; the upper half of his head now sliding in blood-red and brain-gray down the scarlet rock behind him.

Vince turned away, slid and scrambled down the hill till he came to a shelf of rock that turned east. He hurried as fast as he could along the shelf, scraps of burning leaves floating down from not far above, one of them searing his left temple. He flicked it away and squinted through the thickening smoke. The way ahead was warping, rippling in heat and smoke. His eyes were watering and the left side of his face, closest to the heat, felt like it was near cooking.

He noticed a rattlesnake, up ahead, driven by the flames from some lair above, slithering across the rock and dropping down to another tier. It was in a hurry and took no notice of him. He reached an opening between two blocky boulders where there was another game trail offering a way upward.

Vince holstered his Desert Eagle so he could use both hands to climb the steep trail, pulling his way, at times, on the sharp edges of broken boulders. He got a few yards up the steep trail, coughing from a gust of smoke...

Then the fire rushed at him like a living creature of flames charging at its prey, the black smoke its mane; the fire beast was racing down a strip of desert broom on his left and seemed to lunge at him. Flames licked at him and he pulled back, lost his balance, slipped. Thrashing to keep from falling on his back he ended up sliding down the slope face-down. He began to slide, reached to a handhold under a rock on his left, stopped his motion—just as a scorpion was rushing out, disturbed from its winter dormancy by the growing heat of the fire.

Vince gritted his teeth at a sudden vicious pain in his left hand, the sensation a sickening mixture of stinging and tingling and spreading numbness. Vince snatched his hand back, growling at the spreading pain, as the red scorpion, about six inches long, scuttled to vanish under a boulder.

A wave of nausea swept over him and his lower left arm went numb—except for the stung, red and swollen area back of his knuckles. That he could feel.

Finding purchase with the tips of his boots, Vince writhed to his feet, and grasped a boulder with his right hand.

You can still shoot, he told himself, as he looked for another route.

The nausea intensified—and erupted. He vomited against the rock.

Hot smoke swept over him again, and Vince held his breath, squeezing between two boulders on the east side of the trail, sidling onto another long, curving shelf of rock.

This pathway curved gradually north, followed the edge of a crevice in the hillside. To the west, no more than ten yards away, was the nearest fire. He trudged on, coughing as another gust of smoke swept over him; retching from the scorpion toxin and the taste of vomit.

Minutes passed as Vince worked his way around the crown of the hill. Ten minutes? Twenty? It was hard to know, with his head throbbing like this. The roaring of the fire seemed to reach a crescendo… His head throbbed in a sick rhythm with the waves of heat.

He stopped as another frantic scorpion skittered across his left boot. It started up his leg. He kicked out hard so the scorpion was pitched off the edge of the shelf.

Vince moved onward, and in a few wobbly steps—his head was spinning, stomach churning as his body fought to process the scorpion venom—he reached a clearer space, took a breath of pure air, and stopped in his tracks, staring, as about a hundred yards away, Curly and Angel climbed into a Bell 206 red and silver helicopter sitting on a flat smoke-wreathed rocky hilltop, the next hill over. The heli was neither big nor small, the sort used for tourism and industrial transport. Its blades were spinning slowly, churning the smoke from the fire, as the pilot waited for them to take their seats.

Feeling that he was moving in slow-motion, Vince unstrapped the rifle, struggled to get it in place against his shoulder, but his left hand was no longer working except as a kind of dead lump of flesh to lift the rifle barrel up, and his right hand shook as he tried to position the sniper rifle for a shot. The helicopter lifted up, shaking and wavering in the rifle scope.

His eyes still burned and watered from the smoke; his head throbbed. He lost the target in the wobbling scope.

And then the helicopter pitched up, rose as fast as it was able, into the sky…

Angel Lopez's second-hand Blackhawk heli hovering over the palm trees, firing off the missile that went straight for Chris Destry's position.

Vince wrenched his mind from the memory and swung the rifle, looking for the Bell 206, had it for a moment in the scope—and squeezed off a shot. Instantly knew he'd missed…

And then the heli swerved behind a chimney of red rock, and he lost sight of it completely.

Breathing hard, his head spinning, he shifted on the shelf, waiting to get another shot…

But the Bell 206 didn't reappear. The helicopter had flown out of sight. Taking Angel Lopez with it.

Sergeant Fuentes drove the patrol car onto the two-lane overpass. Below, the freeway rumbled and droned through the dusky late afternoon, into Santo Virgil. Fuentes was on his way home. He needed to see his wife, and make contingency plans.

He was worried. He hadn't heard anything from Angel. Just that he'd received the file on Vincent Bellator. With the FBI coming around, asking questions, it would be more like Angel to follow up, make sure that the feds had been properly stonewalled. It made Fuentes nervous when Angel didn't hound him.

Fuentes was thinking about Angel Lopez—when an oncoming pickup truck, in the other lane, suddenly switched into his. It was a big truck; the sort of tall, hulking GMC four-by-four with enormous wheels that looked like they belonged on a construction tractor, and it was speeding up.

In seconds it would hit him head-on.

Heart slamming in his chest, Fuentes veered into the left lane, accelerating to get past the truck, starting to reach for the radio to call for back-up—but then the enormous pick-up sideswiped him, smashing its right front fender into his left, so that the patrol car was knocked out of the lane, across the narrow shoulder and into the thin-steel guard-rails over the freeway.

Yelling in both fear and rage, Fuentes was slammed brutally against his seatbelt, felt his neck painfully twisting, saw the blur of the onrushing guardrails—then a crunching halt knocked the air from him.

Gasping for air, he saw that the patrol car's front end was torn open, the smoking engine half off its blocks, the front left wheel, still in place, spinning over the freeway below.

Angel is trying to kill me, he thought, gasping for air.

Fuentes fumbled at his seatbelt, got it open, and tugged at his gun. It was awkward to get it out. It was stuck in the holster.

But he must get it loose, though it hurt to move, because in the right-side mirror he could see a man coming from the truck. The man had a shotgun in his hand. Angel recognized that crooked nose, that jutting jaw. It was Nicolás Hasta. One of Angel's sicarios. There was no time for back-up. And maybe he couldn't count on some of the other officers. Angel could have gotten to them.

Fuentes twisted his body painfully to get the holster freed up, drew his Glock .44 and twisted himself even more to fire through the rear right-side window as the man bent to look in.

"Demasiado tarde, hijo de puta!" Fuentes shouted, firing the gun

through the glass. Once, twice, three times. But the third bullet hit no one—because the first two struck the sicario in the face, and slammed him backwards, out of view.

The car shifted. Fuentes thought he heard concrete cracking, metal groaning. Mouth dry, pulse hammering, his neck wracked with pain, he turned and crawled over the front passenger seat, and struggled to get the door open. The metal was warped. From the corner of his eyes he saw flames starting from the engine.

No. I will not die that way.

He braced his feet against the steering column, braced his shoulder against the door and shoved with all his strength, one hand holding the handle in the open position. The door squealed and then popped open. He climbed out, dragging himself onto the concrete and paused, on hands and knees, to look at the body of the sicario: lying on his back in a pool of spreading blood, sprinkled with broken glass.

Fuentes got to his knees, holstered his gun, then pulled himself up, using the side of the car. Grimacing with pain, he fingered his cell phone from his coat pocket and speed-dialed his wife. They spoke in Spanish.

"Listen—"

"Are you all right? You sound sick!"

"I got in a car accident. Twisted my neck. I don't think anything is broken. Listen to me, pick me up at the gas station…" He told her precisely which one. It was close to the entrance of the overpass. "Bring the boy. We're all going to Phoenix!"

"Phoenix? Why?"

"There's an FBI office there. I'm going to get us some protection. Don't ask any more questions! Look out the window before you go to the van. If there's no one you don't know out there watching, then you and the boy get to the gas station fast! *Hurry!*"

He hung up, and began to walk, as fast as he could, though every step sent a shiver of agony through him. He trudged doggedly toward the entrance to the gas station.

Fuentes heard the sirens coming. He didn't want to get in an ambulance, or a police car. He didn't want to answer any questions yet. Angel could get to him in the local hospital.

He managed to get in the big hydrangea bushes lining the curving ramp, just before the police cars arrived.

Fuentes waited till they were all up there staring at the body of the sicario, then he went down the slope onto the tarmac behind the gas station. A little store was attached to the gas station, he would wait for his family there. Buy some Tylenol to ease the pain, and call the FBI, tell them to expect him. Tell them that he wanted to make a deal for protection.

And he would do everything possible to see that Angel Lopez went to jail for the rest of his life.

"Who's that big guy on the north end of the fire line?" Chief Delgado asked. He had just gotten to the fire camp to relieve the previous fire chief on the line and he didn't have a sense of the men yet. "He looks like he's been out here too long."

Josephson shrugged. "Hard to tell. He could get a second wind."

Delgado glanced up at the sky. It was dark up there, but the fire-fighters were in the bright, rippling light of the wildfire. Delgado figured it was maybe nine o'clock at night. "How long's he been here?"

"Since pretty early this morning. Insisted on volunteering. He's hardly stopped. I got the EMT to give him a shot of Anascorp when he walked in and asked if he could help…"

"He *walked* in? Wait—Anascorp? He was hit by a scorpion?"

"Yeah. He didn't even mention it but his hand was all swollen and

I saw the sting mark. We gave him the antivenom and some antihistamine, some water and soup and he was ready to go. Big healthy guy like that's not going to die from a scorpion sting."

"I'd still be in bed, was it me," Delgado admitted. "Who authorized him as a volunteer?"

"Uh—I don't know. I didn't have time to ask. He does know what he's doing. He's been really good with digging the firebreaks. Says he volunteered to put out wildfires in Washington. Was on a firefighting team for a while in the army. He's sure been a help. We're getting ahead of it, finally, and he's made a difference."

"What's his name?"

"Uh... Vincent."

"Full name."

Josephson looked uncomfortable. "I'm not sure."

"What the hell! We're supposed to have volunteers here who have been trained and vetted! Who sent him?"

"Well, chief, when you weren't here and we were getting a bit overwhelmed, this guy stepped up and talked like he knew the job. We really needed him! There's that mess over at that Central Arizona Waste, a big fire and guys shot to pieces. Bunch of firefighters out there who would've normally been here with us—"

"We have procedures, Josephson!"

"I know, Chief but—he saved Rucker's life!"

"Rucker? What happened?"

"Cut off by fire, is what. We saw his situation too late. We were trying to open a path to him with the hose but Rucker fell over from smoke inhalation and a pine tree was coming down and this Vincent guy runs through the wet place we made and picked up Rucker—and down comes the pine tree and out comes this Vincent with Rucker on his shoulder."

"Really. Where's Rucker?"

"Hospital. He'll be okay."

"That's good but—I still want to know exactly who this—" Delgado broke off, turning to see three large trucks pulling into the firefighting camp. The men on the line cheered. It was their relief, and an additional firetruck. "Okay, there's the relief. I want this 'Vincent' off the line because I don't know who the hell he is. Also, he looks like he might fall over from exhaustion."

"He's done the hardest work, hour after hour, out there. I had to change out the filter on his breathing mask three times. He had to be talked into taking time to eat a sandwich. What do you want me to do with him?"

"Uh—you're relieved by this new crew, right?"

"Hell, I better be."

"You are. Fire's basically under control. Take this Vincent guy in your jeep wherever he wants to go."

"He said something about leaving a motorcycle off in the desert…"

"Then see if you can take him to it. We owe him, but… I don't want to be breaking the rules. I get blamed if something gets ugly."

"Sure thing, Chief. Glad to. Christ almighty, I'd take that guy for a beer and a steak! Two steaks if he wanted it."

Dierdre had asked to be put in a holding cell just so she could get some sleep. The county sheriff, Cal Bristow, had been reluctant to actually arrest her, after the two neighbors signed a report saying she'd shot Hills in self-defense. And preliminary forensic indications suggested that the police chief had been shot by Hills' gun. Add to that, a round that had wounded Hills looked like it had come from the chief's weapon. Dierdre Corlin had still been an FBI agent at the time—her resignation was official today—and she'd told them about her suspicions regarding Hills and Galway, which were later substantiated in a call to Agent Richard Chang.

But they had to keep her on hand. Dierdre understood that. She'd shot a police officer, and the neighbors hadn't testified under oath yet and the bullet forensics had to be confirmed with lab tests. Hence, they'd kept her sitting around the sheriff's office till three a.m., when they'd found a clean holding cell for her to sleep in.

It was a little past eight when Diedre woke to coffee, a couple of fried eggs and toast, brought by the jailer. Marla was a burly, friendly Native American woman who told Dierdre the D.A. was already meeting with Judge Stein about her situation.

Sitting on the bunk and chatting with Marla about the wildfire in the Rincon foothills, Dierdre had just finished the eggs and coffee when Sheriff Bristow came in, smiling. He was a big bellied man in a dun and black uniform; he had a red face and amused blue eyes, and his smile hinted at good news. He always smelled of cigarettes.

"The D.A. and the judge decided you can go off on your own recognizance," he told her, in a gristly voice. "That, y'see, is owing to all the indications that you're probably not someone who's going to be convicted of anything. *But!*" He stabbed a nicotine-yellowed finger at her. "You'll be summoned to court to clear it all up, sometime in the next couple months, and we expect you to show up!"

Diedre let out a long, relieved breath. "I'll be there, sheriff. Your hospitality here's not bad, but I kind of want to go take a bath and change clothes and look into personal business."

Another finger stab. "And we're keeping your gun till all this is ironed out!"

"That's fine. In fact, I was going to turn it over to the Bureau. I've got to go back and face charges on the Lincoln Memorial affair—"

His smile widened to a grin and he raised his hand in a peremptory stop gesture. "Hold on!"

"Yes, sheriff?"

"I was kinda wondering if you'd heard." He cleared his throat. "Dierdre Corlin, you'll be getting an official notice real quick. The President of the United States has pardoned you and Vince Bellator for that action in D.C.!"

"What!" Dierdre stood up so suddenly the jailer had to grab the breakfast plate to keep it from crashing to the floor. "Oh—sorry Marla!"

Marla turned to the sheriff, wide-eyed. "She did? The president pardoned her?"

"Yep! She pardoned them both, her and Bellator. Of course, the other political party is complaining, but… it's a done deal. You won't be charged, Agent Corlin!"

"I'm not 'Agent anyone' now," Dierdre said ruefully. "Just call me Dierdre. And…"

She felt an urge to thank someone and the sheriff was there. "Thank you!" She shook his hand. "For telling me, I mean! You are the bearer of every kind of good news!"

He chuckled. "That's not usually my job, but I'm glad it was today, Dierdre. But don't forget—you'll be due back here to clear up this whole business with the Stapp police." He shook his head. "I figured those guys were crooked but I never could figure out how to prove it…"

"The president herself pardoned our guest here!" Marla said, shaking her head in wonder. "Wow!" She gave Dierdre a hug. Dierdre was happy to receive it.

She was doubly happy. The pardons meant Vince could come out of the shadows…

But what had happened to him? Where was he now?

From what she could find out from the Sheriff, *someone*—she didn't tell them who—had killed a surprising number of men at the Arizona Central toxic-waste processing station. A young Yavapai man had called in the attack, carried out on the compound by "an unknown person". He'd told the police that one of the buildings likely contained toxic levels of Fentanyl. Men in Hazmat suits found a couple of intact bricks of what looked like dope—and turned out to be pure Fentanyl. One of the guards in the ranch house had survived, saying something about *"El Gran Extrano"*, and the Caidos had given evidence from his hospital bed about the true nature of the compound. Every man killed was a member of the Caidos cartel. No one seemed to know, as yet, what had become of Angel Lopez. The cartel boss had dropped from sight recently. He might be among the bodies still being identified.

The shooter who'd dealt so much death at Arizona Central had not been located.

Lost in speculation, Dierdre went to put on her overcoat.

Had Vince gotten through it all unscathed?

Or had he been wounded—maybe died in the desert somewhere?

If Vince had survived, she had a pretty good idea where he would go…

Chapter Thirteen

Vince Bellator was walking across a battlefield with Uncle Jack.

Jack Sullivan wasn't his real uncle, of course. Vince had always called him Uncle Jack anyway, having known him from early boyhood as a close friend of his father's. He was just someone Vince had trusted—as people, smart and sensitive people, tended to trust Vincent Bellator. Vince's mother had said Uncle Jack was "one of nature's white knights". By degrees, Vince had learned, mostly from his father, and then from stories he heard in the Special Forces, that "Uncle Jack" was a man people looked to get them justice when there was no other way. So long as the cause was genuinely just, and the need dire, Jack Sullivan was there. It had meant Uncle Jack had killed a lot of men, but always armed men; vicious, murderous men. It was hard for the young Vince Bellator to believe those stories—Jack always seemed patient, and kind, and never inclined to talk about guns or combat. He was more interested in fishing.

But now they were walking across a battlefield together. Machine guns chattered; men shouted and other men died. Bullets whistled past them, even passed through them. Vince and Jack were unseen, and untouched. They were here and not here.

It was the Vietnam War. Uncle Jack had served in it as a young man. "You know," Uncle Jack said, "I got in trouble for being reluctant to kill the enemy, in 'Nam—I mean, when I didn't have to kill them. Why not *capture* them, if I could? Some of the brass was all for that. But there were others—the Lieutenant Calleys of the war, who wanted to nail every last VC. I knew the Viet Cong were fighting in something they believed in. Maybe it wasn't such a good cause. But they'd had such hell dumped on them by the colonials back in the day, it seemed like the only way out, to them... Yeah, they were my enemy, I killed them when I had to, but I had some sympathy for them too. I didn't go for communism, but I understood how people could get talked into it."

"So you see my problem, Uncle Jack," Vince said, as they watched a man with a flamethrower pour liquid fire into a Cu Chi tunnel entrance. "It's hard to make the judgment about who should die. And I know people can't go around taking the law into their own hands. But at the Lincoln Memorial—the Neo-Nazis were going to slaughter half a dozen black senators and hundreds of people who'd come to hear the senators speak—"

"And no one else was there to stop them. And now, no one else is stopping Angel Lopez. Sometimes a man has to make up his mind if he's delusional—or if the hand of justice is really resting on his shoulder. Most men could never do what you do righteously, Vince. But you were born to it. You were chosen for it. The hand of justice is resting on your shoulder."

"Who chose me for it?"

"Now that's a big question... It's the one who is doing His best, within the rules of the universe, to help protect the innocent. Come over this way."

Uncle Jack gestured toward a doorway that had just appeared in the thick brush.

Vince followed Uncle Jack through—and the battlefield was gone.

They were standing on a sidewalk looking into a park. Children were climbing a jungle gym in a playground. Their parents sat on benches, watching and smiling. Birds sang in the trees and squirrels chattered instead of machine guns.

"You see those kids, and their folks watching, Vince? All they want is to be a family, living their lives together. Those parents want their kids to grow up safely; to be able to get an education, work a decent job. Have kids of their own, live out their lives in peace. There are some good cops who try to protect them. There are plenty of good soldiers around, protecting their country. But sometimes, with certain kinds of evil… it's just not enough. Then—someone is chosen. *You* were chosen, Vince. But always remember—check your fire. Make sure you know who you're neutralizing, and why. And stay in the shadows, much as you can. Hide from notoriety. Those kids don't have to know you're out there. Just remember that the One who chooses knows what you're going through… Someday, you and I will meet again to talk it all over. But right now, Angel Lopez is still out there, Vincent. And the Russians are behind Lopez."

"Uncle Jack—I've got so many questions. I—"

But Jack Sullivan was melting away into a cloud of smoke.

It was gun smoke that swept away on a breeze.

And then Vince came to. He snapped his head up, blinking, looking around. He was sitting on the porch of the country house, by a thin creek, on a Yavapai reservation in Arizona. It was just past dawn, and it was pretty cold out. But he had his leather coat on, and he was comfortable, a little too comfortable, sitting in the wicker chair, trying to meditate… He'd been listening to Harris's elderly great uncle Chev—it was pronounced Shev—softly chanting a greeting, a prayer of thanks, to the rising sun. And then he'd gone into a dream of some kind. Uncle Jack had been there…

"I went to sleep," he muttered, as Harris looked over at him. Harris had been seated beside him, in a silent state of prayer, a form of Yavapai meditation.

"Did you?" Harris asked, as if he was hinting at something. "You sure you were asleep?"

"Yeah! I was dreaming! I never fall asleep in meditation. Never before, anyway. I don't understand it—I had plenty of sleep last night…"

Vince had been here, at the old farmhouse, for five days. He'd come to see if Harris and his sister were alright and the old man had laved Vince's burns with aloe gel squeezed straight from the desert plant's leaves, and had chanted over him, and waved burning sage, and Vince had found himself agreeing to stay a little while. He was exhausted, scorched with first and second degree burns on his arms and the left side of his face; he had a number of deep bruises. But that was little to Vince Bellator, who had been through far worse, as attested by the scars of half a dozen bullet and frag wounds and knife slashes.

What was wearing him down was the anguish of failure that had gripped him when Angel Lopez escaped—and the feeling of responsibility for the wildfire, though he hadn't started it himself. It had happened because of him. Luckily no one had died in that fire and it had been contained after a few days. Still—wildfires constituted an ongoing series of catastrophes, in the world, now. He hated to add to that misery, even indirectly.

He'd needed time to heal. To find himself again. To see his mission, once more, with clear eyes.

Angel Lopez is still out there, Vincent. And the Russians are behind Lopez…

No doubt it was just a dream. But maybe his subconscious was trying to tell him something.

"Sometimes there are things to be learned from dreams, boy," said the stocky, white haired old man in overalls, gruffly, as he came over to them. Harris's granduncle had been named Chev because he'd been born, in 1937, in the back of a Chevrolet pickup truck. "You got to listen for the message. Now why don't you two lazy bastards make some coffee, help my niece with the breakfast!"

Vince grinned. "I'm on it, Chev. But after we eat and clean up, I'm going to have to head out. I've got to go check on some folks at my house up north. Where all *you* folks are invited to visit, anytime."

"Take you up on that someday, Vince," Harris said.

"Say, Vincent—" Chev said, glancing at the motorcycle near the wooden porch. "You check the carburetor on that Harley for dust? Damn dust out here gets into everything."

"Yes sir, I did, yesterday," Vince said. "Took it out and cleaned it. She's ready to roll."

"Alright, if you think you're ready. Watch your ass on those crazy freeways. Now where's my coffee? Damned lazy bastards…"

Cold and rainy in Washington State. They could smell seawater from the Sound.

"Don't you think, Curly," Renaldo said, in Spanish, "that some of these people are going to figure out we're not surveyors?"

He and Curly both wore the windbreakers—too light for the cold, rainy weather, this morning—that said *Tacoma Surveying*, on the backs. And they both had surveying instruments. When people drove by, they pretended to look through them as if they knew what they were doing. People drove by only rarely, on this tree-covered island, with its few roads and few houses. They could smell the briny water

214

of the Sound, not so far away, and the drippy sap of spruces around them. It all seemed very primeval to Renaldo.

"No, unless they're surveyors themselves," Curly said. He was sitting on a tree stump, shredding a leaf with his fingers as he watched the road. "If anyone comes and bothers us, we'll kill the son of a whore and bury him here somewhere and get on with the job."

"What if the owner of the property sees us? Won't they want to know why we're surveying?"

"We'll make up a story. If he doesn't like it, we'll kill him."

"And bury him in the brush, sure," Renaldo said. He was very unhappy being here. He was far from home, and he was not qualified for any manner of disguise work, and he was not a cartelito soldier, anyway. He would kill someone if he had to, but not in a fight. Walk up behind them and shoot them, that was the best way.

He was puzzled as to why he'd been ordered to come along. They'd said they'd lost a lot of men, but really, there were quite a few more. Why come to him? Angel had gotten someone to run the bodega in Santa Virgil—but it was someone Renaldo didn't know. Maybe the man was stealing from him.

None of it made sense. He was starting to wonder that Angel had some kind of ulterior motive, in bringing him here.

Didn't a man like Angel Lopez always have an ulterior motive?

"We been out here all yesterday and all this morning," Renaldo said. "This Bellator might never come back while we're here. He could be hiding. He could be in, I don't know, Hong Kong or some place."

"We stay here, Renaldo, until Angel says we can leave. Angel calls every four hours. I'll call him if we see Bellator. Or anything that might make us think Bellator is coming here. So just shut up and stop whining or I'll dig a hole for you in the brush and tell Angel you were going to the federals."

"You would do that?" Renaldo was honestly shocked.

"Yes, I would. Are you going to shut up?"

"Certainly. Except if I have to go find a place to pee."

"Do you have to pee now?"

"No."

"Then shut up."

He looked at the road—they heard a car crunching the gravel as it came. Curly stood up, and they both pretended to fuss with his surveying equipment. But they both kept an eye on the road.

A white Honda Civic, fairly new, drove by. The woman driving the Civic glanced at them, and then looked back at the road. She drove on by. Toward Vincent Bellator's house.

"Who was she?" Renaldo asked.

"I don't know. But I'd better call Angel."

Harstine Island was thickly covered by fir trees and thick undergrowth dripping from the recent rain. Driving across it, Dierdre had seen only one house, barely visible through the trees.

It was almost half past noon, and she had been driving since leaving the motel in Oregon, at seven—but only in the last few minutes had she wondered if she were lost. She thought she was probably on the right road, on Harstine, but the name of the winding narrow lane had partly worn off the hand-made wooden sign:

N c l R

That was probably 'Nicoll Rd'—wasn't it?

Dierdre was sure she'd found Vince's house, the instant she drove up in the rented Honda. Because surely that must be Diego and Lupe and the boy Pascual out front. They were just the way Vince had described them. And the chihuahua, quivering on the porch as it barked at her car, must be Superro.

Diego was using a table saw to cut lengths of two-by-four; as he cut them to size, the boy took them and set them on a pile nearby. Lupe, wearing coveralls, was painting stain onto the new porch railings.

They all looked over at her, as she drove up the gravel road and stopped the car.

Dierdre got out, smiling and waving, to put them at their ease. Superro continued to bark.

"Get the dog, Pascual," Lupe said.

Pascual went up the stairs, took the dog into his arms. Superro continued to bark.

"Put him in the house," Lupe said wearily.

Pascual did as he was asked, as Dierdre walked over to Lupe. "Hello, I'm Dierdre Corlin—am I at the right house? Are you Lupe Velasquez?"

"Yes!" The look of puzzled suspicion changed to relief. She put her staining brush down on the bucket. "Dierdre! Dutch told us about you!"

"Yeah," Pascual said, coming down the steps. "He said he thought Vince was in love—"

"Pascual!" Lupe interrupted, almost savagely. "Cállate!"

"Uh—" Dierdre wanted to ask, *Vince was in love with who?* But she said, "Yep, I'm Vince's friend Dierdre. Is he here?"

"No, we don't know when he's coming," Lupe said, shaking her head apologetically.

Dierdre's heart sank. She was so sure he'd be here. But still... maybe she could stay in the area a while.

Only a short time. Just... a practical amount of time.

Waiting for Vince Bellator to show up.

Oh God, she thought. *I've turned into one of those women I never thought I'd be.*

217

"I read about you in the newspaper," Diego said. "Ha! You helped kill the assholes!"

Dierdre shrugged. "Did you also read that Vince and I both were pardoned by the president?" "Hell *yeah* we did!"

"I was so happy for him," Lupe said. "The president is a good woman. She just took the risk and did the right thing."

Then a big-eyed, lissome young woman, barefoot, with long straight blond hair, in a pair of overalls that were too big for her came out of the house, stood on the porch and said, "Ya lunch is almost ready." Then she stared, open mouthed, at Dierdre and said, "Who she?"

Lupe winced at the lack of gentility. "It's Dierdre. Friend of Vince." Lupe hooked a thumb at the young woman. "That's Nilla."

"Hi Nilla," Dierdre said, nodding.

"Hi." It was a dead sound. It carried suspicion, and Nilla's flat, cold gaze, conveyed an instant dislike.

Uh-oh, Dierdre thought. *Is this Vince's girlfriend?*

She found it hard to believe Vince would get caught up with this goopy young thing. But maybe. Some men had strange preferences.

"Dierdre—will you have some lunch with us?" Lupe asked. "We can celebrate the pardons."

"Hey," Pascual said, as if suddenly inspired. "You're, like, an FBI agent, right?"

Dierdre spread her hands. "Um—I was. Actually, I just resigned."

"But while we eat lunch, you could tell us about catching bad guys and shit?"

"Pascual!" Lupe snapped.

"I can tell you some about that, sure," Dierdre said.

"And I'm pretty darn hungry. All I've had today is a croissant and coffee for breakfast."

"Come on in!" Lupe said, with a luminous smile.

218

* * *

Wearing light-green flannel pyjamas from her luggage, Dierdre stretched out to sleep, that night, on a sofa in Vince Bellator's house. She lay there wondering where Vince was. And how this odd crew of people had as been assembled here.

Sleepily, she found herself wondering about the surveyors she'd seen on the road. Something odd about them. Maybe in the Pacific Northwest surveyors had that rough look. Hipsters, maybe. You're no longer in the FBI, she told herself. Got to let go of that state of mind. Seeing perps everywhere… Forget it.

Dierdre closed her eyes. She had only a passing fear that Nilla, who'd been quietly hostile all last evening, would cut her throat as she slept.

Nevertheless, she was relieved to wake up the next morning. She smiled, seeing the morning light glistening on a new fall of snow on the windowsill.

Dierdre got up and raised the blinds to see how much snow had fallen.

It was a light snow, but enough to wreathe the Douglas firs in crystalline ermine, and to make the snow shimmer with the subtle rainbow effect that came when it was struck by early light. Looking at the trees, she found herself thinking of the surveyors in the woods by the road. Something about them nagged at the back of her mind. She couldn't see their faces clearly but one of them seemed familiar, in some way. And both men had worked too hard to look like they knew what they were doing with the theodolite scopes.

Paranoia maybe. But as an agent she'd learned not to ignore those hunches.

As an agent. Which she wasn't anymore. It was painful to think about. Pardon or not, she didn't feel like she could go back to the

Bureau. There'd always be some doubt about her willingness to play by the rules.

She turned to ponder the living room. It was warm enough—Vince had central heating put in—but the room was painfully austere. The living room's only furnishing was the dark blue sofa, a brass cannister for the stone fireplace's poker and ash brush, and a wooden eating tray. There were no pictures on the walls; there was no television—as Pascual had dourly warned her, in a voice tinged by horror.

Seemingly random volumes filled the fireplace mantle: Mark Twain, Thoreau, Emerson, *The Complete Angler*, A Bible, a Koran, the Bhagavad Gita, and much-thumbed volumes of Lawrence's *The Seven Pillars of Wisdom*.

The master bedroom and the den were scarcely less barren; they had one piece of furniture each; a bed in one, a desk in the other, but every wall of both rooms was covered with bookshelves, fully stocked, mostly with biographies, classics, books on science, books on boating, including Coast Guard textbooks, and a baffling variety of reference books. There was no PC, no laptop, but the house did have a satellite dish apparently connected to nothing at all. *The Collected Plays of Shakespeare* was on the desk, open to *Hamlet*.

Lupe had been worried that Vince might have left guns around that her son would find—but she found not a single weapon in the house, "Unless you want to count kitchen knives and the woodpile ax."

There was a large collection of fishing gear in a basement room, along with a weightlifting system that seemed to have been much used; camping equipment, neatly organized in a corner; a washer and a dryer. There was also a vinyl-record stereo in the basement, and about two hundred records. Dierdre pictured Vince listening to the albums while weightlifting. Lupe had been allowing Nilla and Pascual to listen to the old rock and blues albums but Diego had to be there to supervise them.

There was a closet full of clothes in the bedroom, Vince's size, and a few pairs of shoes and boots, including cowboy boots. A dusty gray Stetson cowboy hat sat on the closet shelf. There was a bed and blanket in each of the bedrooms. Only the master bedroom seemed to have ever been used before.

In the kitchen were working appliances and cleansers and plenty of pots and pans and dishes and silverware. A mid-century-style radio sat on a window shelf.

There were no decorations in any of the rooms, except a calendar, a year outdated, hanging in the den.

In an outbuilding turned into a garage was a 1999 Toyota camper and a supply of gasoline. They had the keys for the truck and permission to use it. Vince had made it clear that they could use anything on the property.

In a large metal shed were racks of power tools, buckets of nails and screws, and almost every sort of carpentry tool, systematically organized. Lumber, in three kinds of wood, was stacked in another outbuilding. The remnants of a large truck garden, which seemed to have been well-tended, stretched behind the outbuildings.

"And that's pretty much all there is to it," Lupe had said, after showing her around. "The house is not exactly cozy. It's kind of unfinished. But it's warm and dry. Oh, and there's an attic, but nothing in it. Either Vince liked to keep things really simple or he didn't spend much time here. Probably when he was here, he was just working on the house—and reading."

Working on the house and himself, Dierdre thought.

"Good morning!" Lupe said, coming in with a wooden tray. On it was a mid-century vintage coffee pot, cups, cream and sugar. "It's snowing!" she said excitedly. "We might have a white Christmas! Pascual will enjoy that. He's never actually been in snow before."

"I was admiring the snow, it's beautiful! Oh—some more is coming down! We're used to it in D.C., but it's not like seeing it in a forest."

Lupe put the coffee down on the tray and poured for them. They took their coffee to the window and watched the snowfall. "Have you heard from Vince at all, since you came here?" Dierdre asked.

"One phone call. He didn't say what he was going to do, or what he'd been doing. He just wanted to know if we were all right. And if Nilla had gotten here okay. She's a sort of..." She glanced toward the stairs to see if anyone was there, listening. "... a... what would you say. Waif? I mean, full grown, very experienced in some ways, but still... like somebody's lost little girl. Some bikers were trying to assault her and Vince stepped in and... he didn't kill them, but... he ended it. Then he felt like he was responsible for her. Like they were going to come after her when he left town. And she didn't have a job, so he sent her up here to help us. She actually *likes* working. She does all the dishes, and she can do simple cooking. I was thinking of training her as an assistant cook... I can't see her as a waitress. She's a little rough around the edges. She likes Pascual and they went out with Diego on the boat, had a great time..."

"She didn't seem, you know, happy I was here."

"Oh, she heard something about you from Pascual and—I think she's got a crush on Vince. That could happen pretty easily. Good thing for him he's too young for me—I would wrap him around my little finger and make him my husband!"

Diedre laughed. "Well, I'll get a room tonight in Olympia. Hang around the area a while, check with you, see if we hear from Vince... I wanted to see him after the pardon and... he saved my life, twice, in fact, so..."

"You don't have to explain." Lupe looked out at the woods and shook her head. "Sometimes I think it's crazy for me to come out here. But Vince is just somebody a person trusts. There aren't very many people like that—but…"

"I know what you mean. It's really hard to explain. Just a feeling. Like when you know you're standing on solid ground. You don't have to think about it, you just know."

Lupe nodded. "How do you feel about Huevos Rancheros?"

"My feelings about that dish are close to romantic obsession."

"My Huevos Rancheros isn't like every other—you'll see. My dad's recipe…"

"Can I help you prep? Maybe chop things?"

"Sure. Then I can bore you with the story of my life."

"I would not be bored at all!"

There was a rush of feet overhead and Superro came bounding down the stairs, barking, Pascual close behind. He was wearing pyjama bottoms. "Mama it's snowing!"

"I know!"

"Diego, come see!" he shouted, at the ceiling.

"I bet Diego's seen a lot of snow in his time," Lupe said, getting up. "I'm going to make breakfast, Pascual, you get dressed, and take Superro to see what he thinks of snow. But stay close."

Stay close, Dierdre thought. Lupe—did you notice some surveyors, out near the main road, on the way in?"

"I haven't been out there for days. I wonder if someone plans a new house…"

Dierdre decided not to voice her uneasy feelings about the men. Maybe Lupe would take it as racism, since the men were Hispanic. Probably nothing, anyway…

"Now let's see if I've got all the ingredients," Lupe said, starting for the refrigerator. Then she stopped, lifting her head. Listening.

223

They both went stock still—and turned to look toward the front door. The distinctive sound of a motorcycle…

Dierdre grabbed her suitcase and ran to the bathroom to get dressed and brush her hair. *I'm acting like one of those women frantically getting dolled up for some guy.*

For Vince Bellator? Ridiculous. She needed someone who'd root her in the civilian world. A rich, handsome lawyer. Like David Dreed, who'd proposed to her. Sweet, good-looking, successful guy. Stupid to have said no.

She looked in the mirror, and thought she might put on a little eye makeup. Just a little.

The snowfall was little more than an inch, but the Harley didn't like it, and Vince had to ride with extra care, barely fast enough to keep going down the gravel road. He got to the house just as the snowfall ended.

As he cut the engine, close beside the Civic, Vince saw they'd already constructed a front porch. It was freshly completed, and partly stained. The table saw was out front, covered by a tarp against the weather. He could see sawdust on the ground around it, showing through the thin snow. Recently in use. Diego had been at work.

Then the little dog was at the door, barking, and Pascual, in only his pajama bottoms, waving, and Nilla behind them in her blue terrycloth bathrobe, her feet bare, her breath showing in the cold air. And Lupe… Diego looming behind her…

"Kinda cold for you guys to be hanging around on the porch, isn't it?" he asked, grinning. "'Specially with no shirt or shoes, Pascual."

"Vince—the president pardoned you!"

"I know. I saw it in the newspaper."

"That's how you found out?"

"Yes, it was." He started up the steps, and Lupe said, "Vince—there's someone here to see you! She got here yesterday."

"She?" He stopped halfway up the steps. "Dierdre's here?"

"Ha! Look at him, with his *'Di-eeeeerdre!'*" Pascual taunted.

"Cállate, Pascual!" his mother scolded.

The dog barked at Vince—and then stopped barking when it sniffed him. "Superro recognizes me, I see," Vince said, scratching the dog behind an ear. He glanced up at Diego. "Hey Sarge!"

"Hey Captain!"

"You lathe those banister posts yourself?"

"Yep!"

"They came out great. The whole porch looks good."

"Seemed a good place to start. You had a couple of cinder blocks for a porch."

"I was helping build it!" Pascual said.

"Good work, Pascual," Vince said. He picked up the chihuahua. To everyone's astonishment, the little dog allowed it, and licked Vince's cheek.

"He likes you!" Pascual said wonderingly.

"That's a relief. First time he wanted to go for my throat. You folks have any coffee going?" Lupe said.

"Coffee and breakfast, Vince!"

"Excellent. Hey Nilla, glad you made it. How you doing?"

"Okay." She shrugged glumly. "E'cept my feet are cold."

"You're standing outside on a snowy day in bare feet. That might have something to do with it. Come on, let's get all the barefoot people in the house... Come on, Superro..."

They were in the kitchen, seated around the kitchen table, on various unmatching straight-backed chairs, when Dierdre came in. "Sorry about the chairs, Dierdre," Lupe said, as she went to get the server for the Mexican breakfast. "They're random old things we bought at a Goodwill. Vince only had one chair."

Dierdre didn't seem to hear. She was gazing at Vince, a slight smile on her face. She had put on tight Hudson jeans and red Chuck Taylor high-top sneakers. Her blouse was white cotton, with red floral filigree, unbuttoned enough for some decolletage. Her chestnut-brown hair was in a loose bun on her head. She had just the faintest hint of eye shadow.

Vince swallowed. He wanted to tell her how great she looked, how good it was to see her, and a lot of other things. But they were at breakfast. So all he could manage was, "Hi, Dierdre. There's a place set for you…" He nodded to a seat across from him.

She sat down, her smile broadening a little as she looked at him. "You look… intact!"

"That's the nicest thing anybody ever said to me."

That got a general laugh, and Lupe served the Huevos Ranchero. Which was the best he'd ever tasted. "Lupe, how did you make something so simple taste like…" He shook his head. "It's superb!"

"My mama's a pretty good cook," Pascual said, nodding, sneaking a bit of egg to Superro. The boy had dressed, already wearing his coat in preparation for going out into the snow.

"Lupe gave me many meals," Diego said. "Was always the best food I ever had. She cooks like an angel—she *is* an angel."

Lupe glanced at him, blushing.

"Hey—*I* chopped the onions, here," Dierdre said, deadpan. "Made all the difference."

"Oh surrrrrre," said Pascual.

They ate, and no one asked Vince about his mission, because they knew they weren't supposed to. But he could see Diego, particularly, looking at him inquisitively.

226

They talked about the plans for the restaurant, and the next finishing work to be done on the house, and how Diego had used two-thirds of the money Vince had given him to pay for his new teeth, bridges mostly, that he was going to get in a couple of weeks. And how Superro was going to take to the snow—probably not very well—and how Diego had taken the boy out on the boat, once, and Pascual had only gotten a little seasick. Diego swore the boy had learned a good deal of boat craft… And Nilla said nothing.

Finally, Vince put his coffee cup down and said, "Diego and I and Dierdre have some business to talk—how about, while we're doing the dishes and pots, and putting things away, maybe Lupe and Nilla could take him and Superro outside…?"

Lupe hesitated—then nodded. "Okay!"

Nilla gave another dismal shrug. "Sure. I never been in snow."

As Vince scrubbed the big cast-iron skillet, he filled them in on what had happened at the Caidos compound.

When he finished the abbreviated account, Dierdre nodded, and took another plate from Diego to dry. "I noticed you have some skin peeled off, on your cheek, Vince. And your wrist…"

Vince waved it away. "Superficial burns. Just the top layer of skin. I'll be as gorgeous as always soon."

Diego snorted. "Hell, I got a bunion looks prettier than you, captain."

Vince laughed. "I expect so." He handed the skillet to Dierdre to dry, and said, "When Lopez and his man got away—I thought I had to brief you two. You've both been involved. And I don't know what he's going to do next."

"Vince," Dierdre said, "When you rode in, did you see a couple surveyors, about a quarter-mile from here?"

227

"I didn't see them—but I saw their equipment. Weird they'd leave it out in the weather."

She nodded. "I keep thinking there's something off about them...."

"Vince?" Lupe said, coming in and pulling off snow-caked gloves. She glanced nervously at the windows.

Vince heard Pascual and Nilla coming in the front door, talking to Superro. "What's up, Lupe?" he asked. He had a strong suspicion, already, given what Dierdre had said.

"There are some men in the woods. I saw one of them watching the house with binoculars."

Chapter Fourteen

"You idiots should have stayed where you were and shot him when he rode in," said Angel.

Angel, Curly, Renaldo, Mendoza and De Leon were standing around the white and silver Cadillac parked on the slushy road. Behind it was a plain white van, where two men sat in the front seat and two more were waiting in the back. They were the best killers in Angel's organization. Renaldo knew Angel had to offer Mendoza and Leon and those two in the van extra money to come to this godforsaken place that was sometimes rainy and sometimes snowy, soon before Christmas. They all knew the Caidos cartel was falling apart, partly because of the traitor who'd survived the attack on the Arizona Central Compound—he was talking freely to the State Police—and partly because of Sergeant Fuentes. In the last three days, numerous key Caidos cartelitos in Arizona and New Mexico had been arrested and others were running for Mexico. When a cartel falls apart, Renaldo figured, so does loyalty. Meaning that this was a matter more for money than for loyalty.

"You sure it was this Bellator?" Mendoza asked.

"Saw him in the front window, clear as day," Curly said. "Yeah, it's him."

We should just go in now and get it done, boss," Curly declared. He was wearing a Kevlar vest and holstered on his hips were a MAC-10 and a silenced .38.

"No, we do it tonight, unless we see him leaving before then," Angel said. "I don't want the neighbors seeing something and calling the cops."

"The nearest neighbor is almost a quarter-mile off, boss."

"I don't care. Anyway, I want to go in myself, to kill him personally if I can. In the daylight it's too dangerous. If we can catch him in the darkness..."

"He's got people in that house," Mendoza said. "We could get hold of them, hold them hostage, he might just surrender. We kill 'em all when he surrenders. But it'd make it easier, if he's as dangerous as they say he is." Mendoza was a nervous, wiry man, with a gaunt face stretched out by a goatish beard. He had the MAC-10 they were all issued and a .45 semi-auto pistol. And a Kevlar vest.

Angel and De Leon had one of those too.

"Why does everyone but me have a Kevlar vest?" Renaldo asked.

They ignored his question. Angel said, "If we get that kind of chance, Mendoza, sure we can take hostages. But I doubt he gives it to us. Curly says the house looks like it has a basement. He'll have them down there, secured."

"We could set the place on fire," De Leon said. He had a MAC-10, but in his hands was a big hunting crossbow. A quiver of arrows was strapped on his back. He was a stocky, almost dwarfish man with short graying hair; he wore a camouflage combat outfit, and his face and hands were covered in old blue-ink tattoos.

Angel snorted. "If we set the place on fire, people will see it—or someone in the house will call 911. The cops and fire department will come. No, we have to go at him another way... Let's go to the van and sit down where it's warm. And everyone can hear what I have in mind..."

"There's no window to shoot from in this attic, Captain," Diego said, as he and Dierdre followed him up the raw wooden stairs. "Nothin' up here that I can see. You don't want us to *hide* up here, do you?"

"There actually is something in this attic," Vince said, hunching over to get across the low-ceilinged attic, ducking the hanging single yellow lightbulb. He carried a cordless power drill with him. "I'll show you, Diego."

Vince crouched in a corner, and they knelt near him, watching as he used the drill to bring up eight screws holding down two five-foot-long planks. He reached into a small hole cut in the corner of one, used it to grip the plank and pull it up, partly exposing the steel storage cabinet lying beneath it. He took up the second plank, exposing the cabinet's nine-button keypad. He tapped in the code, Jack Sullivan's birthday, and the box gave out a clicking sound. He raised the lid and they saw the weapons in the cabinet.

"I should have known," Dierdre murmured.

There were two rifles, including the MK18 Mod 1 carbine that Vince needed right now. The compact carbine had a scope, a sound-suppressor and muzzle-brake on it. He'd need quiet and accuracy tonight and the muzzle-brake, which redirected propellant gases, would reduce muzzle recoil, improving accuracy. The scope had a night-vision capability.

"That weapon," Dierdre said. "That's military grade. Did you get that legally, Vince?"

"No."

"Do you think it's a good thing that it's sold illegally?"

"Usually—no. The wrong people would use it. "But for your own use you're cheerfully breaking another law?"

"I either believe in my mission…" He took the MK18 out of the cabinet rack. "…or I don't." He reached for the ammo stored below the rifle. "Happens I do." He slapped the magazines into the guns. He took another silent-kill weapon out of the box.

"Vince is that what I think it is?" Dierdre asked.

"Yep."

"I guess you'd have used those in Delta Force."

"Naturally."

She made an *eww* face. "Grisly."

"But quiet. Very quiet… Diego, pick out a weapon. There's an Uzi there if you want, but I'd recommend the Heckler and Koch, with the scope—good for the mission I have in mind. Just a contingency weapon. I had a good Tango 51 but I gave it to Harris. I think Dierdre should take this Glock."

Late in the afternoon Vince and Diego scoped out the trail from the back of the house, down to the top of the steep stairs accessing the pebble beach and the boat dock. Vince was carrying the MK18 and Diego had the scoped rifle. Dierdre was keeping an eye on the others, listening to records in the basement. Nilla was teaching Pascual to free-dance and Lupe was watching—and trying not to laugh.

Vince and Diego didn't take the trail itself to check it out. They separated at the beginning of the trail, each taking a side of it, and moved slowly down the hill, easing through the brush; stopping often, hyper-vigilant as they looked to see if any Caidos were hiding out here. Sometimes a little snow crunched underfoot; now and then some loosened from the brush as they went by and fell with a soft shoosh sound. But it wasn't enough to get in their way.

They met at the dock, and boarded the cabin cruiser, going down to the little cabin below the deck, so they wouldn't be easy targets from up above.

"Don't seem to be anyone around the trail, Vince," Diego said, sitting across from him. "Maybe those guys Lupe saw were, what you call it, birdwatchers or something."

Vince shook his head. "It's the Caidos. I've been half expecting this. Angel finding out who I am—and where I live. Dierdre was worried there's still a mole in the state department. And Angel's got some kind of relationship with the Russians."

"The Russian mob?"

"Not exactly. The Russian intelligence service. SVR."

"Holy crap!"

"Yeah, that about covers it. I figure the cartelitos are going to put some guys out behind the house tonight. If they get the chance. I don't plan to give them the chance. But I don't want you and the others here."

"Yeah, the plan to send me out in the boat with the kid and the ladies... Kind of insulting, Vince. I should be out there with you."

Vince shook his head. "No. Those people are my responsibility. And Dierdre..."

"Yeah, I've seen how you look at her. Vince let that pass. "I need you to protect them, Diego. Probably they'll be safe out on the Sound. You'll take them down to a waterside restaurant, has a dock, *Penelope's*. I'll tell you how to get there. You guys have dinner and I'll be in touch. It seems safer than having them in the house. I don't want that boy to see anymore killing. He's been through enough. Lupe and Nilla too. They don't have to know about all this. Dierdre's a combat veteran, but I don't want her catching a bullet."

"Lupe wanted to just call the cops, when you saw those guys."

"That could scare them off for a while. But it wouldn't remove the threat. They'd just be back."

"And you're gonna be out there alone tonight? You don't know how many men they've got out there. Angel, that shit-heel coward, he'll have the best men he can find."

"You let me worry about that. If I don't call you by midnight—don't come back to the house. That's when you can call the police."

Diego looked like he wanted to say something more. But he just nodded.

"Diego, you don't have to go along with this. I've got no authority over you. I'm not giving orders, this is a request. You can say no. You can call the cops."

"I know, Captain. But... hell, I'm not going to turn down a free dinner."

"Who said it was free?"

It was dusk when Vince escorted the others down to the top of the stairs overlooking the dock. He watched as they went down to the cabin cruiser, Pascual chattering to his mother and Nilla with excitement. It was a chilly night but the snowfall had stopped, and the breeze off the sound wasn't enough to make the water significantly choppy.

He had his Desert Eagle hidden under his coat. His other weapon was hidden in the brush nearby. Diego's rifle was already stashed aboard the boat. The .45 Glock Dierdre had chosen was hidden under her raincoat.

He had made an excuse to the boy and Nilla—told them he

was going to go meet some people for a discussion on law enforcement. He waved to them now, as Diego and Pascual went to cast off the lines. Nilla was talking to Pascual. They seemed to have become friends.

Diedre just stared up at him, her hands clenching the railing, a stricken look on her face.

Was that the last time he'd ever see her?

Vince forced himself to turn away. He started up the next flight of stairs, that led to the trail. He cut off to the right from the muddy wooden landing and slipped into the brush. He found his MK18 where he'd left it, at the base of a Douglas fir. It was wrapped in a tarp, along with the extra clips. He unwrapped it, stuffed the clips into the inside pockets of his coat. He had his combat rifle, the Desert Eagle, and another weapon on him too.

Vince could hear the cabin cruiser putting out from the dock, the engine beginning to drone as it picked up speed. *Bon Appetit,* he thought.

He glanced up, between the treetops. Flanked by the gray and white clouds, the sky was Prussian Blue. It'd be quite dark, soon. There were several lights on in the house, and he'd left the kitchen radio playing at top volume. Too bad there was no television to turn on. Superro would bark from time to time, which was good. It would add to the illusion of their being at home.

Vince headed south, into the brush between his house, and the neighbor. It was cold and wet and some of the dogwood scratched him. But he was settling into the zone of decision, pure focus on combat readiness. He noticed the discomforts passingly, as information. But most of his attention was riveted on his hearing and his sight.

After a few hundred yards, Vince figured he'd gone far enough to the south. He paused to listen—then changed directions. Heading northeast; hypothetically moving toward the enemy now.

It was dark now. The moon had risen just enough to be a danger to him.

Vince figured the Caidos had their own reasons to wait until dark. And right now, they'd be taking the positions for the attack that Angel had in mind for them. He might be wrong about what they were doing—and he was well aware of that—but Vince saw his mission as stopping the attack before it started. And the best way to do that was to be there first, and come in from their southern flank. He needed to do it as soundlessly as possible.

He tried to avoid the patches of snow between the trees; stepping on snow made a soft squeaking, or crunching, or sloshing; depending on how thick and how slushy it was. He evaded branches, ducking to frog walk under them. Bumping branches made a sound, and made the foliage move. A hundred yards…

Once more, he stopped… and listened.

This time he heard voices, coming from the Northeast. He couldn't tell what they were saying. But he heard just enough to know they were speaking in Spanish. Not loudly.

Vince moved on, keeping to the deepest shadows. He was passing through a stand of spruces now, the sort that made a sort of bell-shape with their branches, low to the ground. That could be used to a man's advantage. Theirs—but his, too.

Here he was treading on an aromatic carpet of fallen fir needles and the thin, tightly wrapped pinecones that spruce trees dropped. Usually it was a quiet carpet to walk on. But sometimes there was a twig buried a little beneath the fir needles—like now. He heard a crackle as he took a step with his right foot. And he froze. If he kept going it'd make another noise as he took the pressure off. And he didn't want the sound of a series of steps. The enemy would think, *Footsteps.*

He waited a full minute, listening and watching; hearing nothing but a faint rustle of the top of the spruces in a light wind, and seeing nothing but the dark slashes of tree trunks, the spruce branches with a light load of snow. Once in a while the breeze would move a branch enough so a little snow sifted down, with a barely audible noise.

Then he gently lifted up his right foot; slowly, so it wouldn't make another crackle. He took another step, listening. Still quiet. He moved on, keeping to the shadows.

Listening. Watching.

"Callarse, estupido!" someone whispered. (Shut up, stupid!) It was a strangely loud whisper from about ten yards Northeast.

Vince froze, listening.

"Yo no dije nada!" (I didn't say anything!)

"Angel dijo—shhh!"

Vince smiled.

"Ve Ajora! Ponerse en marche!"

"No, no!" Then a *thwack* sound and someone yelping. *"Aii!"*

Vincent reckoned one of the men was being driven through the woods by another. A decoy; a sacrificial goat, sent toward the house to distract Vince Bellator while the others moved in from the north and south.

Then Vince saw the silhouette of a man stumbling clumsily in the snow, waving his hands in front of his face as he moved in the general direction of the house. In one of his hands was a pistol, pointed nowhere special.

Vince knelt between two drooping spruce boughs, in the same motion bringing the MK18 to his shoulder, nestling it into firing position—but it wasn't aimed at the guy stumbling through the snow. He looked through the scope—an Armasight Zeus Pro 640 thermal imaging sight, tracking it over to the other man. The other man's voice seemed to have come from...

There he was. The thermal image was a fiery gold, against a blue backdrop. He saw a MAC-10 outlined in the man's right hand; in the left he had a pistol. He had what was probably a Kevlar vest bulking his chest. Definitely this man was a Caidos.

Vince simply laid the crosshairs on the man's head and squeezed the trigger. One shot was enough—with the sound suppressor it was just a whuffing. The cartelito folded.

Vince swept the scope over the forest and caught another heat signature. A big man, with the outline of a hunting crossbow in his hand, moving slowly toward the house. The guy's body profile—very short, wide-bodied--and the crossbow, identified him to Vince. Carlos De Leon. Vince had found the man's kills in the Yucatan and had read the CIA file on him. The bodies of indigenes who'd been giving the cartel trouble. Arrow wounds—but death by torture. De Leon loved to torture wounded victims, when he could.

Vince tracked him, squeezed off a shot—right through the left side of De Leon's head.

The Caidos assassin went to his knees then flopped forward. Without a sound.

Two down, one wandering in confusion toward the house, expecting to be shot down—by someone who wasn't there. Deal with that guy last.

Vince moved off, avoided a patch of snow, hunkered under another spruce. Listened. Thought he heard someone whispering... Moved on again and found himself at the body of the first man he'd shot. Was it Curly?

No. He could see the dead man's staring face in the scant

moonlight, enough to recognize him. Another cartelito from the Yucatan, "Slug" Mendoza.

Vince grabbed the body by an ankle and dragged it into some dogwood bushes. Hiding it reduced the chances of alerting his targets. Then he stalked slowly on. Watchfully. Listening…

There. He heard a footstep crunching snow, not too far away. He glimpsed a man's frosty outbreath in a thin ray of moonlight.

Vince went on one knee, just within the dogwoods, raising the M18 to firing position, and looked through the scope. The heat-signature showed the fiery-yellow outline of a big man, large head shaven. Ballcap. Prognathous jaw. He carried an AR15 automatic rifle with a suppressor and welded atop the suppressor something rarely seen: a custom bayonet.

Vince knew this man too, by reputation. He'd seen CIA images of him in a file. He was an albino from Hispaniola, his face and hands blacked out for night operations. The bayonet was one of his trademarks. He was the assassin Tenzeno, known as *El Espectro*. The Ghost.

Tenzeno was a murderer who raped anyone he could, on an assignment, regarding it as part of his reward for the job. Liked to strangle the children of his prey, even when he wasn't paid to kill them.

Vince aimed—and lost the shot as *El Espectro*, unaware of him, passed behind a tree bole.

Vince circled to the east, glancing around for other Caidos. Seeing no one just yet. He moved quietly into a better position to shoot Tenzeno. The assassin was three strides away now, his back turned. Tenzeno was one guy Vince didn't mind shooting in the back. Vince raised the M18, aimed at the back of Tenzeno's head, squeezed the trigger…

Click.

The M18 jammed.

Probably a badly-made magazine. There was no time to clear the rifle.

If I survive this, Vince thought, putting the gun softly on the ground, *I'm going to find the manufacturer responsible and shove the magazine up his...*

Then he realized that Tenzeno had stopped; was raising his head as if listening. He must have heard the click when the gun jammed.

Vince eased toward Tenzeno, pulling the garrotte from his pocket, opening it with a deft, practiced motion of his hands. Then he took two long fast strides up close behind Tenzeno, whipping the garrotte's piano wire around the Ghost's neck with a split-second motion. Tenzeno was already half turned toward him—but Vince shifted so he was behind the assassin as he pulled the garrote taut as hard as he could, wanting Tenzeno's pain and panic, as the wire both choked and cut, to make the man drop his gun. If *El Espectro* fired the AR15, the sound would alert the others.

Instead, the gurgling Tenzeno whipped the rifle's muzzle back, angling it over his right shoulder, desperately trying to slash Vince with the bayonet. It clipped a bit of Vince's ear.

Remembering the murdered children, Vince used every ounce of strength to jerk the garrote tight in a particular way. He'd used the garrote in a more standard way on other missions, in Iraq and Syria—but he'd been told that if properly operated, and tightened with enough force, the piano wire could...

It did. It took an extra wrenching twist with the garrote...

And it decapitated Tenzeno.

The AR15 fell from lifeless fingers. Tenzeno's twitching body flopped away. His head bounced on the turf, rolled to a stop, its eyelids fluttering.

The Ghost's reeking blood was splashed down Vince's front. Vince's heart was pounding with the effort.

Definitely have to burn these clothes and take a long shower, he thought, as he dropped the bloody garrote and picked up the AR15. It was fitted with a sound suppressor. It just might do.

Glancing around for tangos, Vince wiped blood off the AR15 and moved off into the woods, keeping the thickets between himself and the area the others likely were…

And then a bullet sliced past his neck, close enough it burned the skin.

Vince threw himself flat on the ground as the report of the gun echoed through the woods. The sound gave him a rough approximation of the shooter's whereabouts and he fired four rounds that way, with a spread of a few degrees, hoping to get lucky.

Another shot cracked over his head. He rolled to the left, fired three more rounds toward the shooter as he got to his feet and sprinted to a big Douglas fir.

A bullet scored away bark, splinters spattering his face. But the mark of the bullet on the tree trunk gave him a good sense of the shooter's whereabouts. The guy was under the overhanging branches of a spruce. Vince stepped behind the broad bole of the tree, took the rifle in his left hand and drew the Desert Eagle. No need for quiet now.

He leaned just a little to the left, peering through the semi-darkness, and saw a muzzle flash and ducked back. Felt the tree shudder with the impact of the bullet. But the flash had told him the enemy's position more clearly.

He stepped out and fired round after round, five shots fast as he could get them off. The big .50 caliber bullets crashed right through the thinner lower branches—and he heard a scream of pain.

He stepped back undercover and heard a man groaning, cursing in Spanish. Vince circled around to the south, running, watching for other Caidos. Angel and Curly were still out there somewhere. Or had he just shot one of them?

He came upon the spruce from the southeast side, ducked under the fronds and saw a dead man with an AK47 in his hands. He had been hit twice in the torso and the sizeable .50 impact wounds were still gushing blood. He could barely see the face—but he was sure the man was unknown to him.

Crouching under the spruce, Vince felt exposed now—the others had to know he was somewhere close. Would Angel really be here in person? Maybe he'd done a runner.

But from what Vince gleaned of Angel Lopez, the cartel boss would want to be where he could personally see Vince Bellator dead. Vince had cost him millions of dollars, at the compound. Had killed a great many of his men; made him flee like a rabbit.

Yes. Angel would be here.

Vince holstered the Desert Eagle, took the Ghost's AR15 in both hands, and ducked under the low spruce branches, starting off in a low crouch to the west. The men seemed to have been spread out across the woods; hence Angel and Curly, if they were here, were probably north of him.

After a few steps he heard voices in Spanish—one exclaiming, the other hissing something. Probably telling the first one to shut up.

Vince smiled. He had a partial fix on their position now.

He ducked under the branches, and headed off, keeping trees between him and the approximate location of his enemies when he could

He'd nearly gotten to the road when he spotted Angel. The cartel boss was crouching behind a late-model Cadillac, probably stolen, a MAC-10 in his hand, staring down the road. A car length behind him was a white van. Likely also stolen, to cover their tracks.

Let's keep this simple, Vince thought, as he got to the edge of the tree line. *Just shoot the son of a bitch.*

He glanced around, didn't see anyone else. He was about fifty feet from Angel Lopez.

Vince raised the gun—and Lopez turned toward him. Saw Vince had the drop on him.

And Angel Lopez dropped his MAC-10. "Okay. I surrender," he said, in English. He raised his hands. "You win, Vincent Bellator."

Just shoot him, Vince told himself.

But the guy was *surrendering* to him. He couldn't just shoot him.

Vince lowered the AR15 but kept it pointed toward his target. He walked toward Angel, and said, "Where's your bodyguard?"

"I don't know."

Vince walked closer. "I worked out who he was. 'Rizado' Estrada. Curly. He was there that day. When you shot that family. In Mexico. I was the one up the hill."

"Ah! That was you!" Angel shrugged. "Business—sometimes it's messy."

Vince snorted. "The powerful businessman who simply must murder children," Vince said, coming close.

"You are the man who does so much killing—far more than me!"

"Move over there, between me and the woods."

Lopez obeyed.

Vince circled Lopez, to put the cartel boss between him and the southern woods, where Curly likely was.

"I see you've killed Tenzeno—I know that rifle. And the other men?"

"They're dead. Except for one who seems confused. He ran toward the house."

"That would be Renaldo."

"And I'll take care of Curly. I'll find him after I tie you up."

Stalling, Angel asked, "Why'd you come after me? I got the message—I killed a friend of yours. One of those at the plantation. Maybe the woman?"

"No. Chris Destry."

"I don't know the name."

"You killed him with a ATS missile from your Blackhawk."

"Self-defense, amigo. He was coming after me!"

"You could have surrendered."

"How foolish would that be? I had the edge then."

"Shut up and lay on the ground, hands behind your back. I've got another garrote I can tie your hands with. You're lucky I don't strangle you with it."

Angel nodded, like an understanding old friend, started to go down on one knee as if about to follow directions—but he reached behind and drew the hideaway gun. He lunged at Vince, leveling the .45—

Vince could have shot him. But the memory of that day in the jungle, Angel Lopez ordering the family murdered, crashed over him like an icy breaker, and he found himself stabbing out with the bayonet, thrusting it in deep, under the sternum.

Lopez fired the pistol—but the shot went wild, as he writhed on the bayonet, gasping, his eyes bulging with pain and a kind of cosmic puzzlement. The universe he understood could not permit this to happen to him.

Vince twisted the bayonet. "Drop the gun!"

Lopez screamed and dropped the .45.

Then he wrenched himself back, pulling himself off the bayonet. Blood followed it out, splashing on the road. He went to his knees, clutching his riven belly.

"Curly…" Blood rose in his mouth, and he spat it out so he could talk. "He will kill you."

"I don't think so."

"If… you live… I ask Santa Muerte… to make you… kill Krupin. He knows…" Blood bubbled out with each word. "He knows… your house… The ship… *Love Island* destroys your America… in Mexico… the Russians… Krupin… I hate him… I send you to kill… I send you… Oh, Santa Muerte…"

And then blood gushed from Angel Lopez's mouth, and he choked and went pale. He stared into space—as if he saw something awful Vince couldn't see. Then he fell on his face, shaking… and died.

Krupin.

"Vince, get down!" Dierdre shouted, from his right.

Vince flattened on the road and he heard the booming of the Glock he'd given her.

What the hell?

"Dierdre?" He looked around, and saw one of the Caidos lying on his side, in the tree line to the south. Long curly black hair. Curly Estrada.

Vince got to his feet, as she walked past the Cadillac to him.

"Oh Jesus, Vince—there's blood all over you. We need an ambulance!"

"We don't. It's not my blood."

"None of it?"

"A little bit on my right ear."

She turned to look at the inert bulk of the big sicario lying in the fir needles by the trees.

"Hold on," he said. He raised the AR15 to his shoulder and walked over to the body. Curly Estrada looked quite surprised, staring in death.

"You nailed him right through the throat and the right side of his face there," Vince said, feeling a little dizzy. "He's dead alright. Good shooting."

"Where are the others?" she asked, turning the gun toward the woods.

"I think I got them all. Except one guy. Seemed scared—ran off toward the house."

"Oh—I disarmed him. I took him prisoner. I cuffed him to my car. He seemed kind of relieved."

"Yeah? His name's Renaldo something. He was the one with the bodega, right?"

"Yeah." She lowered the gun. Then she stared at the gutted, still-bleeding body of Angel Lopez. "Oh God. It's him. Did you have to cut him open?"

"It just… worked out that way. I was trying to take him prisoner—because he surrendered. He had a hidden gun…"

She stared at the body, and then shuddered, and looked away.

"Dierdre? What the hell are you doing here? I saw you on the boat!"

"Oh, that…" She pushed a wisp of hair out of her face, an oddly apologetic gesture. "I jumped off the boat, and onto the dock, as Diego was taking the boat out. He wasn't pleased. I told him I had some… some family business. I told him to just go." She gave a rueful smile. "I almost didn't get to the dock. Just about fell in the water. Would have been undignified."

"And I suppose you think you saved my life right now?"

"He had a bead on you, Vince. I yelled to make him look at me and I shot him."

"You know what?"

"Um…what?"

"Just—thank you, Dierdre. I'm glad you were there."

"Really?"

"Really. But now you can help me pick up all the weapons and put them with the dead guys in the tarps. They're already cut up for the bodies."

"Tarps? What about the police?"

"What about them? I can't spend the next two years explaining all this… I'm going to get rid of these cars, and…" He looked at Angel's body.

"And the bodies?"

"Simplest thing. Dump them in the water, way out. There's chunks of concrete from an old building I tore down, out back—we can use those to weigh them down. Me and Diego will do it, once we've got the bodies organized into tarps. I don't want any Caidos diehards being *sure* I killed their boss. They'll think he's fled."

"I shouldn't do that. Help you cover things up."

"You're not an FBI agent anymore. Do you really want the notoriety—more than you have now—of being involved in this firefight? Because your part in it would come out."

Dierdre grimaced, and looked at Curly's body. "No. I guess I don't." She sighed. "It'll be really fucked up, dealing with the bodies."

"Uh… I did decapitate a guy with the garrote."

"You did not."

"I'm afraid I did."

"You clean that up by yourself."

"Done deal."

Then she took a deep breath and said, "Let's get the tarps…"

There was a row of tarps, each with its body, lying in the gravel of the circular driveway in front of the house. One of them had its face exposed. Angel Lopez.

"Angel?" Renaldo said, staring at the dead man's face. Then Renaldo smiled. "That is a relief."

Vince, Dierdre and Renaldo were standing together, looking at the bodies. Renaldo still had Dierdre's handcuffs on.

Vince thought, *She still carries those cuffs? Hard to give up, are they?*

"You're glad he's dead?" Vince asked.

"Yes! He set me up—they were going to use me as a decoy, and let me get killed, while they came at you from the sides and the back... They were using me like I was a pig for slaughter!"

Vince nodded. "That's the cartel. And some of it's still out there. Maybe it'll fall apart. Maybe those guys will join the Sinaloas. But I can't be sure. The smart thing for me to do, Renaldo, would be to kill you. Right now. Because you'll tell the other cartelitos all about this. Some may be sentimental about Angel."

"About him?" Renaldo laughed bitterly. "No! Not at all! Nada! He killed too many men because he was in a bad mood!"

"Maybe. Or maybe it'd be some kind of... obligation to avenge him. Make a name doing that..."

"No. They will be pleased to be rid of him. Like me."

"I don't want them to know he's dead. I want them to think he's running away from the feds. And the federales. That he's hiding somewhere."

"Yes! I will tell them that! I'll say I heard him plan to go to... to Brazil!"

"Will you?" Dierdre asked, making a show of toying with her gun. "Could you keep your mouth shut?"

"Oh yes senora! Always!"

"You know that Fuentes is talking to the FBI?" she asked.

"I heard this."

"Fuentes will talk about *you*," Dierdre said. "Possibly you might have time to sell your store and take the money and go away. Leave the country, before you're arrested. That's if we decide to let you go."

"If anyone comes here again, Renaldo," Vince said, "I'll blame you. I will kill them, like I killed these men. Then I'll come for you. I'll find you no matter where you are. Do you believe that?"

Sweat was rolling down Renaldo's forehead. He was breathing as if he'd just run a half-mile. "Yes! I do believe it! I see what you can do! I heard him talk of you! Yes!"

"Okay," Vince said. "I'm going to take a chance on you. I shouldn't. You should thank this nice lady here. She spoke up for you. Said she thought you wouldn't cause me any trouble."

"Thank you, *senora!*" Renaldo gasped, ducking his head to her. "I will never speak of this!"

"The keys are in that Cadillac," she said, unlocking the handcuffs. "Drive it to the airport. Wipe it down for prints. Just abandon the car there. Then disappear. And do it silently."

"Yes, *si,* certainly!" He backed away, then turned and jogged up the road toward the Caddy.

"I'll get rid of the van before Diego and I head out," Vince said. "We really can't trust him."

"I think he's scared of you, Vince. I think that fear will make him trustworthy. Can we cover Lopez's face now?"

"By all means. Where's the duct tape?"

"It's on Curly's body. I can't believe I'm talking like it's moving day or something and I'm closing up boxes with shoes in it."

"You're done. Go in and have a glass of wine and… whatever you want. I'm going to get the wheelbarrow, start moving these guys into the woods by the trail. Stash 'em till Diego gets back. Don't want to upset Lupe or the kid…"

"Or Nilla?"

"In her case I think she'd just say, 'Huh!' and shrug it off."

A splash as the last of the bodies, duct-taped into pieces of tarps, went into the water to join its compadres. Vince grimaced, watching it sink, weighted down with concrete and the Caidos weapons, into the night-black waters of Puget Sound as Diego held the darkened cabin cruiser in place.

It bothered Vince, dumping bodies like this. It was risky, though it was an inky night under heavy overcast and drizzling rain. Worse, it made him feel like he was doing things the way a serial killer or a mafia hitman would.

Not a warm feeling, he thought, as he looked out over the water. No sign of a Coast Guard patrol, or Seattle Port Police.

"You think anybody'll find 'em in there?" Diego asked, as Vince joined him in the cockpit.

"Not likely. Off Jefferson point here's the deepest part of the Sound. It's a long way down."

"They ain't stoppin' at the bottom," Diego said. "They'll keep going till they hit Hell."

Yeah, that was some consolation, despite the ugly disposal of the bodies. The world was better off without those men in it.

"It's 'bout half an hour before dawn, Captain," Diego said. "We better get outta here."

"Yeah. It's a long trip back to Harstine." Vince was tired.

Diego put the cruiser in gear and brought it about, heading south for Harstine Island. Way at the other end of Puget Sound.

"We going to need fuel, Vince."

"There's a place we can stop, they open about seven-thirty. We can get breakfast there." He was glad he'd taken time to shower and get into clean clothes. He waited another few minutes, then said, "You can go ahead and put the lights back on."

Diego switched on the cabin cruiser's lights and accelerated to twenty knots. "Glad that's behind us."

"Me too, Diego. Thanks for this. It's a risk you didn't have to take."

"I always got your six, Captain."

"I'm looking forward to seeing how you look with those new teeth in. But I bet you're more interested in how Lupe'll like it."

Diego grunted. "You can tell that?"

"Oh yeah. Just keep showing her you're squared away, and staying sober, like you have been. I think she'd go for it, Diego."

"I've been in love with that woman for three years."

They were quiet for a while, listening to the engine, looking at the distant lights; shiny pinpricks on the eastern side of the Sound. "Vince—what Angel said about those Russians. You take that seriously? Maybe he was just trying to get at you one time before he died."

"We called Chang—What he said connects with what the Bureau knows. Up to a point."

Vince remembered every word. *"If... you live... I ask Santa Muerte... to make you... kill Krupin. He knows..."* Blood bubbled out with each word. *"He knows... your house... The ship... Love Island destroys your America... in Mexico... the Russians... Krupin... I hate him... I send you to kill... I send you... Ai, Santa Muerte..."*

The cruiser struck a cross-wave from a distant freighter and pitched enough so Vince had to catch hold of a strap overhead to steady himself. "That part about *Love Island* sounds like bullshit. But Chang said there's a registered cruise ship by that name… And it's owned by a Russian oligarch."

"What do you think's going on out there?"

"I don't know. But I'm going to find out."

"Vince—you kidding, man? You killed Lopez! Let it go!"

"The Russians were behind Lopez. And he said something about them destroying America."

"Probably a lie. He just wants to get you killed fucking with those Russians."

"Could be, Diego. Could be."

But he'd made up his mind. He'd do some research, and stock up on certain weapons…

And then we'll see who kills who…

Five days later, driving the camper through an evening rain to her hotel in Olympia, Vince thought about Dierdre's reaction to helping him roll up dead men in tarps to be dumped at sea. Not an ideal way to win a woman over…

Not that he was trying to win her over.

No, really. He wasn't.

If anything, he was trying to send a message. *This is what happens when you hang around me, Dierdre.* Part of him hoped she kept coming around no matter what. He wanted her, sure, more than he'd ever wanted a woman. But he knew the best thing for her was to stay away.

She'd cussed between gritted teeth, helping him drag the dead assassins onto the tarps. It wasn't that she was so squeamish about bloody corpses—she was a combat veteran. A former law enforcement agent. No, it was the *law* she was squeamish about. She still felt a deep loyalty to the Bureau. And why shouldn't she? These days they were doing good work.

If you want her to leave, he thought, *why are you going to see Dierdre at her hotel?*

Dinner, that's all. Just a farewell dinner between friends.

But his pulse was racing as he pulled up in front of the Olympia Marriot. The valet, a sleek young man in hotel livery, frowned at the battered old camper. But he said, "I'll see if I can find a place for it…"

Vince caught his breath when he saw her waiting in the bar. She was wearing a long, tight, slinky black dress slit to her hips. Her hair was down around her bare shoulders.

He was glad he'd put on his charcoal blazer—his only blazer—and the black pants. And the formal black shoes he hadn't worn in years.

They were almost the only people in the bar. Christmas decorations, almost realistic-looking holly, some gold-plastic bells, adorned the wall above the rows of liquor bottles.

"Look at you," Dierdre said, as he sat down beside her. "Almost civilized. You even combed your hair. More or less."

"It's the Marriot. Slightly fancy."

"Slightly is the word."

"You look…" *Just incredible. Fantastic. Gorgeous.* But he said, "… great."

"You want one of these?" She tapped her cocktail.

"I really want a red ale, with a slice of orange."

They drank, and he asked, "Where's the file on you?"

"On me? There is one. At the Bureau. I'm mixed into your file now too."

"You've read mine. You know I grew up in North Texas. A flower plantation. Providing to florists all over the southeast."

"Horse breeding too, no?"

253

"Yeah but—it was more than a hobby but less than a thriving business. Can be hard to make ends meet breeding horses. Overhead is high. But we had a working ranch too, you bet. I bucked a lot of hay in the barn. I was there for a lot of foaling. I'm half veterinarian."

"So you know all about horses."

"There's always more to know. When I was staying with Harris' family in Arizona, mostly I talked about two things with his granddad. Motorcycles and horses. I learned a lot about mustangs I didn't know."

"Your folks still in Texas?"

"My file's not up to date on that. My mom's there—my dad had a long bout with cancer—we think it was from the pesticide the used to keep the roses and tulips and gardenias lovely. When he figured out about the pesticide, he stopped using them and got the place certified organic. He could charge even more, he said. But he died six months after that. And wait—you're still not briefing me on the life of Agent Dierdre Corlin."

She gave a ghost of a smile. "It almost worked. Okay—Irish Catholic family in Maryland. Not much Catholic in me but lots of Irish. My parents are both professors. He's got a doctorate in American History, she's a sociologist. They argue about what really happened."

"Happened when?"

"Name any time in history at all. That's when."

Vince laughed.

She shrugged. "Not an exciting household. Professor Mom and Professor Dad—my brother, who's now a priest, God help him. And my Aunt Teresa, who's a bit batty. She lived with us till she died from all the cigarettes. A sweet woman, really. Just missing a screw somewhere."

"Where'd the interest in law enforcement come from?"

"I was just… always drawn to it. Maybe because my parents told me a lot of dark stories about history. And all I could think was, some chaos is good but some can't be tolerated."

"I like that. Mind if I use that? Some chaos is good but some can't be tolerated?"

She frowned. "Use it where?"

"Oh, when they interview me on television about the famous FBI agent who was pardoned by the President of the United States."

"You're not going to—!"

He grinned. "No. Not a word. Everyone of your secrets, Dierdre Corlin…" He broke off, suddenly realizing he wanted to kiss her, there and then in the bar. He cleared his throat. "…is safe with me."

Dierdre gave him a long, thoughtful look. She seemed on the point of saying something. Then she looked away and said, "You want to go into the restaurant and order dinner?"

"Rather eat at the bar. In a restaurant I always feel like…" He almost said, *It's harder to watch my back.*

Wild Bill Hickok. That one time he didn't sit with his back to the wall… Aces and eights…

Instead, he said, "You know how I heard we were pardoned?"

"How?"

"I was stopping at a gas station. Went in to get a bottle of water. The guy behind the counter said, 'Hey—aren't you that guy the president pardoned?' The guy points at the newspaper. There's my face on the front cover, and a picture of you right beside it."

Like something from a wedding picture, he thought. Then: *No, you don't, you fool. Forget it.*

"So you feel too exposed in a restaurant? Like…?"

"Like I can't wait for people to forget who I am."

She nodded. "I get that. But I don't know if they ever will. It'll die down some. Let's order something to eat…"

She had a chicken salad, he had salmon, and they talked about their childhoods, and what sports they'd liked and which ones they sucked at, and what bands they liked—she was far more into sensitive-singer-songwriters. He told her how he'd decided that the restaurant would be a building detached from the house, and he had a friend in the area who was an architect, he was interested in doing the design. And they talked about what Lupe's plans for Christmas dinner were.

They avoided talking about dead men in the woods. About that day at the Lincoln Memorial. About the Germanic Brethren and the Caidos.

They didn't agree not to talk about it. They both knew, instinctively, that right now the other wanted to stay away from the blood-splashed shadows.

After a while he found that they were leaning more and more toward one another. That there were long moments where their eyes locked and their gazes seemed to meld.

"Vince," she said, finally, "I've been offered a pretty well-paid consultancy job in D.C. I was wondering what I'd do for a living and I figured I'd be poison and nobody'd hire me—too much notoriety. But… it seems to be the opposite. People are making offers."

"More than one, then. Always good."

"One in Seattle too. The Port of Seattle has a new program trying to interdict drug trafficking. Find ways to know what ships to search, how to find hidden drugs. That kind of thing. They're starting an inhouse security division for narcotics."

He nodded. "Seattle. Not so far from here. You could come down and say hello. Try out the restaurant—on the house—when it's rolling. The boy and Lupe and Diego really like you."

"Nilla doesn't."

"Nilla doesn't know what she likes or who she is yet."

"She likes *you*, big guy."

"In an adolescent kind of way. Nothing's going to happen. Which job you going for? I bet the one in D.C. pays better."

"It does."

"So—you'll probably head out there soon." He did his best to keep his expression neutral.

"Um… not sure. Kind of fed up with D.C."

"Another round, folks?" the lady bartender asked, as she cleared their plates.

Vince looked inquiringly at Dierdre. She shook her head. "No thank you."

He said, "I should get back, see if things are still quiet on the home front. How about I walk you to your room?"

"Mm-hm." She nodded and seemed to be doing her best to keep her expression neutral.

He paid the bill, and they took the lobby elevator up seven floors. In silence.

They were both staring at the floor, because when they looked at each other there was something incendiary in the air, and neither was sure what they should do about it.

Vince walked her to her room, and she got out her key-card, and opened the door, pushed it a little ajar, and he said, "Okay… then. Let us know if you're going to be in Seattle and we'll all…" He found he was having to clear his throat a good deal. "…we'll have you down, if you want to come, go fishing on the Sound and… There are oyster beds in Case Inlet…"

He broke off. She was looking at him with exasperation.

"You're protecting me!"

"What? No! Why would I? Hell, you protected me from Curly Estrada—"

"Exactly, Vince. I did. But you and I have been dancing around each other for a while now. If I'm wrong about that, then I'll go into the room, embarrassed, and you won't hear from me again."

Vince swallowed. "You're not wrong."

"You're trying to protect me. You think I'm going to get hurt, hanging around you."

"I..." He sighed. "Yeah."

"I'm a combat veteran, a pilot, a former FBI agent, and I just shot a guy to save your ass."

"True. But... I've got a lot of enemies. I... You... I don't want you in the line of fire."

"I *live* to be on the line of fire. Just like you do." Then her eyes narrowed, and she said grimly, "Vincent Bellator, I'm placing you under arrest."

"What? Allow me to remind you that you're not in the Bureau anymore!"

"Citizen's arrest then."

"For what?"

"For stupidly blowing a really good time." Then Dierdre reached out, took him by the lapels, and pulled him in for a kiss. His arms went around her of their own accord.

The kiss seemed to go on a long time. It was a kiss that lost track of time. Then Vince felt something shattering in him. What was it that shattered?

Ah yes. It was his resolve.

He pulled back, took a breath, and said, "Where... does the

interrogation take place?" She nodded at the door of her room. "In there. You have the right to remain silent. Anything you say may be used against you in a court of law…"

"Sure, officer. I know the drill." Vince took Dierdre's hand in his. They went into the hotel room, and the door closed behind them.